The Italian Secret

Barry Lillie

Copyright © Barry Lillie 2025

Cover design © Flatfield

The moral right of Barry Lillie to be identified as the author of this work has been asserted in accordance with the Copyright, Designs and Patents Act of 1988.

All rights reserved. No part of this publication may be reproduced, stored in a retrieval system, or transmitted in any form or by any means, electronic, mechanical, photocopying, recording, or otherwise, without the prior permission of the copyright owner of this book.

This novel is entirely a work of fiction. The names, characters and incidents portrayed within are the product of the author's imagination. Any resemblance to actual people living or dead is entirely coincidental.

You can follow Barry on the following platforms:
www.facebook.com/barrylillieauthor
www.instagram.com/barrylillie2

For news about new releases and free content sign up for Lillie's Letters here:
barry@barrylillie.com

This book is for 'the lovely' Annie.
My friend and fellow dragon hunter.
Grazie amore mio.

La felicità non è un obiettivo, ma un percorso

(Happiness is not a destination, but a journey)

Also from Barry Lillie

Willow and the Motorway Horses
52 Weeks
4 Months
Under Italian Stars
One Italian Summer
Lanterns Over Laroscia

To get a **free** copy of the prequel to this book
Lanterns Over Laroscia, go to:
https://barrylillie.eo.page/yz39v

January

Gennaio

Five teenagers packed themselves into one car. Two boys, both eighteen years old and three girls of varying ages. Luciano was driving, and his best friend, Gianni, was sitting beside him with the window rolled down and his arm dangling over the edge.

Flavia was shrieking. She always did when she was excited. The song on the radio changed, and she squealed again, "Turn it up, we can't hear it in the rear."

Gianni drew his hand inside the car and turned up the volume.

Nadia and Pina began singing, both off key, but neither cared.

The car belonged to Luciano's brother. He'd told him to drive carefully before loaning it to him. "Don't drive like a dick,"

"I won't," Luciano had promised. But now, he was driving like a dick.

Luciano pressed the accelerator and, turning the steering wheel from left to right, the car swerved across the road, like a mechanical snake making Flavia shriek louder.

"Stop it, you'll make me throw up," Pina said, as Nadia laughed.

The car straightened up again and with the horn blaring undertook a Fiat, the driver flashing in annoyance and Gianni flipping the finger, his arm outstretched through the window.

Passing the church at Sant'Onofrio, Luciano slowed, crossed himself, then hit the gas again.

"You're going too fast," Nadia shouted as they

approached a hairpin bend and swerving across the road, they almost hit an oncoming car.

Flavia screamed, and Luciano held up a hand, earning a high-five from Gianni.

The car turned right onto Contrada Brecciaio, a long straight road that tempted Luciano, as if it was begging him to speed again.

The girls whooped as air rushed into the car from the open windows at the front. Gianni stretched his arm outside like a one-winged aeroplane.

"I'm bored with this music," Nadia said and leant between the two front seats, trying to change the radio station.

Tyres screeched as a car pulled out from a bar and Luciano crossed onto the wrong side of the road. A car travelling on the other side swerved to avoid a collision. Luciano lost control of his car, veering in a diagonal direction, causing the other to brake suddenly.

There followed a crunching sound, metal on metal and the car behind folded as it came into contact with the one in front.

Luciano straightened up, pressed the accelerator and sped away as Nadia lifted herself up from between him and Gianni and said, "What just happened?"

One

Uno

Riccardo looked up from the vines as a pickup truck pulled into the driveway. Seeing the driver, he called out to Gabby, who came to the door wiping her hands on a towel, the aroma of a roast dinner following her outside.

"Issac," she said as the car stopped and the young Scotsman gave her a big toothy smile. "You didn't say you were coming back."

"The Veneto job has finished."

"The nature reserve in Mesola?" said Riccardo. "How was it?"

"Good, plus it meant I could visit Venice a few times. But after spending months living somewhere so flat, I longed to be near the mountains again."

"I'll make some coffee and you can tell us all about your adventures up north."

The three of them gathered around the kitchen table, and Riccardo added another log to the burner. It wasn't cold, but as the month of March faded out, the breeze carried an easterly chill that took the edge off the spring temperatures.

"So what's next?" Gabby asked as she passed Issac a British sized mug of coffee.

"I've got two features to write for Nolan. And another for an American magazine. That will keep me busy for a couple of weeks, but afterwards, I'll be looking for something local."

"Will you be staying at Tornareccio again?"

"No, my friend has a long-term rental staying there. I'm sharing an apartment in Vasto at the moment."

"Wow, that's quite a distance from here."

"I could use some help here," Riccardo said, "I'm planting more vines, if you're interested?"

"That would be great."

"It's only a couple of weeks' work and the pay is poor."

"I don't mind. Every little helps when you have nothing."

"Will you stay for lunch?" Gabby asked and Issac accepted before following Riccardo outside to see the land he'd cleared ready for the new vines.

A car horn sounded and Gabby went to the door to welcome Rachel and Luca, who had come for lunch.

"I've brought Tiziana's *torta di mele*," Rachel said, holding up the apple tart covered by a cloth.

Luca said hello then sloped off to join the men around the side of the villa and Gabby poured two glasses of wine before salting the huge pot of simmering water, waiting for the pasta that would become the first course.

"Issac's back," Gabby said, sitting at the table, "Riccardo's offered him some work planting vines. He's like Luca, always happy with his hands in the soil."

"Do you think he'd be interested in some gardening work at *Le Stelle*?" asked Rachel.

"You could ask. I'm sure he'd be happy."

"How is work with you?" Rachel asked as Gabby added fresh pasta to the pot.

"I've got a full diary with the magazine, and the creative writing workshops will start again soon. Now that Carlino's guys have finished the studio. I'll show you after lunch."

"It smells divine. What are –"

The men were talking loudly as they entered from outside. Their conversation interrupted Rachel's question, and she laughed, "That's the peace shattered."

Filling glasses with wine, Gabby said, "I was just telling Rachel that the studio is finished."

"Yes," Riccardo said before taking a sip of his wine, "Carlino's men have done a great job. Thanks for the recommendation. Cosmo and Massimo are returning to paint the outside rendering before the summer."

Gabby drained the pasta and, using the traditional Italian method, she added it to the sauce before serving. "This is one of Agata's recipes," she said as she put the large bowl of pasta and mantis shrimps in the centre of the table. "There's a couple of Seppe's small chickens in the oven."

"How is he?" Luca asked.

"He's fine. I don't know where he gets his energy from."

"I think some of these old guys have more stamina and strength than we do," Luca said with a chuckle. "We're too soft."

Their lunch was a pleasant experience, filled with good food and friendly conversation. Issac told tales of his time in Veneto, one that included a scary moment where he stumbled across a family of wild boar with babies. Riccardo fetched more wine from their cellar, and Rachel regaled them all with Rosa's latest exploits.

"Who's for Tiziana's apple tart?" Gabby said as she opened a couple of tin cans and poured the yellow contents into a saucepan.

"What is this?" Luca said. "*Zuppa gialla*?"

"Not yellow soup," Gabby said. "Tinned custard from England."

"Wait until you taste it," Rachel said, laying a hand over his, as Luca looked uneasy.

The apple tart went down well, even when Luca's nose wrinkled, and he protested that it would have been nicer with an Italian *crema pasticceria* rather than what he called synthetic English mud, to which Rachel called him a food snob.

"What is food snob?" Luca asked, and everyone laughed.

Retiring from the table to the sitting room, Riccardo served digestivi; Luca declined as he was driving, and Rachel told everyone about the hotel's forthcoming season.

"We've got eighty-five per cent occupancy booked already. It's going to be a busy year."

"I'm so glad it's working out for you."

"It's hard work, but I'm still loving it."

The crackling of burning logs added to the comfortable atmosphere and more wine flowed until Riccardo said to Issac, "You can't drive back to Vasto now. This wine's stronger than most. Stay the night. We have plenty of space."

"Is this a plan to have me on site tomorrow to start the planting up?"

"You rumbled me," Riccardo said, and once again, everyone laughed.

As dusk crept over the landscape, Rachel and Luca said goodbye and their car disappeared into the evening as a pink stippled sky hung over Perano.

Gabby and Issac were on dishwashing duty as Riccardo topped up the wood burners with logs of seasoned olive wood from the land cleared in readiness for the new vines to be planted.

Spring seemed determined to hold on to a winter chill, and later when Gabby and Issac took their drinks outside, they sat with blankets across their laps.

The sky was changing colour from indigo to black as the last rays from the sun disappeared. Stars became the natural lights that filled the gaps lefts behind from the departing pink ribbons of sunset.

"I love being outside where there's no artificial lighting. You can really appreciate the stars when it's just you and the sky," Issac said.

"I wanted to install outdoor lighting, but Riccardo wouldn't have it," Gabby said.

"Let nature sleep," Riccardo said, joining them and placing a bottle of grappa on the patio table. "I didn't want to disturb the natural rhythm."

"Riccardo thinks the light will keep his vines awake."

"I think nothing of the sort," he said, well versed in his girlfriend's affectionate mockery. "I like to think it allows the wildlife the peace to go about its business without stress."

"Yes. It seems to go about its business all over the place. I'm the one who has to pick it up each morning."

"How are you settling in to being a wine producer?" Issac asked.

"It's all still new to me, but I'm enjoying it."

"And the vines?"

"Luca helped me to plant up the new ones at the side of the villa, and Gabby and I purchased two parcels of adjacent land that needs to be cleared."

The cork from the grappa bottle squeaked as Gabby slid it open, "Riccardo said, last year's harvest was better than in previous years."

"And the wine?"

"We think it should be a good year."

"I'm even thinking I might have a go at making grappa." Riccardo said, taking the bottle from Gabby, "If there is a better segue, I can't think of one."

They held their glasses up to be filled, and after chinking the rims, swallowed the fiery liquid in one mouthful.

Gabby exhaled loudly and held out her glass for another top up, and said, "I'll have another, then I'll get the room ready for you."

"No," Riccardo said as he poured more of the lethal spirit into her glass, "you two catch up, I'll sort Issac's room out."

Watching Riccardo enter the villa, Issac said, "He's very domesticated."

"Oh yes, very much the modern Italian male."

"Is it your influence?"

"No, he just likes to have control. Me, I'd just put some sheets and blankets on the bed for you to make it up yourself," she sniggered. "But Riccardo likes everything done to his standard, and who am I to complain?"

"I'm so grateful to you for letting me stay over, and for the work."

"You're welcome. Finding locals to work is difficult, as they're all busy at this time of the year getting their own plots ready."

Gabby sat and listened as Issac told her about his job up north and how he wanted to stay in Abruzzo for the year, explaining that he'd enjoyed travelling around the country working, but now he needed a period of stability.

"Will you put down roots," Gabby said, as she laughed loudly. "Did you see what I did then? Put down roots and you a gardener."

"I got it," Issac said, his teeth and the whites of his eyes the only things she could see in the darkness. "Don't give up your day job. Oh, and by the way, it's landscape specialist."

"Ooh, get you."

Riccardo heard their laughter as he returned and told Issac his bedroom at the rear of the villa was ready whenever he was. "I've left the bedside lamp switched on for you. So you know which room it is."

"I think we should have one more drink before bed," Gabby said, and both men agreed and held out their glasses.

***

Issac rose early and stood looking out of the window. The sky was the colour of a smudged pencil in a sketchbook with no clouds to blanket the earth from the cold. In the distance, he could see the town of Perano, a hotchpotch of houses that looked precariously balanced on the hillside like Jenga blocks.

He guessed the Maiella would still have its coating of winter snow and presumed that higher in Passo Lanciano skiers would make the most of the last runs before the thaw.

He could hear activity downstairs and pulling on a sweater, he made his way down to the kitchen to find Riccardo putting the Moka pot on the stove. "Morning,"

"Coffee?" asked Riccardo, already reaching for another cup.

"Thanks. Would you like me to rake out the wood burners?"

"It's already done. The last of the warm ash is outside cooling before I scatter it around the vines."

After breakfast, Issac zipped up his jacket and went outside for a walk. He was interested in seeing the new land that his hosts had purchased.

He strolled past the area prepared for the new plants; it looked like a large rotavator had turned the stony soil and, following on a hand tiller, had laid out parallel lines ready for the fresh grapevines. The border that divided the parcels of land was still visible. A defined line of unkempt grass and brambles that had separated the spaces between the neighbours. There were large holes where he thought olives must have grown. Riccardo had already said he'd sold some to local farmers who had come with their diggers to remove them. It always amazed Issac how they could take such a brutal pruning and moving yet still bear the fruit that delivered the green peppery oil. As he wandered through the land, between more of the gnarled ancient olives, he recalled the previous year when he'd tried to explain to Will at the writing group how olives were not trees but shrubs, and that most Italians referred to them simply as plants.

Entering a shaded area where several oak trees had taken root, cyclamen were abundant, their purple flowers standing out from the leaf litter. In a patch of rough scrub, he spotted the yellow flowers of winter aconites, doing their best to soak up some early spring sunshine.

In this type of setting, Issac was at his happiest. Being surrounded by nature filled him with joy. He touched the leaves and grasses as he moved through the undergrowth, contemplating the hard work that would be required to repurpose and cultivate the land abandoned for decades.

He wandered into a small copse of young oak trees and bent down to study a small patch of porcini mushrooms, wondering if he should pick them and take them back for his hosts. Deciding to leave them, he settled on asking Riccardo if he planned on leaving some land wild. *Maybe he could set aside a patch for pollinators*, he thought, as he stood up startling a Jay, its blue wing bars flashing as it screeched its annoyance at being disturbed.

Coming out of the oaks, a flat expanse of land met him with regimented rows of olives, obviously the border to someone else's land.

He turned around and walked around the perimeter of the land before making his way back to the villa. Looking in the distance, he wondered if Perano was close enough to walk to. *I'll ask when I get back.*

At the villa, Issac saw Luca's car in the drive and found him unpacking a wooden box filled with what looked like bare-root vines. Passing them to Riccardo, he inspected each one before dropping it into a large bucket of water to rehydrate the roots.

"Pleasant walk?" Riccardo asked, looking up and seeing him.

"Yes, thanks. I enjoyed it."

"There's nothing better than a morning stroll with nature to set you up for the day," Luca said.

"Is there anything here I can help with?"

"You could cut the ties from that other box of vines," Riccardo said, nodding towards a pair of scissors.

"So, how will you be staying in Abruzzo?" Luca asked.

"I'm not sure I have to find for a job if I want to stay."

Issac shrugged, then added, "I'm going back to Vasto this evening. So, I'll start looking tomorrow."

"Rachel has said there could be some occasional work at *Le Stelle*. If you're interested?" Luca said as Gabby appeared around the corner.

"Aah, Issac, you're here. Can I have a word?"

"Sure," he said and followed her as she turned and made her way back to the villa.

"Part timer," Riccardo joked, calling after him.

In the kitchen, Gabby poured two English sized mugs of instant coffee and placed them down on the dining table. She opened a tin of biscuits and pushed it over towards Issac. "Custard creams and bourbons all the way from the homeland."

Issac reached in, took two and looked across at Gabby as she stirred a sweetener into her drink. "Riccardo and I have been talking," she said as she took a custard cream and dunked it into her coffee. "We didn't want to be presumptuous. We're not aware of your living arrangement at Vasto. Whether you're staying with a close friend…"

Issac shook his head, wondering where the conversation was heading.

"Riccardo and I think if it is okay with you, you could move in here."

"Really?" Issac's eyebrows flitted up into his hairline.

"Yes. Whatever you're paying in Vasto, we'll match it. There's paid work here for you until you get sorted out and you can use the writing room for your freelance projects."

Issac was stunned. Unable to speak for a long moment until Gabby said, "Well?"

"That's so kind. I'm overwhelmed."

"Don't be. You'll have to do your share of the cooking."

He returned her smile and accepted the offer just as Riccardo's head appeared around the doorjamb and enquired, "Any chance of a fresh coffee?"

"I'll make it." Issac said, rising from his seat.

"So, has he said yes?" asked Riccardo.

"Yes, he has," said Gabby.

"*Buona scelta.* Good choice. By the way, it's one sugar for me."

Two

Due

Looking through the double doors of the *porte-finestre*, Salvatore Pasquini gazed at the patio and across into the overgrown wilderness beyond. He sighed loudly. Another morning had slipped by without stimulation. He checked the clock on the wall and counted. Two hours had passed since breakfast, another three before lunch.

The room was hazy with smoke, and logs crackled and spat in the vast open mouth of the fireplace. These were the only sounds in the room where he felt imprisoned.

The hospital had discharged him a week ago, and almost at once when he'd returned home, he understood how much his life had changed. And that change did little to lift his mood. In the hospital, dosed up on painkillers, he'd had little time to remember the accident in which he'd lost his left leg. But now it was all he could think about.

The doctors had told him it would take time for him to adjust, and he understood that. What they hadn't told him was how desperate he'd feel, and that desperation grew bigger with each new day.

He was grateful for the prescriptions that kept his pain at bay, but sometimes, just briefly, he felt like his leg was still there. A phantom limb that mocked him, feeding his depression until his past demons returned and he felt the thirst that he'd been a slave to return.

"You cannot go back to your old life," Doctor Colucci had told him. "We've done all we can here at the hospital, but now it's up to you to stay sober." She had also told him that at forty-nine he had the insides of someone at least twenty years his senior.

Forty-nine, he thought, *forty-nine and now I need someone to care for me like they would an ancient nonno.*

Salvatore knew his rehabilitation would take time, and time was all he had now. Endless hours and monotonous days where he'd sit looking outside, watching the birds that visited the garden. Some mornings, he was envious of the birds. Jealous of their flight, while he was weighed down with sadness. He succumbed to the darkness of depression, like a murmuration of starlings as it swept over him, breaking and returning in swathes of iridescent beating wings.

He turned his head, listening as a scooter sounded outside. Nadia had returned from her job at the stables.

"*Papà?*" she called as she came inside the villa and opened the door to his room. "*Papà*, the fire." She moved to the fireplace and, taking a poker, she pushed a log back inside the grate and opened the damper to allow the smoke to be sucked up the chimney. "Didn't you notice how smoky the room was?" she said, opening the *porte-finestre* to let fresh air into the room.

Salvatore shrugged. Of course, he had noticed, he just hadn't cared to move. Everything seemed to be too much effort.

Pulling a blanket from the sofa bed where her father had taken to sleeping, Nadia wrapped it around his shoulders and told him it was cold outside. "I have fresh bread from the bakery in Selva. We can have it with the leftover soup from yesterday. Would you like that?"

"Yes," her father replied, his voice just a whisper.

"*Caffè?*" He shook his head. Too much coffee made his nerves jangle. Nadia gently kissed his cheek and left the room.

Salvatore could hear his daughter as she bustled around the kitchen. Yesterday he'd listened as she'd prepared a large pan of minestrone with orzo and although his appetite had dwindled, he'd enjoyed the vegetable soup. So much so that he'd eaten the last of yesterday's bread.

"We have some chicken leftover from dinner last night," Nadia called from the kitchen. "I'll add it to the soup?"

"Whatever you feel best," he said, knowing she couldn't hear him.

Another thought followed another sigh. *Nadia shouldn't be tied to her father working as a nursemaid and cook. It's no life for a nineteen-year-old.*

As he waited for his lunch, Salvatore decided he'd spent too much of his time sighing. Sighing and thinking.

***

Nadia shredded the cold chicken and added it to the pot of vegetable soup, then added a handful of broken dried pasta to make it go further. She looked over at the Lavazza coffee tin where they kept their housekeeping funds. Earlier she'd taken the last five euro note to buy bread from the *panificio* in Selva and to top up the tank of her scooter.

As the soup heated through, she cut slices of bread and splashed them with a few drops of olive oil before adding mortadella, folding the pink slices of meat into a mound. After preparing a tray, she carried her father's lunch into his room. His head was resting on his chest, sleep had crept up on him, so she placed the tray down and shook him gently by the shoulder; hoping the action wouldn't cause him to call out in fear, as he did at night when the nightmares came. Salvatore opened his eyes slowly and gave his daughter a fragile smile. "I have brought you your lunch. A fresh mortadella sandwich and minestrone," she said.

"Where is yours?"

"In the kitchen *papà*." She lied. They hadn't sufficient funds to buy enough of the pink meat speckled with pork fat for both of them. Nadia would make do with the reheated soup.

She wheeled his chair over to the small table beside the

fireplace and applied the brake before placing the tray in front of him. As he ate slowly, she made up his bed. Her father had taken to sleeping downstairs in the *salotto* and she thought the sofa bed he used must be uncomfortable. The doctor had told her he needed undisturbed sleep if he was to recuperate fully and a proper bed was what he needed, but how would she be able to bring it down from his upstairs bedroom?

She looked over and noticed he'd stopped eating and was watching her. "Is something wrong, *papà?*"

Salvatore paced his spoon down and wiped his mouth with a napkin and said, "I have been thinking. Maybe you should take a job."

"But I have a job *papà.*"

"Two days a week isn't enough to support you."

"I also have a job looking after you."

"Looking after me isn't a job, it's a trial. A sentence. I want you to meet new people. Make friends. You're too young to be trapped here with me."

"I'm not trapped, *papà*, I enjoy looking after you."

Nadia bit down on her bottom lip. She knew what she was saying was untrue. How could she tell her father the truth? He was right; she did feel trapped?

"You could go back to school, finish your final year."

"I don't want to go back to school."

"Well, I think you should look for a position with more hours and maybe you can put some money aside for your future."

"There's plenty of time for that. Besides, where would I find work? There are no other jobs in Laroscia."

"There must be work in Casoli, a shop maybe, or a bar. We need more money. The insurance I receive hardly keeps us afloat."

"It's too soon to leave you alone, and we can't afford any extra help."

"I worry about you. *Mia cara*. I cannot let you waste

your life here looking after me."

Nadia knew the tear was forming long before it rolled down her father's cheek. She picked up his napkin and wiped it away. *"Ti amo papà,"* she straightened up, "Stop worrying about me, and finish your soup before it goes cold."

Three

Tre

Riccardo and Issac were already outside sorting through a delivery of fertiliser that had arrived earlier when Gabby came down for breakfast. She'd filled the Moka pot and lit the gas underneath it when her phone beeped. Taking it from her pocket, she read a text from Rachel. She looked up as she heard boots being stamped outside the front door, and Riccardo entered the kitchen. "Rachel's friend Louise is coming over to stay," she told him.

"Louise?"

"The friend who helped her when she first came to Sant'Andrea after her husband, Marco passed away."

"I remember you saying. Didn't she design the website for *Le Stelle*?"

"Yes, she's a marketing consultant in the UK. She's coming over for a holiday." The Moka pot bubbled, the steam below forcing its way through the compressed ground coffee. She reached up and took three small coffee cups from a cupboard and placed them on the table before removing it from the stove.

"Don't forget, I have to see Ennio up at the stables this morning."

"More legal work?"

"Yes, sadly, I still need to keep up my freelance work."

"Freelance work?" Issac said, entering the kitchen.

"Yes, until the vines can bring in an income, I need to swap my work boots for lawyer's shoes occasionally."

Riccardo opened a packet of crema filled cornetti and offered them to the others.

"Not for me," Issac said. "It's at breakfast time that I

miss a square of Scottish Lorne sausage the most."

"A bacon and egg butty for me," Gabby said with a smile.

"You're both barbarians," joked Riccardo.

***

Nadia was outside polishing the brass door handles when Riccardo's car pulled into the driveway. He saw her look up as he pulled on his jacket and walked towards the villa. He'd changed his clothes and now wore a suit but looked informal without a tie.

"*Buongiorno, signore*," Nadia said.

"*Buongiorno,*" Riccardo replied.

Ennio Barone appeared in the doorway and asked Nadia if she'd please make some coffee for his visitor.

"*Certamente il signor Barone.*" She dipped her eyes and disappeared inside.

In the kitchen, Valentina was sitting at the breakfast bar, flicking through a magazine.

"Signor Barone has asked me to make coffee for his visitor."

"I'll make it." Valentina said, rising from the stool, "Could you plate up some pastries and take them through to the sitting room? Tell them I'll follow with the coffee."

Nadia did as requested and as she walked into the sitting room, she heard Riccardo ask how things had been since the fire.

"We're getting back to normal. Who'd have thought something made to bring happiness could create such sadness?"

Nadia recalled hearing about Valentina's birthday celebrations and how Chinese lanterns were lit. She was told the guests had cheered as they rose into the night sky and floated away.

Sadly, nobody expected one would sail into the Dutch barn

and set the stables alight.

The sirens had woken the entire village, and everyone had gathered around as the groomsmen removed the trekking ponies. But it had been thirteen-year-old Alina's bravery that had saved the prize thoroughbreds. For weeks, the village had been rife with tales of the young girl's courage.

Nadia shook the memory from her head as Valentina appeared with the tray of coffee and, placing it down, she greeted Riccardo.

"Thank you for coming," Ennio said. "I know you do very little legal work now, but I hope you will assist me."

"I'll do my best. What is it you need?"

"There's two things. One is quite simple. We want to purchase some more land and need the transfer of ownership for that to be completed quickly, before we can then outline a proposal to build. Which is the second thing."

"What are your plans?"

"Ennio and I want to develop the business," Valentina said. "We want to make the stables a place where families can come to and enjoy. An area for children and also somewhere for people to eat."

"Come, let me show you." Ennio stood up and Riccardo followed him out to his office to look at the plans that they'd had drawn up.

***

As Riccardo returned home, Gabby met him outside. "Can you fetch some wine? Lunch is almost ready."

He crossed the yard to the storeroom and picked up a couple of bottles. Walking back, he watched a curl of smoke as it escaped from the chimney and listened to the flapping of bedsheets drying on the washing line. These simple things brought a smile to his face.

Since he had put his demons to rest, he enjoyed the deep

love he now had for his family home. The established vines were looking good, but there was still a lot of work to be done. Trellis wires needed to be checked and tightened if required and the new canes needed to be tied in and mulched. The pruning was complete and the early April sunshine was encouraging the bud burst and new leaves were appearing.

"Something smells good," he said, placing the wine on the kitchen table.

"Gnocchi with a lamb ragù."

"I didn't know you could make gnocchi."

"I can't. Issac made it, and the ragù."

"Looks like asking him to move in was a win-win situation."

Over dinner, Riccardo told Gabby and Issac about Ennio's plans for the stables. "They're quite ambitious,"

"A children's playground *and* a bar and restaurant. Do you think they'll get permission?" said Gabby.

"I can't see why not. I'd argue that it will bring new jobs to the village, and I can't see the *comune* refusing after they'd previously given them the approval to build the stables."

After lunch, Riccardo sat back in his seat and patted his stomach. "That was excellent, but now I'm too stuffed to go outside to continue with the planting."

"The new vines are all hydrated, so they'll tolerate being put in the ground a day later." Issac reached over and refilled Riccardo and Gabby's glasses.

"Have you heard any more about Rachel's friend?"

"Yes," Gabby said, "She's arriving next week and staying until after Easter. I'm looking forward to meeting her."

Riccardo looked closely at Gabby; he could sense she was nervous about Louise's visit, and he hoped her old insecurities wouldn't get the better of her.

Four

Quatro

Salvatore experienced another restless night; he hadn't slept well since the accident. The screeching of brakes and broken glass had tormented his dreams again, waking him often. It was during these moments of fitful sleep that his body craved alcohol.

He'd been dry now for ten weeks, two of those spent in the hospital at Chieti where he'd had his left leg amputated. The doctors had stressed on his discharge that he must stop drinking; he didn't think he could. He'd been a slave to the spirit for years, but his mood had changed with the loss of a limb and he couldn't muster up any enthusiasm for anything, even drinking. Not that the desire didn't torture him. Every morning he woke up feeling good, happy he'd got through another day. He liked the fact that now he went to sleep rather than passed out and awoke instead of coming around. But the days weren't easy. At midday, the shakes came; not as pronounced as when he'd first abstained, but they were still a reminder that he was far from free of his addiction. After dinner was the worst. As the day slowed down his cravings increased, the taste in his mouth became sour and his brain hungered for alcoholic sedation. He was determined to beat it, even if some days, he imagined he was in a fugue where he had lost awareness of his identity. Some mornings, while looking in the shaving mirror, he thought the man looking back at him was someone else. Maybe it was? A new man. The man he'd failed to be the first time around.

He looked at the clock; it was still early but there was no chance of catching up on his sleep and so he pulled himself into his chair and opened the *porte-finestre* that led out into the garden.

He tried to remember how the garden once looked, but the images were gone, trapped somewhere between drunken forgetfulness and trauma. The patio once was a wide space with pots of vibrant flowers, now it was uneven and mossy. The lavender hedges were old and woody, straggly old plants that had long since stopped flowering. Rosemary and sage had grown into giants, taking over the borders, and brambles and ivy strangled what remained.

The roses his wife had loved once bordered a central path that was out of control, and the occasional blooms topped stems too tall and thin to support them.

Salvatore could see no further. He knew the garden stretched down to the lane at the top of the village leading to the village of Verratti, but in a wheelchair, it would be impossible for him to move through the undergrowth.

He hated that over the years he had lost so much, his wife, his dream and now his garden.

Of course, the accident had changed him, not just physically, but mentally. No one would have expected anything less. At first, he thought it was yet another tragic event in a life littered with them, but being a pragmatic man, he knew he'd spent decades in denial and sobriety had made him face up to his failings.

A sound high in the trees caught Salvatore's attention, the fluting whistle of an Oriole. He looked up and glimpsed the secretive, yellow bird with pitch black wings. A rare sign that summer was moving closer. He wheeled himself to the edge of the patio, hoping to get a better look at the bird, but his motion scared it away.

Disappointed, he reversed and one of the front wheels caught in a rut. He shook the chair, tried to move it back and forth, but the wheel had become securely lodged.

Frustration got the better of him and he forced the chair backwards and it started rocking. He tried to steady himself but over corrected and the chair tipped onto its side. Tipping him onto the paving where he landed heavily on his left side, the pain shooting through his body and winding him.

He lay for a few minutes until his breathing returned to normal, angry at his own stupidity. "Anyone with a gram of sense would know not to come out here," he said as he pulled himself into a sitting position. Unable to free his chair, he shuffled on his bottom backwards towards the *porte-finestre* doors.

Salvatore didn't know how long he had sat outside before Nadia found him. "*Papà*, what are you doing outside?"

"The door locked behind me. I couldn't get inside."

Nadia went to retrieve his wheelchair as he shuffled his way into the *salotto* and plonked himself in an armchair.

"What happened?" Nadia asked.

"What do you think happened?" he replied tersely, rubbing away the pain in his amputated leg.

Without answering him, she left the room and returned with antiseptic, a bandage and gauze. "Do you need me to dress your leg again?" she said as she wiped antiseptic across a graze on his cheek. He jolted his head away and as he raised his voice and said, "For the love of God, stop fussing, girl," Nadia flinched and his heart plummeted.

How can she be afraid of me? He thought, *She must know I'd never harm her.* Unaware that over the years, he already had.

He tempered his attitude and said, "I woke early. It was a pleasant morning."

"But it's not safe in the garden. The paving is loose, and the overgrown borders are impassable. Not to mention snakes."

"Snakes don't scare me."

"They should."

He saw Nadia shiver at the thought and laughed a little. "For years, people have feared our snakes when they are more frightened of us. The only ones that pose a danger are the small vipers that hide among the logs for our fires."

"Whatever. You need to be more careful."

Nadia rose and went into his bathroom, where she moved his shower chair into the centre of the cubicle and turned on the water before leaving. "I'll make coffee while you shower."

After he'd cleaned himself up, he entered the kitchen and watched as Nadia sliced bread and lay out slices of *prosciutto* and *provolone* for his breakfast. He looked up as the horn from the *poste italiane* van announced the mail delivery. He went to the window but was too late to see the lady who drove the white van with its iconic yellow and blue livery. As Nadia poured herself a cup of coffee, he wheeled himself back to the table and took a slice of bread and some cheese. "It's nearly eight-thirty," he said. "Nadia, you'll be late for work."

"I'm not going today. I need to look after you. You hurt your leg when you fell."

"I'll be fine. You can't let signora Barone down."

"I'll explain tomorrow. Now eat your breakfast and then I'll turn on the radio for you. There's plenty of things need to be attended to here."

Salvatore looked out of the kitchen window as his daughter pegged the washing out in the sunshine. On the radio surrounded by modern tunes he didn't recognise, an old song started playing and each note conjured up a memory.

Cristina was shading her eyes from the sunshine as she tipped her head back and laughed. Behind her was one of her favourite persica roses.

Salvatore couldn't recall the name but remembered the soft yellow pastel-coloured petals with a red centre.

He wheeled himself into his room and looked out over the garden, trying to remember where his wife had planted the rose. No matter how much he sieved through his memories, he couldn't remember where it had grown, and as the song faded out, so did his memories.

***

Nadia finished attending to the washing and walking back to the house she stopped beside the *cassetta* and collected the mail. She recognised the logo on the envelope and pushed the letter into her apron pocket, thinking she'd leave it until her father's mood had softened before she showed it to him.

Coming into the kitchen again, she boiled the kettle and took a mug of camomile tea through to her father. Seeing him gazing out of the doors, she asked him if he was okay.

"*Si, cara mia.* I was just trying to remember something."

She put his drink down and he murmured, "Can you remember your mother's roses?"

"A little." Nadia did remember. She recalled how after her mother had gone, she had tried to take over tending to the garden, until her father's anger forbade her to continue, leaving it to grow wild over the years.

"Of course, my darling, you were a small child when she went away."

"I was twelve, not so little. But I remember she loved her roses and would fill the vases you made with them."

Nadia thought about how when her mother had left, her role had changed. She'd gone from daughter to a surrogate mother. Over the years, this change had annoyed her; angry that her teenage years were framed with subservience. Now those thoughts had changed, and the secret she was pushing down into her core forced her into a newer, more passive role of servitude.

"If only she had loved us, too."

"Please Nadia, let's not dwell on this again."

"But *Papà.*"

"We both know why she left."

Salvatore reached out to his daughter, and she allowed him to pull her close, his head resting against her ribs. "She loved you, Nadia. It was me. I spoiled that love."

Pushing away from him, she said, "I have made you some tea."

She turned away from him for fear he'd see the sadness in her eyes and after she'd told him she was going to wash the breakfast dishes; she pulled the door closed behind herself as she left the room.

Five

Cinque

Ennio was spooning the crema off the top of his coffee while Valentina warmed a cornetto for her breakfast. Looking at the clock, she said, "I certainly hope Nadia has a good excuse for not turning up yesterday. I think she should have at least called to say she wasn't coming to work."

"Perhaps she was unwell."

"I don't know, but I shall ask her if she turns in this morning. There's much to do, especially with Santino coming home from school for the holidays."

"Alina will be happy to see him."

"She will. She's been practising her jumping on Tempesta and is eager to show him."

The outside door opened and as Nadia stepped inside, Ennio swallowed his coffee and made his excuses and left the room.

"I'm so sorry I couldn't come in yesterday," Nadia said as Valentina tore tiny pieces from her pastry and popped the flaky morsels into her mouth. "I got up in the morning and found my father sitting outside. He had fallen on the patio."

She related the story, and Valentina listened, unspeaking until Nadia dipped her eyelids.

"How is Salvatore today?"

Nadia had expected a recrimination but lifted her eyes to see Valentina was concerned. "He's much better, thank you."

"I'll ask the cook to prepare something warming for you to take home for him."

"Oh, signora, there's no need to do that."

"It's not a problem. Can you make a start on the breakfast dishes and I'll organise something with the cook?"

Nadia was working at the sink when the door opened and Ennio Barone walked in. "My wife tells me your father had a fall yesterday."

"Yes sir, but he's much better now."

"If you need to take him to the doctor, let me know I'd be happy to drive you there."

Without warning, Nadia started crying. Loud, heaving, breathy sobs and Ennio called for his wife.

Valentina gathered Nadia into her and, stroking her hair, spoke soothingly before instructing her husband to put a pan of milk on the hob.

Ennio looked confused, and Valentina directed Nadia to a stool and went to heat the milk. "Men can be useless at emotional times," she said to Nadia as she placed two mugs of hot chocolate on the breakfast bar. "Now, what are these tears for?"

"You and your husband have been so kind to me. I don't deserve such kindness."

"Why do you say that?"

"Because I didn't come into work yesterday."

"You've already explained why. Is something else bothering you?"

"It's just so hard. I try my best, but some days by the time I've finished the chores and taken care of father, there is no time left for myself."

"Have you considered getting some help?"

"We can't afford it. And yesterday, this letter came."

Nadia removed the crumpled envelope from her pocket and handed it to Valentina who removed the letter, read it, then returned it and said, "I see."

"We are barely getting along on the paltry amount from father's insurance company, and now this."

"Have you spoken to him about it?"

"Not yet. He's been so depressed lately; I dare not upset him more."

Valentina nodded to the hot chocolate that remained untouched. Nadia picked it up and sipped before turning back to her employer.

Valentina sniggered and took her phone out and shocked Nadia watched as she took a photograph.

"Look," she turned the phone around and Nadia saw her image complete with frothy milk moustache and laughed.

"That's better," Valentina said, pulling a tissue from a packet in her pocket and passing it to the girl.

"I'd better get off," Ennio said, looking at his watch for an excuse to leave the room where he wasn't feeling comfortable.

"Say hello To Gabby and Riccardo for me." Valentina called after him as he left the kitchen. "So, are you feeling better now?"

"Yes, Signora," Nadia replied, "I'll get back to the breakfast dishes."

"They're not important. I can load the dishwasher. If you need to go home, I think we'll manage without you today."

"Thank you, but I'd rather be here." Nadia got down from the stool and began loading the dishwasher.

***

Riccardo shook hands with Ennio before showing him around the winery. "Gabby's in her office. I'll take you over in a moment."

"It looks like everything is falling into place."

"It is now I've got this young man helping me." Riccardo introduced Issac to signor Barone, who asked him if he was enjoying being in Perano.

"Yes sir," Issac said, "I've just returned from working near Venice." Ennio listened as Issac gave him a potted history.

"And is this your speciality?" Ennio opened his arms, gesturing to the vineyard.

"Not really. I'm an aspiring landscape gardener."

"Well maybe you could pop into the stables and look at where we could dress it up a little."

"Oh, sorry, I wasn't touting for work."

Ennio could see the young gardener was blushing. "My wife was saying only last week that she'd like more flowers in the courtyard. Come along and have a chat with her. Riccardo will give you directions, I'm sure."

A door opened, and Gabby stepped outside. "I thought I heard voices… Ennio, how lovely to see you."

"You too. I called to drop off some paperwork for Riccardo."

"Gives me an excuse to take a break. Come through." Ennio said goodbye to Issac and followed Gabby inside her office.

"I think I've just embarrassed Issac."

"He's quite sensitive, but I'm sure he'll be okay."

"Is he a talented gardener?"

"I think so. He'd like to make a name for himself as a landscape designer rather than just be a man who looks after gardens at ex pat holiday homes."

"I've invited him to come and look at the stables."

"I'll bring him over this afternoon if that's okay?"

"Sure. I've an appointment in Lanciano, then I should be back there after lunch. Why don't you all come over for aperitivi? I'm sure Valentina would enjoy that."

Ennio said goodbye to Issac and Riccardo and as his car left the driveway Gabby told them both that they were going to the stables for drinks later.

"He seems like a nice man," Issac said, "asked me to speak with his wife about doing some work."

"Well, if his plans for the stables get the go ahead, I'm sure there'll be more to come." Riccardo said.

"Yes," said Gabby. "You never know where it will lead.

I'm sure Ennio and Valentina have a lot of wealthy friends who you could work for."

Issac blushed again.

***

Alina was sweeping the stable floor when Gabby's car arrived and dropping the brush, she rushed outside to greet her. "*Ciao* Gabby."

"*Ciao* Alina, *come stai?*"

"I am well. I've been decorating Ferro's stall for Sonny. He's coming home from school."

Alina took Gabby by the hand and led her inside the stable block as Riccardo and Issac unloaded two boxes of wine from the car's boot and made their way to the villa.

Inside the stables, Gabby saw the banner that Alina had pinned to the door of Sonny's horse's stall.

"It's to welcome him home. I made it."

"Yes, I can see that. I'm sure it will make him smile."

"Alina?"

Hearing her name being called, Alina popped her head outside and called, "*Si, signora Barone?*"

"Would you like an *aranciata*?" Valentina asked.

"Yes, please."

Valentina disappeared back inside the villa and Gabby walked over to where everyone was sitting around a patio heater. Ennio was opening a box that Riccardo had brought over and he removed a bottle and studied the label.

"That's a punchy red, around thirteen point five proof," Riccardo said. "The other box is a softer cerasuolo."

"Thank you. Valentina likes a rosé."

On cue, Valentina appeared, followed by Nadia, who was carrying a tray. "Aperol spritz and a special one for our young guest." She looked around and then called Alina, who appeared at the stable door, waved and then ran over to join everyone. Nadia handed her an orange drink that looked just like everyone else's, with slices of orange and lemon and two paper straws.

Alina said hello to everyone and shyly asked Issac, "Who are you?"

"I'm Issac."

"He's a gardener just like you," Ennio said.

"So *you're* Alina the gardener." Issac said and Alina looked confused, "Luca told me all about you. He tells me you have a lovely garden. I'd love to see it."

"You know Luca?"

Issac nodded and Gabby whispered to Riccardo that she thought Alina had a bit of a crush on the *Le Stelle* gardener. "Did he tell you about our competition?"

"The watermelons?"

"Yes, that's right. I've started mine already." Alina placed her drink down and rushed out of the gates and across the road.

"I think if you agree to help us with the garden displays, you'll have an eager assistant." Valentina told Issac when Alina reappeared with a plant in her hand.

"This is one of my watermelons. But you must keep it a secret from Luca." Alina handed Issac the pot with the small plant.

Issac put a finger to his lips and said, "It's our secret." And Alina giggled. "Tell me Alina, do you call this a *cocomero* or an *anguria*?"

"Nonna calls it a *cocomero*. Why?"

"Well, when I was working up in the north, the people there call them *anguria*."

Alina looked confused. "That's silly," she said. "They won't taste any different with a different name… will they?"

"You're right," Ennio said. "They'll taste the same no matter what people call them."

"Except mine will taste nicer than Luca's." she crossed her fingers and held them up for everyone to see and the people around the table laughed.

Issac excused himself from the group and allowed Valentina to show him around. She pointed out where she thought pots could stand and also led him to a patch of dry earth beside the gates and explained she wanted it to look welcoming. "I have ordered terracotta pots they should be here soon."

Issac took out his phone. "I'll take some photographs and then I can work out a plan to show you."

"Thank you. I'll return to the others and I'll ask Nadia to bring you a cold beer."

Six

Sei

Since his accident in January, Salvatore had become somewhat reclusive. He knew it was irrational, but the wheelchair embarrassed him. His brain told him it was required for his recuperation, but his pride said something different. He felt ashamed that he could no longer walk unaided and had even said to Nadia that without his left leg; he was now only half a man. Depression was reeling him in, and the monotonous days that trudged by only added to his feelings of loss.

Following his fall, Nadia had forbidden him from going into the garden. She had said, "If you must go outside, then sit at the front of the house where the path is level."

Once again, he'd woken after a fitful night in a room as dark as his mood. He knew he needed to push himself to prevent his melancholy from taking hold of another day, so he wheeled himself up the hallway and reaching the front door; hesitated before opening it. An irrational fear rose in his chest. Would the neighbours see him? Would they stare at him like he was a freak?

He opened the door slowly and looked out onto an empty piazza. His was the only occupied house at the top of Laroscia. The villa opposite was a holiday home, its owners coming from Calabria in the summer to escape the intense heat of southern Italy. The owners had abandoned the house next door five years ago; moving north for work and the remaining empty houses in the square were in various stages of decay.

Attached to Salvatore's villa was a small building, one storey with a shuttered façade and a chain around the front door to prevent access. He wheeled himself over to the front door and lifted the chain and pulled it, as if checking it was secure. This was something he'd done many times over the years, ever since he'd closed up his studio. Never once had he stepped back inside.

The sound of a car approaching took his attention and, looking up, he recognised the red Alfa Giulia. The car belonged to his lawyer, Dante Zampieri.

"*Avvocato*," Salvatore said as the man in the smart suit walked towards him.

"*Buongiorno Signor Pasquini.* You got my letter?"

"What letter?"

The lawyer wrestled his briefcase open, perched it on his knee and removed a sheet of paper which he handed to Salvatore.

"I've not seen this."

"Not to worry, you have a copy now."

Dante followed Salvatore inside the villa and waited as Salvatore read the letter. A pot of coffee bubbled on the stove and stirring sugar into his, Dante said. "I'm sorry I can do no more."

Salvatore shook his head and said, "What happens now?"

"I have used the money you gave me, and without more, I cannot continue with your case."

"How much more do you need?"

"Sal, can I speak honestly?"

"An honest lawyer?" Salvatore attempted a small laugh, but Zampieri didn't smile.

"I don't want to take your money, Sal. I think it will be difficult to claim compensation from the driver's insurance company. The driver is still claiming there was a third car involved."

"There wasn't."

"Sal, think about this. The insurance company has an expensive legal team who will defend the claim."

"But you said I had a legitimate case."

"And you do. But they will dig into your past and use their findings in court."

"Are you saying they will say I was drunk? Because I wasn't, the carabinieri did all the checks, and I was under the limit."

"Yes, but they'll argue because of your history with alcohol this was a rare occasion."

To stop himself from raising his voice, Salvatore put the letter on the table and rubbed a hand across his mouth.

"They'll also say your own insurance company has already compensated you."

"The small monthly payment we receive is hardly enough for my daughter and I to live on. Is this it? There's nothing more you can do?"

"I've already said I will need more funds to continue with your case and, as a friend, I'm saying to you. There is no guarantee you will win."

The lawyer concluded his visit and, along with Salvatore's hope, his car disappeared down the lane and, for a long while, Salvatore stared at the spot where he'd last seen it. He had no more money to give Zampieri. What little he had; he needed to support himself and Nadia.

"Are you alright?" a small voice asked.

Salvatore opened his eyes and saw a girl standing outside his house. "I must have fallen asleep."

"Nonna does that too."

"It happens when you get old." Salvatore smiled and she took a couple of steps closer and he noticed her limp.

"You're Nadia's father?"

"You know my Nadia."

"Yes, I see her at the Barone stables."

"So you must be Alina?"

"That's right Signor Pasquini."

"Please call me Salvatore. You're the brave girl who saved the horses from the fire."

Alina nodded, then said, "I'm picking flowers for Nonna." She held up the small bouquet of wildflowers she was holding.

Salvatore reached forward and plucked a margherita and offered the yellow daisy it to her.

"*Grazie*," she said, taking the flower and adding it to the others.

Salvatore nodded behind Alina and said, "Here's Nadia."

"It must be lunchtime. I should go home Nonna will be cross if I'm late."

Nadia and Alina swapped greetings, and Salvatore said, "I need to ask you something, Nadia," as Alina skipped down the lane.

"Is something wrong, *papà?*"

"Come inside."

In the kitchen, Salvatore showed his daughter the letter Dante had delivered, and she told him she had kept it from him because she was worried it would upset him.

"It has. Avvocato Zampieri says there's nothing more he can do."

"We'll manage, *papà*. We have each other, and as you have said, I'll look for another job. Until then, let me make lunch."

***

Sitting at a table in a piazza, Rachel looked across the road at the queue of people outside a pizzeria that was doing a steady trade in takeout. One girl behind the counter was using scissors to cut the pizzas into squares as another served the customers.

"They look busy," she said as Gabby joined her with two glasses of frizzante.

"Every time I come here; they have a queue outside."

"Must be good pizza," Rachel said. "Let's try a slice

after our drinks."

The sun was getting warmer with each new day, and the friends were sitting in a shaded spot. There would be plenty of time to top up their tans when the summer arrived.

"Are you all set for Louise's visit?"

"Yes. We pick her up from the airport tomorrow. She's coming alone as Ben is working, but he'll join us before *Pasqua*."

"I'm looking forward to it. I've not spent Easter in Italy before."

"It's a busy time at the hotel. We have lots of Italian families booked in and Tiziana and her kitchen staff will need a holiday themselves afterwards."

"Riccardo said, unlike in England, most shops will close."

"Yes, and some bars. Easter weekend is not the time to suddenly find you've run out of milk."

Gabby recognised the young girl who walked past their table and entered the bar but couldn't place where she'd seen her before. "Will you be bringing Issac for our Easter lunch on the Saturday?" Rachel said, cutting into Gabby's thoughts.

"Yes, he's happy to be invited."

"We'd have liked to have it on the Sunday but the hotel will take all our attention."

The girl returned and caught Gabby's attention, and she recalled who she was. "Nadia?" Gabby rose from her seat and the girl saw her. "We met at the stables." Watching the confusion fall from her eyes, Gabby asked if she was well.

"Yes, thank you."

"Not working today?"

"No. A friend told me this bar was looking for someone, but they have no vacancies."

"Are you looking for more work?"

"Yes. I only work two days a week for Valentina, so need a second job."

"Do you have experience with bar work?" Rachel asked after Gabby had introduced her.

"No, but I could learn."

"What do you do for Valentina?"

"Mostly cleaning and making beds, housework."

"We have a temporary vacancy in housekeeping coming up, if you'd be interested."

"Where?"

"*Le Stelle*. A hotel in Sant'Andrea." Rachel watched as Nadia was thinking about what she'd said.

"It's quite a long way away from Laroscia."

"Yes, it might be too far to travel for just two weeks' work. I was just thinking out loud."

"Can I think about it?" Nadia asked.

"Certainly. Take this and call me." Rachel took a business card from her wallet and handed it to her.

"Thank you. I'll speak to my father. It was nice to meet you."

As Nadia walked away, Gabby said, "She seems to carry so much sadness."

"Remind you of anyone?" Rachel smiled, and Gabby knew what she was inferring. "Shall we have another drink before a slice of pizza?"

"You bet," Gabby said.

Seven

Sette

Rachel was bobbing impatiently from foot to foot at the arrivals gate at Pescara airport. She almost screamed when she spotted Louise but held it together. The airport was full of people waiting to welcome back friends and family. She spotted quite a few Brits that she had met since she'd been living in Sant'Andrea and didn't want to appear silly.

Luca was waiting outside in the car. He wanted to give the two friends some space to say hello.

It had been over a year since Louise had last visited, and despite their weekly telephone calls, Rachel had missed her best friend.

Once they were together, their arms wrapped around each other and regardless of the people whose paths they blocked, they hugged and ignored the tutting and loud exhales of breath.

"I have missed you so much," Rachel said when they broke free. She reached over and took Louise's hand and dragged her out into the evening air.

"It's warmer than I expected," Louise said.

"Don't let Luca hear you say that. He thinks it's positively polar."

Luca stepped out of the car and hugged Louise before he took her cabin bag and loaded it into the boot. "*Andiamo,*" he said, "we go and return to the hotel where it will be warm."

Louise laughed, and he asked Rachel what he had said that was so funny?

"Nothing." She kissed him before she slid into the rear seat with Louise. "I've some prosecco chilling at the hotel."

"If you hadn't, I would be very disappointed in you."

Kicking her shoes off and swallowing half a glass of bubbles, Louise groaned with pleasure. "I have missed this so much." Looking around the apartment, she said, "It's looking lovely in here now. It looks, lived in."

"It's my happy space," Rachel said, dropping onto the sofa. "I know it's above the hotel, but when I'm here, I feel separated from it."

Luca entered the room and told Louise he'd put her suitcase in the spare room. "I suspect you have so much talking to do," he said before he made his excuses and left the friends to their chatter.

"You look happy together," Louise said.

"We are. He's still got his apartment in Lanciano, and we spend the occasional night apart."

"So he's not moved in then?"

"Not yet. We're happy with how things are for now. What about you and Ben?"

"Oh, you know us; we plod along just as we always have."

As Louise changed her clothes, Rachel told her she'd organise a table in the dining room for them. "Come join me when you're ready."

When Louise arrived, she found the dining room full of guests enjoying dinner and spotted Rachel at a corner table overlooking the garden, illuminated by lights that cut through the twilight, creating an ethereal glow. Glasses of wine had been pre-poured and Mirella waited on them, serving up Tiziana's *gnocchi di ricotta e spinaci*, small green balls of spinach and ricotta cheese in a melted butter sauce with shavings of pecorino, followed by *sogliole in salsa piccante,* a tender fillet of sole with piquant sauce of capers and anchovies.

"I see the food's still fantastic," Louise said after dinner as Mirella served them both a small tumbler of *limoncello*.

"Yes. I'm very lucky to have Tiziana. The hotel guests leave lots of excellent reviews about her cooking."

"I'm so pleased you've made this such a success. I just wish I'd been around last summer."

"Nonsense you had your own business to build up. How's that going?"

"Steady. I've picked a few good clients."

"Well, I'm happy with your services. I'm hopeless at marketing. I'm sure without your help *Le Stelle* wouldn't be as successful as it's been."

"Louisa!" a rasping ancient voice called across the room.

"Rosa, you old witch," Louise said, standing up with open arms for the old woman to come into. "I'd have thought you'd be in bed by now."

Rosa looked at Rachel to interpret, then replied, "What and miss your return."

Rachel signalled to Mirella, and with a practiced nod, she carried over a small bottle of genziana. Louise shuddered, remembering the drink from her previous visits as Mirella poured a glass of the urine coloured liquid for Rosa.

"Rachel told me you will stay for *Pasqua*."

"Yes, I'm staying until the end of April."

"*Mannaggia, che palle.*" The old woman frowned and with cupped hands gestured as if she was holding two oranges, then cackled with good humour.

"Don't tell me what she said, I can guess," Louise said before she turned back to Rosa. "And Ben is coming soon, too."

"*Un rivestimento d'argento*," Rosa replied.

Louise looked at Rachel, expecting a translation, and laughed when she said, "A silver lining."

"Cheeky old witch," Louise said, and hugged Rosa close and kissed the top of her head.

The threesome talked well past the dining room's closing time after most of the hotel's guests had retired to their rooms.

***

When Louise woke the next morning, she lay in bed listening to the sounds from outside the open window of her bedroom. The birdsong was lively and, from down below, she could hear the kitchen staff going about their morning routines. The noise didn't distract her from her relaxation. In fact, it enriched her waking, reaffirming she was on holiday.

She got out of bed and, looking out of the window, she could see Luca was already at work, tending to the produce in his orto. A young man in a hotel uniform was cleaning the swimming pool; Rachel had said it was reopening at Easter and a van arrived with a delivery of freshly laundered bedsheets. Looking past the orto, she noticed the citrus trees close to the gazebo were in blossom and promised herself a walk among them later to breathe in their perfume. She remembered when Luca had first planted them and now, a year later, they looked perfect.

A telephone rang in the sitting room and she pulled on a dressing gown. Rachel's phone was on the coffee table beside the empty wine bottle and glasses from the night before. Before she reached it, the ringing stopped. She turned to go back into her bedroom when it rang again. This time, she picked it up and answered the call intended for her friend.

"*Pronto*," the caller said twice and Louise thought, *just my luck, an Italian… well, what else could they be?*

None of the words made sense to Louise, but she caught the caller's name. "I'll – tell – Rachel – you – called," she said, in the annoying way tourists speak to waiters, thinking, if they break up the sentence and speak slowly, they'll understand.

After her shower, she picked up the phone and headed

downstairs. Rachel was behind the reception desk with Silvana, who looked up and gave her a steely stare. *She still looks as abrasive as a nail file,* Louise thought.

"Have you had breakfast?" Rachel asked.

"No, I'll maybe have an orange juice outside."

"You must eat," Silvana said, and moved from behind the desk and said, "*Vieni, vieni.*"

Louise handed the phone to Rachel and before she followed Silvana into the dining room, said, "A girl called. I think she said her name was Nadia."

Louise devoured sweet pastries and strong coffee before she walked outside to see how the gardens had changed over the past year.

She wandered over to where Luca was sowing seeds in a drill; he looked up as she neared him and asked if she'd slept well.

"Yes, it makes such a change to be in the countryside rather than in a town."

"I understand, even in Lanciano, there is much noise that you don't have here."

Louise smiled. She'd always liked Luca's sentence structure. It made him appear more interesting, and dare she say, more romantic.

"Ben, he comes soon too."

"Yes, he'll be here in a week's time. What are you sowing?"

"Lettuce. It's a hard job keeping up with the kitchen."

"That's a downside to success; more work." Louise left Luca to his work and headed down the garden towards the gazebo, inhaling the citrus perfume from the colonnade of lemon and orange trees.

At the gazebo she stepped inside and stood looking out over the rolling hills into the distance; there was something magical about this setting, she thought and vowed to share it with Ben when he arrived. But for now, what she wanted most was to take a walk down to the beach at the end of the lane and dip her toes in the Adriatic. She wanted a few minutes to empty her head of the work related thoughts she had left in England, to soak up the new experiences that the holiday would give her.

Eight

Otto

Issac was unpacking his gardening tools as Alina called from across the road. He waved to the young girl, and she promised she'd come over to say hello after breakfast.

He looked at the collection of terracotta pots that Valentina had had delivered, inspecting each one and deciding what plants they would accommodate and where he'd position them.

The front door opened and Nadia walked outside with a tray and he smiled as she told him the pot of coffee was for him. He watched as she walked back inside the villa; he looked at her posture; she seemed to be weighed down, as if carrying an invisible load.

Valentina appeared from the stables and beckoned him over to a table where there were several polystyrene trays of plug plants. "I asked the garden centre for an assortment of summer bedding. I hope it's sufficient."

"I think there'll be more than enough for the planters. Maybe I can use some elsewhere. I have created the design for the border on my phone."

"I look forward to seeing it." She looked up as a groom led her horse Ametista out of the sables, its hooves ringing on the flagstones. Issac let out a low whistle.

"He's impressive, isn't he?" Valentina said as she fastened the riding helmet strap under her chin.

"He certainly is. I'd be far too scared to climb up on his back."

"He's a powerful stallion, but also very gentle."

"*Buongiorno.*"

Valentina looked around and saw Alina. "*Ciao Alina,*"

then turning to Issac she said, "Looks like you have a junior assistant."

The comment relaxed Issac as he'd heard that Valentina could be fierce. Gabby had told him how when she first met signora Barone, she'd been spiky, almost mean, but the fire that had destroyed most of the stables and put the horses' lives in danger seemed to have mellowed her.

Valentina rode away, leaving Issac and Alina looking at the trays of small plants. The girl pointed to a section and said, "*Sembrano tageti francesi.*"

"That's right Alina, they are French marigolds."

They passed a few minutes where he pointed to the plants and asked her if she knew what they were and, impressed with her knowledge, he asked for her ideas about planting up the pots.

The gardener and his young assistant were sitting at a table outside sieving seed compost into trays when Nadia came over to deliver lunch. "*Panini morbida con caciacavallo.*" Issac looked at the tray of soft bread rolls and Nadia asked what they'd like to drink.

Minutes later, she returned with cans of *limonata* and after she'd left Issac and Alina were sitting eating their cheese sandwiches and drinking lemonade in the sunshine.

Issac asked Alina about the fire and she told him what had happened. "I remember it was frightening, and I was in hospital afterwards." He enquired about Sonny and she told him all about her friend, who was coming home from school for the holiday and how when he was back, they'd go out riding down to the river. "Do you ride?"

Issac shook his head. "I'll tell you a secret. I'm a little scared of horses."

"Sonny can teach you. He taught me."

"I'm not sure. I like my feet on the ground."

After their lunch, Alina listened as he showed her where the new border would be and how he hoped it would look. He watched her face light up when he showed her the screen on his phone where he'd uploaded his initial design.

"This will be nice for my nonna. That is her bedroom." Alina pointed across the road. "She will see it every morning when she wakes and opens her shutters. My bedroom window is at the back and looks over my orto. Come, I will show you."

They were leaving when Nadia returned for their empty plates and Alina told her she was taking Issac to see her orto and olive grove. "Sadly, my olives are as overgrown as yours."

"My olives. How do you know what they look like?"

Alina blushed and told Nadia about the adventure she'd had with Sonny in the summer. "One day, we went to explore and walked through your garden. We went inside your *frantoio*. I'm sorry."

"That's okay. You're right, the garden is an overgrown mess. It used to be beautiful when it was my mother's. I wish for my father it could be beautiful again."

Issac imagined he saw an extra weight being added to Nadia's sadness as she carried their dishes back to the house.

After being introduced to Nonna, she allowed Alina to show him around her garden. He commented on the neatness of her flower borders; she pointed out which areas were for cut flowers for the house and which were purely for the garden's appearance. Issac commented on how well she had designed the orto. He stopped to pick a tender young leaf from a row of lettuces and said it was tasty.

"See this lavender," Alina said, pointing to a row of five plants that bordered a path, "I took these cuttings at the hotel last year with Luca."

She was especially proud of her wigwam of bamboo canes she'd constructed ready for the borlotti bean seedlings she had started on the kitchen windowsill. "Would you like to help me plant them?" she asked and Issac nodded.

As Alina went inside to collect her tender young plants,

he walked into the small olive grove at the rear.

He noticed that grass and weeds covered the ground, pressing right up against the olive trunks, competing for water and goodness from the earth. *This will need to be removed,* he thought, pulling up some wild borage.

Alina called him and he returned to the orto and together they planted the beans.

"I think your olives need pruning," he said. "Would you like me to come and do it for you?"

"I'd much prefer it if you could show me how to do it."

"Yes, I can do that, but first we need to sort out all the weeds and grass."

"I think there's weedkiller in the shed." Alina said.

"You don't want to use that; it'll poison the soil. What it needs is hard work, to remove it by hand."

"I'll make a start tomorrow," Alina said, looking glum.

"I'll help you after I've been at the stables in the morning." Issac replied and Alina's smile returned just as Nonna called to say she had squeezed some fresh orange juice.

***

From the kitchen window the following day, Nadia watched as Issac's pickup parked in the driveway and he unloaded a small cultivator. He wheeled it over to the border he was about to work on and pulled on ear defenders and started the petrol engine.

As he turned the soil over, bending occasionally to remove large stones, Nadia couldn't stop herself from watching him. His shoulders were broad, and the fabric of his shirt became taut each time he leaned over. She thought that for a young man who was obviously strong, his waist was quite small. This gave him an inverted appearance, almost triangular and balanced upon long legs.

"He's handsome, isn't he?"

Valentina's voice caught her off guard and Nadia stammered, "I... I... don't know."

"There's no harm in admiring." Valentina said with a smile, and Nadia relaxed a little. "Why don't you ask him if he'd like a cold drink? It's quite warm this morning."

Nadia stood to the side for several minutes, waiting for Issac to see her. As he did, he switched off the machine and removed the ear protectors.

"Sorry I didn't see you there." He said.

"Signora Barone sent me to ask if you would like a cold drink."

Just then, Valentina placed a tray with two glasses and a jug of lemonade on the patio table and called them both over. "It's a lovely morning. Why don't the two of you take a break and enjoy a drink?"

Nadia's heart leapt in her chest. Why was Valentina doing this? Was she setting her up? What if Issac doesn't want to share a drink with her? After all, she's just a local girl, and he's a well-travelled English man.

"That would be lovely," Issac called back and turning to Nadia he said, "Would you like to join me?"

She nodded and silently followed him to the patio. He waited until she was sitting before he reached over to pick up the jug. Nadia reached over too and their hands brushed against each other and she felt the blush rise in her cheeks.

"I will pour. After-all it's a woman's job."

Issac picked up the jug and poured, his eyes fixed on her face. *Have I upset him?* She thought.

"The borders between male and female roles have yet to become as blurred in Italy as they are back home."

She returned his smile, realising he wasn't upset with her, and she accepted the glass he handed to her. "Where in England are you from?" she asked.

"I'm not from England," Issac said, and cutting her apology off, he added, "I'm from Scotland."

"Now I know why you sound different to Gabby and

Rachel."

"Aye lassie, I'm a braw wee laddie." He smiled as she looked confused by his dialect driven reply. So far, she'd only heard him speaking Italian, and this was even stranger to her ears than the English people she'd heard speaking around town.

As the sun moved across the blue sky, they chatted. He asked her about life in Laroscia, her response being, "It might be quiet, but I like it here. I don't think I would enjoy living in a busy town like Casoli."

Issac smiled. He thought how different Casoli was when compared to the great Scottish cities of Glasgow and Edinburgh. "Tell me about your father's garden, Alina's nonna said it used to be beautiful."

Nadia's eyes skimmed the table's surface, and her posture changed. "It was my mother's garden. She loved it so much and every evening when she returned from work, she'd be out there looking after it."

"And doesn't she care for it any longer?"

"No. She left seven years ago, when I was twelve."

"I'm sorry." It was Issac's turn to blush and Nadia noticed his cheeks take on the colour of apples.

"You wouldn't know." She quickly changed the topic and asked him if he enjoyed being a gardener.

"I had my first patch of earth in my grandparents' garden as a small boy and ever since then, it's been the only thing I've ever wanted to do. I'd love to build up a business here in Italy."

"Will you work for the holiday homeowners?"

He paused and took a sip of his drink before he said, "I want more than weekly grass cutting and planting pots in the summer. I'd love to be involved in designing gardens, for private homes and maybe hotels."

"Is this job at the stables the only one you have?" Nadia asked him.

"I'm working at a vineyard in Perano too and I also have

some work at a hotel in *Sant'Andrea*."

"I have some work at a hotel there, just casual over Easter."

"*Le Stelle?*"

"Yes."

"*Anch'io.*"

As Issac had told her, 'me too'. Valentina called, and Nadia excused herself and returned to the villa, happy that she'd see more of the Scotsman.

Nine

Nove

Gabby was nervous as she waited for Rachel and Louise to arrive. She'd changed her clothes twice. Originally, she had aimed for a natural girl in the Italian countryside look but decided it looked too contrived and so changed into jeans and a simple blouse.

Riccardo had already asked her twice if she was okay and she knew he could sense she was tense. Meeting new people had always been difficult for Gabby. "Think back to how easy you found it to make friends when you were in Bomba." Riccardo said, and she knew he was right. She had found fitting in with her new neighbours relatively easy once she'd put the mistrust of strangers that stemmed from a difficult upbringing aside. Besides, Rachel had pre-warned her, saying, 'Louise is an acquired taste, but on the whole she's harmless.'

A car horn sounded, and Riccardo used it as an excuse to escape into the winery. Gabby checked her hair in the mirror and opened the front door.

Rachel climbed out of her car; the red tones of her newly coloured hair shining in the morning sunshine. Louise was a complete contrast. Shorter and curvier with a blunt blonde bob that could have looked severe on a less friendly face.

"So, you're Gabby," Louise said, reaching out and pulling her into an embrace. "Sorry I'm a space invader."

"Louise has never known how to deal with personal space," laughed Rachel.

"That's okay. Lovely to meet you. I've heard so much about you."

"All lies. Disgusting filthy lies." She laughed and Gabby

felt Louise intended for her to join in.

She breathed a sigh of relief when Riccardo appeared.

"Who's this walking image of sexiness?" Louise said, moving towards him and Gabby watched him falter before he held out his hand and she smiled, knowing he felt similarly uncomfortable.

"Hi, I'm Gabby's partner."

"Well, hello Gabby's partner." Louise moved forward and accepted the customary air kisses.

"This is Riccardo," Gabby said. "He's been to fetch us a bottle of wine."

"Wine, you say. Well, in that case, he can hang around. There's nothing better than wonderful wine and a handsome waiter."

"I'm sorry… I have to be…"

"It's okay, Riccardo, she's just messing with you." Rachel said.

"Sorry, I get nervous about meeting new people." Louise said.

"Do you?" Gabby questioned.

"Do I hell. I'm always full on. I've no other settings for my personality."

"Yes," Rachel said, "Inappropriate is Louise's middle name."

Gabby noticed Riccardo had disappeared, leaving the bottle of wine on a windowsill and so picking it up, she held it aloft and said, "Shall we?"

With a glass of wine each and a slice of cake that Tiziana had sent from the hotel, the three women were soon deep in conversation. Louise thanked Gabby for looking out for Rachel and was told in return it was the opposite, that Rachel was the one who'd looked after her when she'd first arrived in Abruzzo.

"Well, I'm quite envious of you both living here in sunshine with handsome Italian men." Louise picked up the empty wine bottle and said, "Why is it wine evaporates so quickly in Italy?"

Gabby relaxed when going to fetch another bottle; she'd overheard Louise say, "Gabby's nice, isn't she?" and her fears dispersed.

The afternoon passed with gossip and tales of deeds both good and bad that Rachel and Louise had been entangled in. Gabby listened as they told her about their old job working together and in return, she told Louise about her previous summer in Bomba.

"Gabby was one of Alessio Narducci's models at his last fashion show." Rachel said.

"I wasn't really a model. I literally stepped out of a box onto a stage."

"I've seen some of his creations worn by A-listers on Instagram I'm sure he dressed some celebs at the last Met Gala. What was he like?"

Gabby smiled and said, "What's the phrase? Oh yes, an acquired taste."

The women looked up as the sound of Issac's truck entered the courtyard and Louise moved to the window and looked out. "Now there's a strapping lad if ever there was one."

"Be careful," Rachel said.

"Issac is quite shy," Gabby added.

"And," Rachel said, joining her at the window, "He's far too young for you."

"I don't need new shoes, but it doesn't stop me window shopping."

"Do you need to rush back to the hotel?"

"No, Silvana and Mirella have everything in hand," Rachel said. "Why?"

"Now Issac is home. Why don't you stay for dinner?"

"Okay, no more wine for me, or I won't be able to drive back."

"That's a bonus," Louise said, and they both looked at her. "That means more wine for me."

Issac introduced himself to Louise before going for a shower and Gabby began cooking dinner.

As Riccardo gave Louise a tour of the vineyard and winery, Issac was sitting talking to Rachel about his day. He told her he was going to restore Alina's grove. "It is small, just a dozen olives, but hopefully enough to harvest and add in with a neighbour to get a couple of bottles each year."

"I'm sure she'll sort something out. Alina's very capable for someone so young."

"I also had a chat with Nadia, who works at the stables. She told me she had picked up some shifts at *Le Stelle*."

"That's right. Gabby and I met her when she was looking for work in a bar."

"There seems to be something sad about her."

"I thought that, but nothing I could put my finger on."

"What are you two talking about?" Riccardo asked, coming back into the villa with Louise.

"Issac was telling me he met Nadia, the girl who's got some temporary work at the hotel."

"Dinner's ready," Gabby called and one by one they filed through to the kitchen.

Gabby's dinner was simple, and as Riccardo uncorked a bottle of wine, she dished up *rigatoni all'Amatriciana* and pushed a small bowl of freshly grated *pecorino romano* into the centre of the table. "I've put some pork chops in the oven," she said as she took her seat.

The atmosphere was convivial, and the conversation flowed easily as the diners enjoyed their meal. Rachel told everyone about her plans for the Easter lunch and Riccardo told Issac he'd now planted the last of the vines.

"I guess you won't be needing me, then?"

"Don't forget, I need you at the hotel."

"That's good. The job at the stables will finish in a week's time."

"What will you do then?" Louise asked.

"I'll be helping a friend restore their olive grove. It's less than a week's work, no payment, but it'll keep me out of trouble."

"Can I ask? What is your plan?"

Leaning forward, Louise listened as Issac repeated what he'd told Nadia earlier that day. "And how do you find your work?"

"Mostly word of mouth. Originally, I was taking a kind of gap year, bumming around and gardening. But now I know it's here where I want to be."

"From experience, I know you'll never make a fortune getting jobs from casual recommendations. Do you have a marketing strategy?"

"Louise works in marketing," Rachel said, butting into the conversation.

"I'm not touting for work," Louise said. "Just curious."

Issac looked down at the table and replied, "I've no plan. I wouldn't know where to start."

"Let's talk one day. I'll give you a few pointers that might help."

Issac smiled his thanks and Louise said, "Come on Riccardo. We've eaten and it must be time for *digestivi* before Rachel drags me away."

"I'll fetch the grappa," He said, rising from the table and casually tossing Gabby a wink.

All was good with her world and she thought, *why did I start the day off feeling nervous?*

Ten

Dieci

Alina was sweeping up the compost from the driveway as Issac placed the last of the terracotta pots in position. "Do you think Valentina will like it?"

"Yes," Alina replied, "but maybe swap those pastel anemones for the orange tulips."

"I think you're right," he said, moving the pots around.

The villa door opened and Nadia appeared with a tray of drinks and panini. "Valentina said I had to deliver you lunch at this hour." She placed the tray down and walked to look at the finished display of pots.

"Do you like it?" Alina asked.

"Yes, it's cheered up the driveway."

Issac thanked her and with Alina he retired to the patio and sitting in the shade of an umbrella they ate the lunch that the cook had sent out.

"What will you do now this job has ended?" Alina asked.

"I've some work in Sant'Andrea, but before that, we can repair your olives. In fact, shall we start this afternoon?"

Alina didn't have time to answer as Valentina's car pulled into the drive. Issac watched as she got out and walked over to the assembled pots. She removed her sunglasses and said, "This looks fabulous. Thank you, Issac."

"Glad you like it," he said. "I couldn't have finished it without Alina's help."

"Yes, I was coming to that." She held out a cardboard box to the girl. "This is for your contribution."

Alina looked inside the box and gasped before she removed a shiny new trowel and hand fork.

"Look," she said, holding the tools up for Issac to see.

"There's something else," Valentina said, and Alina dipped inside and removed an envelope.

"What is it?"

"Open it and you'll find out."

Alina ripped open the envelope and her face opened up with a huge smile as she looked at the voucher.

"It's for *Verdeaventino,* the garden centre on *Contrada Vicenne.* You can use it for new plants for your garden."

"Can I show nonna?"

"Of course." Alina said, thank you, and as fast as her leg would allow, she ran across the road to show her gifts to her grandmother.

"Would you like me to explain what I've planted in the border by the fence?"

Valentina followed him and listened as he explained how the jasmine would cover the fence, creating a hedge like effect. "There's two loropetalum on either side which will give you reddish - purple leaves to match with the purple ears of the French lavender at the front and its silver foliage should complement the white agapanthus behind it."

"It sounds lovely," Valentina said. "I'm looking forward to it filling the space."

"I'll dot some annuals in to give it some depth throughout its first summer," Issac said.

"I've been speaking with a friend with a property outside Roccascalegna. She's looking for someone to landscape the land at the front of her villa. I hope you don't mind; I've given her your number?"

"Not at all. Thank you, that's very kind."

"We've been more than happy with your work, Issac, and when our proposed building work is complete, we'll be asking you to design the outside spaces."

Valentina pressed her key fob and the boot of her car rose silently and reaching inside, she removed a wooden box and handed it to Issac. "I hope this is appropriate. I had to order it online."

Issac took the box and turned it around to discover it was an expensive single malt whisky from Scotland.

"Thank you, signora. This is…"

"Special, I hope."

"It certainly is."

***

Valentina had sent the leftover bedding plants to Alina and Issac had delivered them before he started using the petrol rotavator in the olive grove. As she pottered about in her garden using the new tools, she kept looking over, waiting for Issac to tell her it was safe to come and help.

On the outside table, Nonna had placed a net cloche over a jug of lemonade and a plate of *Baiocchi*, Alina's favourite chocolate sandwich biscuits.

After laying out pots of impatiens, she confirmed she was happy with the arrangement of colours and got down on her knees and began planting the border.

"Alina," Nonna called. "Use the kneeling mat."

"Yes, nonna," she said with a sigh and got up to fetch it.

"You should always use the mat," Issac said, joining her, "I think I might have some old knee pads you could use. Mind you, they'd probably be too big for your little legs."

They moved over to the table and shared the biscuits and lemonade before Issac led her into the grove and handed her a pair of thick gloves that looked ridiculous on her small hands. "You'll need these, as some weeds are spiky."

"What do we do now?"

"We pick out the weeds, shake off the soil, and drop them into the wheelbarrow."

Expecting her to complain, she surprised him with a broad smile.

Several hours later, they had cleared most of the clumps of weed from the small grove and piled them into a mound to dry.

"We'll burn the weeds at a later date." Issac said as he lifted the rotavator onto the back of his truck. "Do you think you could show me where the wild garden is you told me about?"

"Yes, it's just up there." Alina pointed up the lane. "I'll just tell Nonna where I'm going."

Issac had spent enough time in Italy to be aware of how quiet the streets were in the afternoon. Families usually relaxed after a long lunch before going back to work in the early evening. But the quiet of Laroscia was slightly unnerving. There were no people outside, gardens were empty and the further up the village they moved the fewer houses appeared occupied.

They skirted around a three-storey house, its empty windows looking down at them as it blocked out the sun, casting a shadow that seemed to follow them along a slender lane that opened out onto a piazza. There were a handful of abandoned properties, another secured with metal shutters, and a villa with smoke coming from its chimney. Alina pointed and said, "That's signor Pasquini's house."

The villa must have been grand once, Issac thought, looking at the large house with an exterior that required some attention. The difference between the shuttered villa, and this one, was obvious: the closed-up house had kerb appeal with pots of succulents and cacti that could tolerate months of neglect, yet the front garden of the Pasquini home had become overrun with weeds, it's neglect obvious. It had a short path bordered on both sides by trees that had long since grown out of shape, and its wooden window boxes were in a sorry state of disrepair.

A slim driveway led around the side of a squat building that was secured by a chain and padlock. "Follow me," Alina said, moving along the narrow passage which led them to the rear of the properties, and Issac saw the vast garden that belonged to the Pasquini villa. It came out from behind the villa and spread out on either side, leading up to the woodland at the top of the village.

There had once been a chain-link fence, but this was now broken in places and rusted.

"This way," Alina said, stepping over a fallen part of the boundary, and Issac found himself in a wild place. "Sonny said he thinks wild boar broke through the fence."

"Probably attracted by cachi in the autumn," he pointed to an Italian persimmon tree.

Issac noted that ryegrass covered patches of the land dotted with the grey leaves of borage and underneath the pernicious arum. Brambles ran rampant alongside ivy and young saplings that had been unattended grew through paving, lifting the stones that showed there had once been an ordered pathway.

"Over there is the *frantoio*," Alina told him, pointing out the ramshackle building that had once converted the family's olives into oil.

Pushing onwards, they moved closer to the villa and, coming through what was a knotted tangle of thorny branches that Issac assumed had once been rose bushes, they stopped when they heard banging and they looked at an angry face looking back at them. A fist banged against the *porte-finestre*, rattling the glass and they could see a man shouting, his words trapped inside his house.

"That's signor Pasquini," Alina said. "People in Laroscia say he's a bad man, one who is always angry."

Issac could see the man behind the glass was indeed angry, and he turned to Alina and said, "I think we should leave."

"I don't think he's as bad as people say. When I first met him, he was really kind. He gave me a flower to add to a bunch I had picked for Nonna."

Eleven

Undici

Issac was standing with Luca at the hotel's boundary fence. They were watching two men as they cut the grass beneath their olives while a dog ran around chasing birds. "I cleared the ground around Alina's olives last week,"

"How is she?" Luca asked.

"She's well. We got caught trespassing." Luca listened as Issac told him about their exploration of the garden at the top of the village. "It must have been very grand once, but now it's a mess."

"I can imagine. This place was wild when Rachel first moved here. If left alone, nature can very quickly to take back control."

"Too right, there's always something that needs attending to in a garden." As if a testament to what Issac had said, Luca had spent the morning clipping the grass beneath the citrus trees that led to the gazebo, while he'd made minor repairs to the fence.

The two men walked back to the orto and as they put away their tools, Rachel called to them. She was standing on her apartment balcony as she told them that lunch was ready.

They entered the hotel through the rear door and Silvana stopped them before they passed the hotel kitchen through to the reception area.

"Boots off," she said.

"Why?" Issac said.

"Because these floor tiles have been cleaned."

"It's best to do as she says," Luca said, bending down to unlace his boots.

"Not in here. Outside." Silvana ushered them both back out and as she watched them remove their boots, she said, "Now come in through the front." The door was closed to any protestations, leaving them to make their way around the building to the main entrance.

Walking into Rachel's apartment, she looked at the two men in their stocking feet and sniggered, "Silvana?"

"Yes," Luca said.

"And she made us we leave our boots outside before letting us into reception," added Issac.

"Okay, wash your hands and then we can eat."

"This hotel is full of bossy women," Luca said with a smile.

"Be careful what you say," Louise said, holding up a wooden spoon. "I'm trained to kill with one of these."

Rachel placed a basket of bread in the centre of the dining table and everyone gathered around. Louise brought over the pan she'd been stirring and served everyone *mezze maniche* with a creamy spinach and gorgonzola sauce.

"This is divine," Issac said, taking his first mouthful. "Did you make it?"

"Did I heck." Louise said. "It's Tiziana's from the kitchen. I just stirred it for effect."

"She's also sent spinach and salmon for our second course," Rachel said, reaching for a slice of bread.

"Issac has been helping Alina tidy up her olives," Luca told Rachel.

"Who's Alina?" Louise asked, and she listened as they told her the story about the fire.

"Luca is having a watermelon competition with her," Rachel said.

"She sounds like a little minx." Louise said.

"She's lovely."

While Luca helped Rachel to clear the table, Louise asked Issac how his job was going at the stables. He explained that it had finished now and apart from his work at *Le Stelle* and Riccardo's vineyard; he had nothing else lined up.

"Valentina has recommended me to a friend who wants some landscaping."

"What you need to do is get your name around."

"I've told him he should speak to Penny. She might need another gardener."

"I appreciate it, Rachel, but I want to do more than just cut lawns for holiday makers."

"What you need is taking in hand, young man," Louise said with just a hint of naughtiness in her tone and as the young Scot blushed, she laughed, knowing her intention had worked, and said, "Take your mind out of the gutter. I'm talking about marketing advice."

Rachel passed a bottle of wine and a corkscrew to Luca and said, "Looks like we'll need some lubrication as Louise tells Issac how to make his first million."

Everyone except Issac laughed, and Louise took a notepad from her handbag and started firing questions at him.

A couple of hours later, Issac was leaving the hotel with a handful of scribbled notes and a list of things he needed to organise.

"I'll need a progress report next time we meet," Louise called after him as his pickup moved out of the hotel drive.

That evening, sitting at the kitchen table in Perano, Issac was going through the notes, thinking that much of what Louise had said made sense, even if her delivery had been extreme.

"Wine?" Riccardo said, holding up a bottle.

"Please."

Placing a glass in front of him, Riccardo looked at the sheets of paper laid out and said, "What are you working on?"

"They're Louise's notes." Issac saw his friend's

confusion and elaborated, "She pointed out where my business needs to be headed."

"I thought business was good."

"It looks promising, but Louise thinks I'm missing a few tricks, and this is her plan for me to expand and become more successful." He pushed the papers towards Riccardo.

"Photos. Business cards. A-boards."

"I understand I should already have most of the things on her list, but do I really need a website?"

"Makes sense," Gabby said, coming into the kitchen. "Sorry I wasn't eavesdropping. There are plenty of free website providers out there. You don't need something with lots of bells and whistles."

"Gabby's right," Riccardo said, "Start off with something simple and as the business grows, you can upgrade. What you will need is your own domain name. It'll make you look more legitimate."

"I just want to plant things and get dirt under my fingernails."

"We'll give you a hand." Gabby looked at Riccardo and he nodded.

"Once it's set up, all you'll need to do is update your calendar and check emails."

"And this A-board thing?"

"They're just advertising boards you put outside where you're working. There's a place in Pescara that makes them."

Issac emptied his wineglass and said, "Next you'll be saying I need to design a logo."

"Good idea," Gabby laughed, rolling a pencil across the table towards him.

The following day, as he helped Alina, Issac spotted Nadia in the Barone's driveway. She waved to him and wiping his hands down the front of his jeans; he crossed the road to say hello.

"I need to apologise to you," he said.

"What for?"

"Last week, I was in your garden without permission."

"Oh, it was you. My father said someone had been there."

"I was just looking around. I didn't mean to upset him."

"It's okay. He's forgotten about it now."

"It's a sizeable space. I can see how it must have been beautiful." He watched as Nadia's eyeballs rolled upwards; a signal she was remembering something. "Do you go into the garden?"

"Not any longer. I'd like to make the patio safe for my father's wheelchair, but I don't know where to start."

"Would you like me to look at it?"

"I'm not sure. I can ask my father." Nadia looked across the yard and said, "I'd better get back to my chores." After giving Issac a smile, she went inside the villa.

With the collected weeds from Alina's grove burning, Issac leant on the fork and processed the suggestions he'd had from Louise. She'd expressed the importance of taking photographs and he knew he needed to get permission from Valentina to take some of the work he'd done at the stables. "Pity I didn't take some before I started," he muttered to himself.

"Before what?" Alina asked, looking up and wiping a smudge of dirt across her cheek from the gloves she was wearing.

"I was thinking aloud," he said.

He forked some more weeds onto the fire and said, "Alina. What do you know about signor Pasquini?"

"Just that he drinks too much and had a serious accident last January. Nonna says he is argumentative, but as I said last week, he was very nice when he spoke to me."

As he turned over the soil and Alina pulled up the last of the weeds from the grove, Issac was turning over an idea in his head.

Twelve

Dodici

"What plans do you have for today?" Gabby asked Issac as he poured himself a coffee. His hair was still wet after his morning shower and it dripped onto the shoulders of his T-shirt.

"Nothing much. I might look over some notes I've written for a magazine feature I want to pitch to Nolan."

"Well, if you need to use the writing studio, feel free."

"Won't you be needing it today?"

"No. Riccardo is taking me to Pescara. We can pick up your A-board if it's finished. We're meeting up with Louise and Rachel, as Ben is arriving today, so I'm afraid we won't be back for dinner. Is that okay with you?"

"Sure. I'll look after myself. You go have fun."

After Riccardo and Gabby had left, Issac was working in Gabby's office, but he couldn't shape his notes into coherent sentences. The same thought was repeating in his head, dislodging every other thought he was holding onto. Eventually he gave in to it and grabbed his pickup keys and drove to Laroscia.

Arriving at the Pasquini villa Issac saw that Nadia's scooter was outside and happily assumed she was home.

He parked up and walked up the path that was strewn with weed filled plant pots and untidy borders.

"What are you doing here?" Nadia said, opening the door before he'd reached it.

"I've come to take a look at the patio. If I can make it safe for your father, I'd like to."

"Why? He won't want your charity."

"Believe me, I'm not being charitable. Can I speak with

him? I can explain."

"Who's at the door?" Hearing her father's voice, Nadia turned around.

"It's okay *Papà*."

"You!" Salvatore was now at the door, peering out. "You were in my garden last week. Why were you there?"

"Yes sir, I was," Issac said, "and I'd like to apologise."

"Nadia has already passed on your apology, so why are you here now?"

"Issac was leaving *papà*."

"You know this man, Nadia?" The door was now fully open and Salvatore's wheelchair was sitting on the threshold.

"We both work at the stables," Issac said, stepping forward and offering his hand to signor Pasquini.

There was an awkward moment of silence as Salvatore ignored Issac's hand, before he said, "You still haven't explained why you were in my garden."

"I'm sorry, *papà*. I asked him to look at the patio." Issac looked across at Nadia, and she gave him a tight smile, an explanation for the white lie. "He thinks he can repair it for us."

"We can't afford the repairs."

"There will be no cost signor Pasquini."

"So it's charity, is it?"

"No signor. Can I come inside and explain?"

"Very well, but that's not an assurance I'll agree to your suggestion."

Nadia wheeled her father into the *salotto* and excused herself by saying she'd make coffee. Issac entered and instantly noticed the room was dark; it felt almost hostile. The shutters on the windows were still closed despite the time of day and at the *porte-finestre* hung heavy curtains. Against one wall was a table lamp illuminating a slender table with a dusting of wood ash from a fire that had long since died. Salvatore pointed to a high-backed chair and

Issac sat down.

"So, if you want to repair the patio, you must be a builder?"

"No, sir…"

"Less of the formality. Call me Salvatore."

"I'm a garden designer." Issac said, "Or rather I hope to be. I've been working in Italy for over a year, and now I want to set up my own business."

"Running a business is hard work with no guarantee of success."

"I understand that, sir… sorry, Salvatore. I'm good at what I do, but I need to have examples of my work to show to potential clients."

"You want to bring people here?"

"No. I want to take photographs of the work before and after that will show what I can achieve."

The door opened and Nadia entered with a tray of coffee and after putting it down; she opened the drapes. Sunlight cut through the gloom and Issac could now see Salvatore in more detail.

He had severe features. A narrow face with a sharp nose and small, almost black eyes. His cheeks were ruddy, and this confirmed the notion that he was a drinker. He was unshaven, with thick black hair beginning to grey at the temples and a long neck that rested upon broad shoulders. *He must have looked imposing when standing up*, Issac thought, doing his best not to look at the space where a leg had once been.

"Shall I show Issac the patio?" Nadia said, ending the silence that had crept into the room.

Salvatore wheeled himself away from the double doors, allowing Issac to follow Nadia outside.

On the patio they didn't speak. Issac looked at the uneven surface while she pulled seed heads off the long grasses growing through the paving. Looking back at the house, Issac could see Salvatore was watching them both intently.

"I think I can restore it." Issac said to Salvatore when he returned to the villa. "The paving needs to be lifted and re-laid."

"And you'd be willing to do this work for free?"

"I'm sure we could make you lunch while you are here," Nadia interjected.

"Yes. I'd like to do this for you and Nadia, if you'll let me."

"Nadia, we need fresh coffee." Salvatore said and when she'd left the room, he fixed on a smile and leant closer to Issac and said, "You wouldn't be doing this because you have your eye on my daughter would you?" He gave a small laugh, but Issac didn't believe the man in the wheelchair was joking with him.

After another coffee, Issac said he'd return the following day to measure up and make a few notes and as he left the Pasquini villa, he could feel Salvatore's eyes on his back as he said goodbye to Nadia.

Gabby and Riccardo were already home when Issac returned. He took off his boots and placed them outside the front door before walking into the sitting room. "I thought you two were going to be home late," he said.

"So did we, but it turned out that Ben missed his flight and has booked himself on another for tomorrow." Gabby said.

"Louise was livid," Riccardo said. "Mind you, she did say it was typical of Ben."

"So, what have you been up to today? I thought you were working on a feature in the office."

"I was, but I couldn't concentrate. Something Louise had mentioned was tapping my head and so I went to see signor Pasquini at Laroscia. I'm going to repair his patio."

"Nadia's father?"

"Yes, he can't use it at the moment with his wheelchair

and so this will give me a chance to get some photographs for my website when I get around to creating it."

"I can help you if you like," Riccardo said, "and feel free to use any of the building materials left over from the restoration of Gabby's office." He moved to get up from his chair. "Wine anyone?"

"You stay there. I'll fetch it and thank you." Issac went into the kitchen thinking things were starting to look up for his fledgling enterprise.

Thirteen

Tredici

The sky was as blue as the irises in the borders of Alina's garden; the sun was high but the gentle breeze that swayed the flowers took the edge of the morning heat. Looking across at the stables, Issac noticed Nadia's scooter parked up and hoped she'd come outside so he could speak to her.

"Are you looking for Nadia?" Alina said, creeping up on him.

"No. I was just…" his words tailed off as he saw her laughing at him behind her hand.

"Come along, trouble. Let's get to work." He opened the pickup's door and she lifted herself into the cab, making him realise how sometimes her left leg made her movement less fluid. Climbing into the driver's seat, he said, "Have you got a pencil?"

"Yes," she replied and held it up for him to see.

"Brilliant. I think you'll make an excellent apprentice."

"Apprentice," she scowled at him. "I'm not the apprentice. I'm a co-worker."

"That's told me," he said with a smile.

When they arrived at the villa, Salvatore was waiting for them. At first, he was confused to see the young girl he'd met previously with Issac but he gave her a welcoming smile when she'd explained that she was there to help.

Outside, Alina looked at the patio, occasionally stepping on a loose paver and shaking her head. "This is really bad, isn't it?"

"It is," Issac said. "I think it will need to be taken up and re-laid. I was thinking it would probably be better if it's set in concrete to stop the pavers sinking into sand."

"What about this border? Will it be too low for signor Pasquini?" Alina was standing looking down at a strip of earth at the edge of the patio where weeds were flourishing. "Maybe we could build a wall here."

"That's a good idea Alina." Issac said, "or maybe a raised bed with flowers and herbs that will be at the right height for signor Pasquini's wheelchair."

"Come with me." Alina took Issac's hand and led him through the garden towards the derelict olive mill. She pointed to the stones that lay around the crumbling building. "Could you use these?"

"I think I could. I'll need to ask signor Pasquini first."

Issac and Alina returned to the patio and finished measuring it when Salvatore opened the *porte-finestre* and told them he'd got drinks for them. Inside the room where he slept, Salvatore had placed a Moka pot of coffee on a tray alongside a can of orange soda and some biscuits.

Issac told him about Alina's idea and Salvatore said he was happy for them to do whatever they wanted to do. "Nadia is constantly nagging me to get outside in the fresh air."

"Once the patio is safe, you'll be able to do that." Alina said. "I grow lots of things from seed. Would you like me to bring some of my flowers for the garden?"

"I couldn't take your flowers."

"It's okay I always grow too many. Maybe I could put them in the pots on the side of the piazza."

Salvatore just smiled. He didn't respond and Issac wondered if it was his pride that stopped him from accepting Alina's offer.

"This is beautiful," Alina said and, turning Issac saw she was looking at a ceramic bowl on the table that had been dusted since his last visit. "The decoration is really nice."

"You think so?"

"Yes, it's pretty."

"Well, why don't we make an exchange?"

Salvatore wheeled himself over and picked up the small dish and handed it to Alina. "You can have this in exchange for your flowers."

"I shouldn't. Nonna wouldn't be happy if I took it."

"I'm sure Issac could explain that it is a gift."

"It must be expensive, though."

"Not at all. It's just one of many I used to make years ago."

"You made this?" Issac watched as Alina's eyes widened in wonder. "Do you still make them?"

"No. Not any longer." Salvatore's voice trailed off into a whisper and Issac thought he looked uncomfortable with Alina's question.

"Thank you for the coffee," Issac said, rising from his seat. "Come on Alina, we need to go now. Let Signor Pasquini get some rest."

They were leaving the villa when Salvatore said, "Alina. I hope you'll come again with Issac."

"I will and I'll bring the flowers next time."

When Issac's pickup pulled up outside Alina's house, a teenage boy was standing outside, "It's Sonny," Alina squealed, "he's back home." The pickup had barely stopped before she opened the door to get out to greet him. Issac watched as the two young friends embraced and, after shouting goodbye over her shoulder, they disappeared into the stables. About to turn the key in the ignition, he spotted Nadia leaving the villa. She was putting on her crash helmet when she saw him and waved. She placed it down on the seat of her scooter and walked over.

"Have you just come from seeing my father?"

Issac said he had, and that he and Alina had made some plans for the work they would be doing. "But it won't be for a couple of days as I'm working at *Le Stelle* tomorrow."

"I start my casual job there on Saturday."

"Are you going all the way to Sant'Andrea on your scooter?"

"Yes. I went to school in Francavilla so it's not much further than I've travelled before."

"Why don't I take you when I go?"

"I'm not sure. My father might have something to say about that."

Issac recalled the subtle warning from Salvatore.

"I could meet you in the car park at the bar in Guarenna. I can leave my scooter there."

After arranging a time, Nadia went back to her scooter and Issac drove away, unaware of the huge smile on his face.

***

The arrivals gate at Pescara airport was heaving with people. The air was full of voices, all speaking loudly and excitedly. Italians gathered, ready to welcome family members from overseas who had travelled to spend the Easter holiday with them. The evening air was quite warm for the time of year, and to avoid the claustrophobic atmosphere in arrivals, Rachel and Louise waited outside.

"I hope I didn't offend Issac when I gave him some marketing tips."

"I don't think so. He seemed genuinely happy you shared your expertise with him."

"He's a nice young man, so I hope he can make the business work. It's never easy, starting from scratch, especially in another country."

"Tell me about it," laughed Rachel, remembering her experience of discovering the hotel and setting up her business.

"You seem to be doing okay," Louise said.

"We are, but a lot of it's down to Penny and her contacts and, of course, your marketing."

"I think it's mostly down to the service. That's why people come back. Not photographs and bylines on a website."

The air filled with the whooshing sound of a landing aeroplane, and looking at her watch, Louise said, "Looks like Ben's here."

There was the usual crush of people hugging and saying hello in the foyer as others tried to skirt around them and leave. One family had taken root in the entrance and were greeting each other enthusiastically, blocking the automatic doors that opened and closed with every fresh hug of a new arrival.

"He's here," Rachel said, pointing past a young man who was unashamedly kissing his girlfriend, slowing down the flow of people coming from passport control.

Louise shouted to get Ben's attention and, beaming, he pushed past the kissing couple to be enveloped in his girlfriend's arms. "You two hadn't better start snogging," Rachel said, and Ben pulled away from Louise and hugged her, too.

The queue of cars snaked its way along the narrow lanes separating the parking bays as each driver waited their turn to deposit coins in the barrier to exit.

"Luca's across the road." Rachel said,

"Well then, what are we waiting for?" Ben pulled up the handle on his cabin bag. "I'm looking forward to a cold beer when we get to the hotel."

"I hope that's not all you're looking forward to," Louise said, snuggling up to her boyfriend as they crossed the road to greet Luca who was waiting in the supermarket car park.

Fourteen

Quattordici

Sonny stumbled in the doorway as Valentina manoeuvred him outside, and he tugged at her hands covering his eyes. "Mamma let me see."

"Not yet Santino, I have a surprise." Valentina guided her son over to the paddock before removing her hands with a flourish.

"Wow!" Sonny exclaimed, looking at Alina sitting on Tempesta's back. The surly black horse looked calm as it waited for instruction from its rider.

Alina gave the horse whose life she had saved a gentle squeeze with her thighs, and they trotted sedately over to Sonny. "Watch this." Alina clicked her tongue and Tempesta turned and cantered towards the first of the jumps, clearing it and the subsequent ones with ease.

"Bravo," Sonny shouted, "You have tamed the beast."

"We have an understanding." Alina patted Tempesta's thick neck and muttered her thanks as she brought the horse to a halt, and Ennio helped her down from the saddle. "We've been practising while you've been away at school."

Sonny hugged his friend and pulled her towards the stables. "Let me get Ferro tacked up and we can go for a ride."

"You know that riding Tempesta outside the stables is not possible." Valentina said. "He is a thoroughbred. A very expensive competition horse that you can't take out with the trekking ponies."

"Yes Mamma," said Sonny.

"Ferro can wait. Come with me I have something to

show you." Alina said. It was her turn to pull at Sonny, and she moved him outside and across the road.

"How was it?" Nonna said, as the two friends entered the rear garden.

"Alina was brilliant." Sonny said. "She had complete control of Tempesta."

"The fire forged a bond between the two of them, I think," Nonna said. "They both saved each other's lives."

Fidgeting, Alina was impatient to show Sonny the changes she'd made to her orto.

After he'd complimented her watermelon plants and told her the tidied up olive grove was looking better, he said, "What shall we do now?"

"I haven't finished yet; I have something else to show you." Alina led him by the hand; and as they wandered up the hill to the top of the village, she listened to his stories about life at his school, away from home.

As they walked, she kept stealing glances to the side to take in the changes her friend had undergone away from home. He must be at least two centimetres taller, she thought, and he has hair now on his top lip. Maybe he'll start thinking he's too old to be my friend. The gap between seventeen and fourteen feels wider than it did last year when I was thirteen.

Entering the piazza, Sonny said, "Where are we going?"

"There," Alina pointed to the Pasquini house.

"The house of the angry man?"

"Signor Pasquini isn't so bad. You'll see." Alina marched up the path and knocked on the door.

Nadia opened it and said, "Alina, are you here to see *papà*?" then spotting Sonny said, "Hello Santino, what brings you here? Does your mother need me?"

"No. I've come with Alina."

Sonny's head turned as he heard a man's voice, "Is that Alina?"

Salvatore appeared behind his daughter in the doorway. *"Ciao cara, vieni, entra."*

Alina stepped forward, then beckoned Sonny to follow.

"So who is this?" Salvatore said.

"I am Santino Barone, but my friends call me Sonny."

"Well, I hope after your visit I shall be able to call you that too, young Santino."

"I wanted to show him the garden now Issac, and I have started work."

"Very well, you take him outside and I'll ask Nadia to make drinks."

Outside, Alina laughed when Sonny performed an exaggerated exhalation. "I told you he was okay. Look at the work we have done." She pointed to the weeds and grasses that they had cut down and piled up, ready to burn once dry. She showed him the *frantoio* and the pile of stones they had chosen for the raised bed. As they walked around, she pointed out the plants that years of neglect had covered with weeds.

"It looks much better now." Sonny said.

"We're going to fix the patio so that Salvatore can sit outside."

"That will be good, but won't the weeds come back to take over?"

"Of course they will. But I'm hoping he'll let me come to help keep it like this."

Salvatore's call cut through their conversation as he summoned them inside for glasses of orange juice.

Sitting on the sofa that doubled as Salvatore's bed, Sonny told him about his schooling in Turin. "I only have one year left."

"Then what will you do?"

"Mamma wants me to go to university, but I'm not sure what I want to do with my life."

"You must miss your family when you're in Turin."

"Yes sir. I know it is a privilege to go to my school. It's

very well thought of. My parents say it will give me a good start in life, so it's worth missing my family to be there."

"It shows that they love you very much. Family is important. Without family, you are like a single leaf in a river, separated from your tree and moving without a rudder."

"I have time to think about things before I need to decide on my future, and *Papà* says I can take a year off to come home and ride my horse."

"Sonny is an excellent rider," Alina said.

"Is that so?"

"Yes sir. So people say."

"Please call me Salvatore and if I may, can I call you Sonny?"

Alina watched Sonny's face light up; she knew he was enjoying the conversation, and she listened as he talked about Ferro and his love of being with the horses.

"I think I'd really like to be a jockey. If I can stop growing." Sonny gave a small laugh and continued talking about the three thoroughbreds and how Alina had jumped Tempesta that morning. "She's very tricky," then realising, he corrected himself, "The horse, not Alina."

"I'm not so sure," Salvatore said with a wink.

Alina screwed her face up and then laughed.

"You must always do what makes you happy," Salvatore said, "Like Alina here with her love of plants and gardens. But never lose sight of the important things like love, family and –"

"*Papà*." Nadia interrupted. "You need to rest, and I think we should let Alina and Sonny get on with their day."

Salvatore looked at his daughter and nodded, and after the teenagers had promised to return, he allowed Sonny to shake his hand and everyone said goodbye.

Fifteen

Quindici

Nadia was already waiting for Issac when he arrived at the bar in Guarenna. She looked like a hotel worker, dressed in a black skirt and white blouse. "*Buongiorno*," she said as she opened the pickup's door and climbed into the passenger seat. Issac returned her greeting and as he drove away, she gave him a sideways glance. There was something about the Scotsman that attracted her to him. Was it his pale skin and red hair that intrigued her? It certainly set him apart from the other men she knew. Or could it be the fact he wasn't Italian that made him more attractive to her? *Is that what this is*, she thought, *attraction?* If so, it was something new, something she'd not felt before. She'd had boyfriends in school, but nothing serious and now she found she couldn't stop thinking about Issac although she barely knew him.

"Are you looking forward to working at *Le Stelle*?" He asked her.

"Yes, but I'm a little nervous. I've never worked in a hotel before."

"You'll be fine."

The conversation stalled until Nadia said, "Alina came to visit my father yesterday. She brought her friend Sonny along with her."

"I hope she wasn't bothering him."

"No, not at all. He enjoyed their company. It was nice to see him engaged."

"It must be hard for him, stuck in at home with nothing to do."

Nadia shrugged, and they travelled the rest of the way in

silence until they passed Rosa's little house in Sant'Andrea.

"Look at those rose bushes," Nadia said.

"They belong to Rosa. That's her house."

"My mother loved roses."

"I've seen them in your garden. They need pruning to bring them back to life. Maybe I can do that after I've fixed the patio."

The pickup parked around the side of the hotel and Issac walked Nadia inside and introduced her to Silvana, who checked her watch and said she was expecting her.

"I'll see you later," Issac said and went to find Luca as Nadia watched him disappear out of the main door.

Silvana took Nadia upstairs and introduced her to one of the hotel room stewards, (the job title Rachel preferred to chambermaid). "Martina will show you what to do."

After Silvana had left, Nadia said to the girl, "She looks fierce."

"Silvana is strict but fair," said Martina, leading her into a bedroom. "I'll show you what we need to do."

"Have you worked here long?"

"Almost a year. It's a nice place, not like the hotel I worked at before."

Martina showed Nadia how to refresh two rooms before she allowed her to try one for herself. She was cleaning the bathroom sink when the door opened and Rachel walked in. "Hi Nadia, Sorry I wasn't there to meet you when you arrived. Is Martina looking after you?"

"Yes, signora Balducci."

"Please call me Rachel. We're quite informal here at *Le Stelle*."

Rachel told her a little about the hotel and apologised for the position being temporary. "We could stretch to an extra two or three days if you're available," and asked Nadia if she had any experience of waiting tables.

"I've a little experience. I worked in a bar on the weekends while I was at school."

"Also, I should have asked; do you have plans for Easter?"

"No."

"I'll ask Mirella to come and talk to you later."

After Rachel had gone Martina said, "The hotel is going to be busy during *Pasqua*, every room has been booked."

Secretly, Nadia hoped she'd be downstairs waiting tables rather than refreshing bedrooms.

The morning slipped by quickly, and Nadia enjoyed working with Martina, and at lunchtime, she followed her outside for a break. The experienced room steward showed her around the grounds, pointing out the wedding gazebo and told her that Rachel and her friends were having their Easter dinner in the citrus grove on the Thursday before Good Friday.

Nadia looked down through the colonnade of lemon and orange trees and thought it would be lovely to eat lunch with friends there.

***

With Nadia away from Laroscia for the day, Salvatore thought about the advice he'd given to Sonny the day before. *'You must always do what makes you happy'* and taking his own advice, he ventured outside.

He wheeled himself over to his studio and removed a key from his pocket and unlocked the chain that was fed through the door handles. Once inside, he closed the doors again and just sat looking around.

He took in the wheel and kiln that had stood unused for years. On the far wall was a shelf of powdered glazes and oxides and on the table beneath were unfinished bowls and dishes in various stages of decoration. Over the years of being locked, every surface had accumulated a layer of dust and the pages of Salvatore's sketch pad had yellowed and curled at the edges.

He tried to remember the last time he'd worked in the studio, but his recollection was hazy. All his mind conjured up were incidents of anger and disagreements with Cristina. Arguments about unpaid bills, unfinished orders and mostly his drinking. As his mind filtered these moments through his consciousness, he realised his wife had been right to leave him.

"I was a terrible husband," he said sadly as he slowly moved across the floor to a workbench where his tools lay undisturbed. Brushes and diddlers lay discarded alongside callipers and rubber kidneys.

Again, he tried to recall how he had worked in the studio, even picking up a square diddler sponge and turning it over in his hand, hoping a memory would surface, but nothing came. He moved to his sketchbook and flicked through the drawings, but he couldn't remember sketching any of the floral studies in the pages. And wondered if he still had the talent to draw such intricate designs.

A dish decorated with irises, painted but unglazed, grabbed his attention. Could this be the last piece of pottery he had made before Cristina had walked away and he had closed up the studio and drank himself into oblivion?

His studio had once been full of ambition. A chance to make a name for himself, but he had failed to deliver on his dream and now all he could feel in the room was grief, a sadness that pushed down onto his shoulders, threatening to crush him.

Escaping, he went back outside and was locking up again when he wondered how Nadia was getting on at the hotel. His chest puffed out with pride as he thought about how she had grown into the young woman she was now; life hadn't been easy for her and he knew his actions were mostly to blame, and that was why he had vowed that under no circumstances would he ever let her down. He slipped the keys into his pocket and locked away that promise in his heart as he saw Alina and Sonny come into the piazza carrying trays of what looked like plants.

***

As the afternoon progressed, Nadia continued to refresh guests' bedrooms with Martina, and occasionally they'd stop and look down at the orto where Issac and Luca were working. Martina had admitted she had a crush on Luca and also said she thought Issac was handsome. Nadia, however, kept her own counsel.

Mirella sent a barman up to ask Nadia to come to see her and, following him down the staircase, she saw Rosa talking to Rachel and Louise; they were sitting in the tub chairs and Nadia thought they looked happy as they laughed together.

In the bar, Mirella asked her a handful of questions and then, checking a rota, organised what shifts she could cover.

"Could you carry this bottle over to Rachel, please?" Mirella said, and Nadia wondered if she was being tested.

"Do I have to pour it for them?"

"No, just remove the cork. They'll look after themselves."

Nadia did as instructed, and before she returned to helping Martina, Rachel took her into the kitchen to meet Tiziana and her staff, making her feel important.

***

Rachel topped up everyone's glasses and said, "Rosa, will you be joining us for lunch on Thursday? I hope so." She watched as a smile formed on the old woman's face and her dark eyes shone like the glass stars embedded in the reception area's ceiling.

"You want me? Is it not a lunch for family and close friends?"

"Yes, and you are one of my closest friends, so I'd like you to be there."

"I'll have to select one of my old gowns for such a special occasion."

Rachel glanced across at Louise and smiled. She'd told her friend all about Rosa's extravagant dressing up last summer when she had a photoshoot and interview with the magazine that Gabby worked for.

"It's going to be quite informal. Luca said he'd set up a long table between the citrus trees."

"Oh, that'll be fab," Louise said. "Just like in the movies when they screen Italian dinners with everyone sitting at a long table eating outside."

"Who else is coming?" Rosa asked as she picked up her glass of wine.

"Gabby and Riccardo are coming and they'll bring Issac."

"The new gardener?"

"Yes."

"Can I sit next to him?" Rosa said with a girlish grin.

"Rosa! He's far too young for you." Rachel laughed before she told the old woman the names of the other guests.

"It'll be nice to see Mole and Ivan again," Louise said, "And Sprog… what's her real name again?"

"Olivia."

"That's it. She's quite a handful, I remember."

"She's in double figures now, not so much the little girl."

"I remember Ivan. Another handsome man." Rosa said. "He can sit on my other side."

And laughing, the three women enjoyed their afternoon drinks.

***

That evening, as Issac drove Nadia home, she told him she felt everyone had welcomed her and told him that Silvana had shared a few kind words with her after inspecting her work.

"I'll be working during *Pasqua*," she said. "Mirella has given me five shifts, starting on Thursday."

"That means I can give you a ride, as I'll be going there on Thursday."

"Are you working again?"

"No, I'm invited to lunch with Rachel and Luca's friends."

As the pickup moved towards the crossroads at Guarenna, Issac mentioned the ceramic dish Salvatore had given to Alina. "Your father said it was one he had made."

"It was his dream to design and make pottery. He was good at it, but the business didn't work out."

The pickup pulled into the car park belonging to the bar and Issac asked, "Why didn't the business work out?"

"It just didn't," Nadia said and quickly she opened the door, jumped out and went to collect her scooter.

Watching Issac drive away, she felt angry with herself for her rudeness, but what could she have said? If she told him the truth, would it change their friendship?

Riding into the piazza, Nadia instantly saw pots of flowers outside her house. Frothy stems of cosmos replaced the weeds and marigolds, their yellow and orange heads already blooming made the two window boxes look cheerful.

Her father opened the door for her and she smiled and said, "Is this Alina's doing?"

"Yes, she came this afternoon with Sonny. She removed all the weeds while he washed the pots and together, they refilled them and planted up the display you can see now."

"It looks lovely. What are these?" Nadia pointed to some limp stems planted along the paved driveway.

"Alina said they're cornflowers. She said they need to be watered every day until they perk up."

Nadia wanted to ask her father about the ceramic dish he'd gifted to Alina, but as she hadn't been home, he'd know she had spoken to Issac and for now she wanted to keep her new friendship to herself.

"Come inside, and tell me how your day was," Salvatore said and Nadia noticed he was looking a little less gloomy.

Sixteen

Sedici

After lifting the uneven paving slabs at Salvatore's, Issac unloaded the sand and cement and the work on the patio began in earnest. The day was cool, a cloudy sky hung over Laroscia keeping the sun at bay, making the task easier.

Salvatore had given Issac permission to do what he thought would work and as he levelled the ground, ready for footings, Nadia made coffee for the two men.

Sitting in the doorway, Salvatore said, "Did you see the flowers that Alina planted for us?"

"Yes," Issac said. "They certainly brighten up the front of the villa."

Nadia carried the drinks into the *salotto*, and Issac joined Salvatore. As the men drank their coffee, Nadia went into the garden. They watched as she leant over an unruly border and plucked an emerging rosebud, its colour showing through the tight petals.

"Do you think you could salvage any of the roses?" asked Salvatore.

"I think I could try. They might not flower for the first year after a hard pruning."

"I wish I'd not let the garden become so overgrown. I've found some photographs to show you." Sal pointed to the table where the dish he'd gifted to Alina had sat. Issac went over and collected them and flicked through, looking at the neat and well-maintained outdoor space. "Take them with you and look at them at your leisure."

Nadia returned and saw the photographs and asked, "Will you try to recreate the garden as it once was?"

"I don't want it to be how it was," Salvatore said. "I'd

like Issac to design a new layout. Something new with no memories." Salvatore put down his coffee and reached inside his pocket and removed an envelope and handed it to Issac. "I know it's not much, but I'd like to contribute to the restoration."

Issac looked inside the envelope at the few euro notes and had a feeling that he'd offend Salvatore if he declined the offer, so thanked him, slid the photographs beside the cash and put them away.

The light was fading after Issac had laid the final paver and as he washed his hands, he could hear Nadia singing in the kitchen. He looked inside and, for a few seconds, just watched as she prepared the evening meal. She'd tied her dark hair back, revealing her neck, and Issac found himself transfixed at the sight of her golden-coloured skin.

Turning around, she looked shocked to see him staring at her and he faltered and, tripping over his words; he made a clumsy attempt at asking if she'd need a lift to the hotel the following day.

"Oh… Yes… The lunch in the garden." It was Nadia's turn to stumble over her words. "Can we meet at the bar again?"

Issac agreed to keep their arrangement as before, especially after accepting the payment from Salvatore. The last thing he wanted to do was upset him.

"The patio is looking good," Salvatore said, coming into the kitchen. He fixed his gaze on Nadia and Issac hoped he wasn't suspicious.

"Let it settle for a few days before you go on it." Issac said. "I'll come back to finish the raised bed. Thanks for the photographs. I'll study them and return them after *Pasqua*."

He excused himself and didn't feel like he'd taken another breath until he'd turned over the engine of the pickup and headed back to Perano.

Gabby was preparing dinner as Issac entered the kitchen.

"There's some wine open." She nodded towards the bottle on the table. "I needed some for the sauce. That's my excuse and I'm sticking to it." She gave a small laugh, then said, "How was your day?"

"It was good. I laid all the pavers for Salvatore's new patio, so it'll be safer for him in his wheelchair."

"Riccardo's deciding on some wine to take tomorrow. He spends longer picking that, than I do choosing what to wear."

"I'll just grab a shower and get changed before dinner."

"Okay. It'll will be another half hour yet."

After dinner, Issac laid out the photographs and was studying them when Riccardo sat down opposite him. "I wanted to say thank you for offering to be the designated driver tomorrow."

"It's the least I can do after you donated the sand and cement I used today. I wanted to ask if I could borrow your brush cutter again after Easter. I want to cut back the weeds in the Pasquini olive grove."

"So, you're continuing with the project?"

"Yes. Salvatore gave me some cash towards the job, hardly enough to cover the costs, but I want to do this both for him and for my business plan."

Issac pushed the photographs over the table and together they looked and discussed them over a fine red from the Di Renzo vineyard.

"Did you speak with Seppe?" Gabby said, coming into the room.

"Yes. He's expecting us." Riccardo said, "He told me not to fuss, he'd walk, but I told him we'd collect him."

Issac remembered he'd promised to pick up Nadia and as he told the others, he explained about their clandestine arrangement. He watched Gabby raise her eyebrows to Riccardo. She made no comment, just said, "I'm looking forward to it and we finally get to meet Ben."

Seventeen

Diciassette

Thursday morning delivered a clear blue sky that brought out the birds who sang in the olives and the bees that buzzed among the spring flowers that reached up towards the high yellow sun that warmed the Abruzzese countryside. It was a perfect day for *all'aperto* dining. Gabby watched Riccardo as he watered his vines and smiled when she remembered she had once used the phrase eating *al fresco* for their picnic beside Lake Bomba and he'd explained that although universally people use it to mean eating outside; 'in fresh air' in Italian slang it actually means 'in prison' and being in prison wasn't something she wanted to experience on a day like today. She looked at the outfit she'd chosen for the day, a long-sleeved blouse in aquamarine, and a pair of navy culottes for protection from the early mosquitos that seemed attracted to her ankles. Riccardo had chosen jeans and a shirt; free from his legal practise, he tended towards informal attire mostly and not only did he look more relaxed, but Gabby also felt he had become the same.

Coming into the kitchen, she saw Issac filling the Moka pot, and she placed her coffee cup next to his and smiled.

"Cornetto?" he said.

"Not for me. I need to save space for lunch. You know how long an Italian celebration meal can last?"

"I need something or I might fade away," he joked as he dropped a sweetener into Gabby's cup.

"Rachel said the main course will be lamb, as it usually is at Easter."

"I expect Tiziana will deliver many fabulous dishes

today." Issac poured three small cups of coffee and said he'd take one out to Riccardo before he went for a shower. "Will Rachel expect us all to dress up?" he asked at the doorway.

"Smart casual should be okay," replied Gabby. Unable to resist it, she looked at the apricot cornetto Issac had laid out for himself and picked it up, took a bite and carried it outside to sit and take in the morning.

She liked the regimented vines that were now sporting their young foliage. There was something about the ordered rows that pleased her. It suited the way she worked, methodically and with care. She gave Nolan a thought; thinking he'd have liked to be here today, probably dressed in something as inappropriate as his conversation.

"You look miles away," Riccardo said, placing his empty coffee cup down beside her.

"I was just thinking I must call Nolan soon. I need to check in with the features team, too. But it'll keep until after the Easter weekend."

"Come with me," He held out a hand, she took it and together they walked around to the land that Issac had cleaned up and behind the newly planted vines facing the view of the town in the distance she saw a small square space that was marked with wooden pegs. "Issac is going to build us a small, covered seating area here." Gabby shook her head slightly and Riccardo explained, "It won't be as grand as the gazebo at *Le Stelle*, but I thought we could have somewhere away from the front of the house and back from the road. Somewhere special just for the two of us."

Gabby reached up and kissed him. "You old romantic."

"Who are you calling old?" He slapped her on the bottom and, running away, she laughed as he chased her back to the front of their villa.

***

Most of the guests had assembled in the hotel's reception area when the Barone family arrived with Alina and her grandmother. Rachel left Luca's side and walked over to welcome them. After customary air kisses, she turned to Alina and her nonna and said. "I'm so pleased you both came."

"Thank you for the invite," Nonna said. "It was most kind of you to think of us."

"Hello trouble," Luca said, joining them.

"I'm not trouble," Alina laughed before she asked him how his watermelons were coming along.

"Do you think I'd be crazy enough to let you see them?" he said, tapping the side of his head.

Rachel watched as her guests mingled and introduced themselves. The atmosphere was buoyant and occasionally she would hear Louise's laughter cut through the conversation.

Issac was talking with Ennio and Sonny Barone and Alina had made friends with Sprog, who was still happy to be known by her nickname.

Penny was chatting with Mole and Ivan and Rachel thought it odd to see her without *Sale* her little dog, who had passed away in the winter at the grand age of fourteen.

In the doorway stood two men, one tall with an enormous moustache covering half of his face and the other small and rotund, with shiny black eyes and a rosy complexion.

"Massimo. Cosmo." Rachel called, moving towards the brothers. "It's so good to see you again. We're both so pleased you could come today." The builder brothers hugged her, and both placed a kiss on each of her cheeks, saying they had been happy to receive their invites. "My wife sends her apologies," Cosmo said, "She's away caring for her mother at present. But she sends her love."

With everyone finally assembled, Rachel called out to get their attention and told them all, "Mirella is serving prosecco in the gazebo."

***

Louise thought the table setting was just like it would be if their lunch was being featured in a movie, a rom-com maybe. On the grass, between the citrus trees, a long table with a crisp white tablecloth was waiting for them, with the plates and glassware already laid out. A little further on, Mirella was waiting under the gazebo. A prosecco cork popped, and the wine fizzed in flutes as Nadia handed glasses to the guests. "This is perfect," she said to Rachel.

As everyone chatted, Mirella opened two bottles of red wine and two of white and Nadia placed them on the table for the lunch guests to help themselves and a waiter appeared and whispered something to Rachel, who asked everyone to take their places.

Rosa kept her promise and made sure she had Issac sitting next to her and on her other side was Alina's nonna; the old women had much to catch up on.

Louise saw Ben leaning into Luca and whispering and she wondered what they were talking about. It would have to wait as the waiters had arrived with plates of antipasti. Once everyone was served, the conversation became punctuated with the sounds of cutlery on china as the party enjoyed the assorted cheeses and cured meats.

Luca and Riccardo took charge of the wine, one serving red, the other white. After the antipasti, everyone was served a small portion of *pallotte cacio e uova*, the traditional Abruzzese cheese balls in tomato sauce, before the waiters brought out dishes of ox cheek ravioli with sage butter.

"This is divine," Gabby said, and everyone agreed with her.

Today is a run through for the Easter lunches we'll be serving. Tiziana has been making ravioli for the past twenty-four hours.

"So you're saying we're guinea pigs?" said Louise.

"Who cares when the food's this good?" said Riccardo, who gave his uncle Seppe a wink across the table.

When the waiters had cleared the diners' plates, they had a brief respite between courses and their conversations mixed with the soft music that was coming from the gazebo's sound system.

Again Louise saw Ben whispering to Luca and this time she said, "What are you two cooking up?"

"Nothing," Ben said a little too quickly before he diverted his attention towards his empty glass.

Silvana appeared to ask if the main course could be served and, within minutes, plates of roasted lamb with garlic and rosemary appeared. Penny was sitting beside Valentina and grilled her about the stables. Louise nudged Rachel and whispered, "She never takes a day off, does she?"

"Penny is constantly in work mode. Ennio and Valentina want to extend the stables and add a bar, a restaurant and a children's area. Penny's probably looking for a potential business opportunity."

Dolce arrived and disappeared in seconds and Nadia and Mirella delivered bottles of digestivi to the table as the waiters cleared the empty *zabaglione* glasses.

The three older guests retired to the comfy chairs that were set up around a small table, while along with Sonny and Olivia, Alina ran off to the bottom of the garden.

While people enjoyed their after-dinner drinks, Ben left the table and stood beside the gazebo with Luca. They were talking animatedly and nodding their heads. Louise nudged Rachel and said, "What's going on with those two? They've been whispering to each other most of the morning."

"Probably talking about man stuff."

I don't think so, Louise thought. *Ben has no interest in gardening and Luca's never so much as picked up a gaming control.*

The two men broke apart, and Ben walked to Louise and held out his hand to her. "Will you come with me?"

"Where?"

"To the beach."

"We can't leave. It would be rude."

"Just for a few minutes, then we can come back." She watched as he looked back over to Luca, who rolled his eyes.

Something is going on, she thought. "Very well, but just for a few minutes."

They walked down the lane in silence, past Rosa's cottage and on to the steps that led to the private beach.

Standing on the sand, with the almost silent hush of lazy waves, Ben took Louise's hand. "I have a confession," he said.

"Yes," Louise replied frostily.

"I didn't miss my flight the other day I had to change it for a reason."

"What reason?"

"This one," she watched as Ben removed a small box from his pocket and went down on one knee. "The jeweller was a day late resizing this." He opened the box, and the sunlight caught the diamond sending a coloured spark upwards. Louise's heart leapt in her chest as he proposed to her and as he slid the ring onto her finger, applause sounded, and she turned to see her friends clapping at the top of the steps.

"Is this what you've been whispering to Luca about?"

"Yes, he knew. I asked him to keep it a secret. I was going to propose in the gazebo, but he thought it best to do it here, away from the other lunch guests."

On the walk back to the hotel, Rachel, Mole and Gabby clustered around Louise, looking at the ring.

Arriving back at the table, Rosa called over to Louise, "Well, let's finally see the ring."

"Rosa knew?"

"Yes," said Ben with a shrug of his shoulders.

***

News of the proposal spread through the party until it was Valentina's turn to congratulate the couple and gaze at the diamond on Louise's finger. "Ennio," she called to her husband. "This calls for champagne." Instantly Mirella left the party to fetch a bottle and Valentina turned to Nadia and said, "Are you enjoying working here?"

"Yes, Signora. It's only for a few days. It won't stop me working for you."

"I'm not criticising Nadia. Tell me, how are things at home?"

"Avvocato Zampieri has said he can't represent my father any longer in his compensation claim."

"What will he do now?"

"I don't know. I'm worried he'll slip further into his depression."

"Maybe things will change soon."

"I hope so. At least with Issac working on the garden, it's given him something else to focus on."

Hearing Nadia explain about the arrangement her father had made with Issac gave Valentina an idea.

***

As Valentina walked away, Rachel joined Nadia and asked if she'd enjoyed her shift at the hotel.

"Yes, Signora."

"Please, call me Rachel."

"Yes, Rachel."

"I've noticed you and Issac can't stop looking at each other."

"I'm sorry…"

"It's okay. Are you seeing each other romantically?"

"No Sig... Rachel, we're just friends. It felt strange serving him over lunch, though."

"Well, why don't you join him for a drink?"

"I couldn't. I'm working."

A champagne cork popped loudly, and everyone cheered.

"Yes, you can. Mirella will take care of everything for now."

Eighteen

Diciotto

A week had passed since the Easter lunch and Gabby and Riccardo had spent most of the time at home in Perano. Issac had divided his attention between the vineyard's needs and the Pasquini garden. He'd also taken Nadia out one evening but stressed it wasn't a date, which led to him being ribbed by Gabby, but joking aside, Riccardo could see their houseguest was smitten. This morning, he was in the kitchen taking a telephone call, with Gabby hovering in the background listening in.

"Good news?" she asked as the call ended. "I heard the name Barone a few times. Was it about the permissions for the stables' intended extension and land purchase?"

"I think Ennio will see it that way. We can complete his land purchase now that the *comune* has given permission for the restaurant and children's area."

The conversation faltered when Gabby's phone rang and it was Riccardo's turn to hear a one-sided conversation.

"That was Rachel." Gabby said, ending the call. "She and Luca have been busy looking after the guests who were staying for *Pasqua* and Tiziana's menu was a success, with quite a few people booking again for next year."

"That's brilliant news."

"She's on her way over with Louise. They're going into Lanciano to do some shopping and I said I'd go with them. Is that okay?"

"Sure. I'll take a drive over to see Ennio and Valentina."

While Gabby got changed to go out, Riccardo called Ennio to give him the good news and said he'd call over.

Arriving at the stables he smiled when he spotted Issac

talking to Nadia at the gate, "Thought you were supposed to working in Salvatore's garden," he called to him good-naturedly.

"I am I just needed to speak with Nadia about a planting scheme."

"Planting scheme. Is that what they call it nowadays?"

Ennio came out of the villa to greet Riccardo and invited Issac to join them for a drink, "You might be happy with Riccardo's news, I know I am."

Nadia offered to fetch the drinks and disappeared inside and returned with glasses and three bottles of Nastro and left the men to their conversation.

Issac listened as Ennio told him the council had granted permission for his project to go ahead and Riccardo explained that if the notary had an appointment free, they could complete the land sale by the end of the week.

"How will this involve me?" Issac said.

"Because the land will need to be cleared. I thought of you working for Salvatore Pasquini. If there are any plants or shrubs you could use, then you're welcome to them before the bulldozers come in."

Issac looked across at the land earmarked for the new café-bar and asked about the olives.

"They'll need to be moved; we'll probably keep half of them and what's left you're welcome to," said Ennio. "Why don't you take a look and see if there's anything you can recycle."

Issac thanked signor Barone, and taking his bottle of beer he walked over to survey the land.

Riccardo remained with Ennio and together they arranged a meeting with a notary in Lanciano and called the seller to make sure he'd be there on the day. Riccardo was walking back to his car when Valentina came into the yard and asked if she could speak with him. "It's a little sensitive," she said.

Riccardo listened as she told him about her

conversations with Nadia and her father's predicament and asked if he could help.

"I'm not sure. I've never met the man and he may take offence if I offer my services."

"Please excuse me for a moment." Valentina went back into the villa and ten minutes later, she returned with Nadia. "I have explained my idea to Nadia, and she says she will introduce you to her father."

"At lunchtime, I go home to fix him something to eat," Nadia said to Riccardo. "I can speak to him then and let you know what he's said."

"Is Issac working for your father this afternoon?"

"Yes. He's going to have lunch with us, too."

"Very well you can send your reply home with him this evening."

Nadia thanked Riccardo and went back inside, and as he opened his car door Valentina said. "She is such a sweet girl. I'd really like to help her, so I will cover the cost of your consultation."

"That's very generous of you."

***

The three friends strolled down *Corso Trento e Trieste*, their heels clicking on the geometric black-and-white tiles. "You'd think I'd got used to the hot weather by now," Rachel said, removing a battery powered fan from her handbag. "Let's find somewhere to have a drink, preferably in the shade."

"*Caffe ai Portici?*" Gabby offered.

"Perfect, we can sit under cover in the entrance and watch the world go by."

"Better still, I can show my ring off as people come and go," said Louise, flashing her diamond in the sunshine.

They chose a table in the walkway and while Gabby went to the bar to order drinks, Louise leant into Rachel and said. "I've been meaning to ask, rather than go back to England with Ben tomorrow; would you mind if I stayed on for another week, maybe two?"

"Of course you can," Rachel said with a smile. She was more than happy to have her madcap friend staying with her for longer.

The two friends hugged each other as Gabby returned to the table. "What's going on here?"

"Louise is staying for a couple more weeks." Rachel said.

"What about work?"

"I've got my laptop with me and I can move any meetings to video calls."

"Well, it's a good job I ordered a bottle of prosecco. Now we have something to celebrate."

As a waitress poured their drinks at the table, she spotted Louise's ring and hearing she'd only recently become engaged complimented her before leaving the women to raise their glasses in a toast to staying on in Italy.

"Have you and Ben set a date yet?" Gabby asked.

"We've not got that far. I think I need more time to get used to the idea of taking Ben on. We've not finished his training yet." Louise laughed. "I'm sure I'd be better off with a rescue dog."

"Stop it." Rachel said, joining in with the laughter, "You know you love him."

"I must do, or I'm as mad as he is. No sensible woman would take him on."

With the laughter and friendly conversation fizzing like their drinks, the thoughts of shopping faded away and the three friends ordered a second bottle.

***

Nadia was nervous. *How will father react to a stranger hearing his personal business?* She thought as she poured dried pasta into the pan of simmering water.

"Nadia?"

"Yes *Papà?*"

"Come see what Issac has done with the patio."

Nadia left the kitchen and walked into the *salotto*. Her father was outside in his chair on the patio, pointing to a raised bed that Issac had planted up.

"There's basil and oregano for the kitchen, and along the edge he's put in some lettuces for us. What do you think?"

"These are pretty," she said, running her hands over an orange nasturtium.

"They are nice and peppery in salads," Issac said.

"The leaves?"

"And the flowers. I thought a little salad and herb bed would suffice until I've created the mini orto on the other side of the garden."

Nadia smiled. She was happy with how things were progressing, both in the garden and with her and Issac's friendship.

After she'd set the dining table and took a bottle of lemonade from the fridge and set it down, Nadia asked them to come inside for lunch.

Pointing to the steaming bowl in the centre of the table, she said, "*Tortiglioni con ragù di salsiccia.*"

"Sausage ragù," Issac said washing his hands at the sink, "Perfect food after a morning gardening."

Nadia placed a bowl of green salad next to a small jar with oil and chillies. "There's homemade *olio Santo* too, if you like it spicy."

"Holy oil, did you make this?" Issac said, opening the jar and taking a sniff of the marinated chilli peppers. "It smells funky, but delicious."

"No *papà* makes it. What is funky?"

"It means warm and comforting."

"Warm and comforting is one way to describe it," Salvatore said.

Nadia laughed after Issac had added oil to his lunch and gulped cold lemonade to quench the fire on his tongue.

With lunch over, Issac returned to the garden, and as Nadia washed the dishes, she spoke to her father. She explained about Riccardo. "He's a lawyer; Avvocato di Renzo. He works for Ennio Barone and has offered to speak to you about your claim."

"Have you discussed my situation with signor Barone?"

"His wife saw I was upset about the letter from Zampieri. She asked what was wrong. I'm sorry, *papà*, I didn't tell her intentionally."

"And what does this... Avvocato di Renzo think he can do?"

"He just said he'd speak with you. No promises. But it can't hurt to get a second opinion."

"Second opinion? Is this what Valentina Barone has told you to say?"

"No, *papà*." Nadia's shoulders began to rise and fall. She knew she'd upset her father and, facing away, she let the tears fill her eyes.

"Very well, *mia cara*." Salvatore's voice softened. "I will speak with this other lawyer."

Nineteen

Diciannove

Riccardo followed Issac to Laroscia, and after shaking hands with Salvatore, he followed him inside his home. "Do you mind if we speak privately?"

"Of course," Riccardo said.

Salvatore opened the door of the *porte-finestre* and asked Issac if he could give them some privacy.

"I can go to the bar in Guarenna. Shall I take Nadia too?" Salvatore hesitated and his daughter interrupted.

"Yes, I'll keep you company. You can tell me about your other plans for the garden." She leant in and kissed her father on the cheek and told him she had already made coffee for him and Riccardo.

Once they were alone, Salvatore poured the coffee and started telling Riccardo about the accident.

"It was late afternoon, January, so the light was fading and I was driving on Contrada Brecciaio. Do you know it?"

Riccardo nodded.

"I stopped at the bar…" Salvatore noticed the lawyer's eyebrow rise. Voluntarily or not, he was used to this reaction. "I went to the bathroom and bought myself a coffee. When I left, the road appeared clear and so I drove out of the car park. Suddenly, a car swerved across the road and collided with me head on."

"And this other car was I'm assuming on the wrong side of the road?"

"Yes. The carabinieri confirmed this."

"This sounds like a fairly straightforward claim. Why has it faltered?"

"My previous lawyer says it's because of my history."

"Your history?"

"It's something that is behind me now." Salvatore thought Riccardo looked uncomfortable and guessed he'd heard stories. "I used to drink," he said, then quickly backed up his statement with, "A carabiniere breathalysed me while I was trapped inside my car and I was clean."

"Had your drinking previously been a problem?"

"Yes," Salvatore's voice was almost inaudible. He felt his shame flushing his face with redness and diverted his eyes towards the floor. "You don't need to know the full story, but the drink ruined my life. I'm not proud of it and I'm sober now."

"And you're worried the insurance company will use this against you?"

"Yes. Zampieri said it could affect my claim."

"A good lawyer would use the medical evidence from the crash to argue this is irrelevant."

Salvatore lifted his eyes and looked at Riccardo. "So it wouldn't be applicable?"

"Not if the roadside breath test and the blood tests refute you had any alcohol in your system at the time of the accident."

A silence fell on the men, and Riccardo stood up, offered to make a fresh pot of coffee, and left the room.

When Riccardo returned, he saw Salvatore looking out of the window. "Is Issac making a good job of the patio repair?"

"Yes, you can go outside and look if you like. He's also built a salad and herb bed."

"I can see from here. It looks good. Issac also works at my vineyard."

"Vineyard? I thought you were a lawyer."

"I am, but currently, I'm trying to build up my old family business, so I'm only taking on a handful of legal cases at the moment."

"Would you be able to help me?" Salvatore said, and as

an afterthought, "I doubt it, because I couldn't pay you until the settlement."

"If there is a settlement."

"Yes, exactly."

***

Nadia chose a table in the covered area outside the main bar, here she could look out of the windows and watch for anyone passing on the road outside. She was acutely aware that her father had become protective of her since her mother had left and his asking her to spread her wings had become a contradiction that perplexed her. Looking across at Issac as he ordered drinks at the bar, she smiled inside. His simple manner differed from the other boys she'd been friends with previously, and she enjoyed being with him. After growing up with an intense father, Issac had a calmness that was different, and she liked different.

He walked over to the table, followed by the barman, who placed snacks on the table and said hello to her and enquired after her father before leaving Issac to take his seat.

She reached across and took an olive from the dish and popped it into her mouth.

"It's nice in here." Issac said.

"Yes."

He picked up a small slice of bread covered with a slice of salami. He slid the small *bruschetta* into his mouth whole and after swallowing, he said, "I love how in Italy, bars provide these nibbles."

"Nibbles?" Nadia asked him.

"Bar snacks."

"Oh, yes."

Why had things suddenly become uncomfortable? The conversation stilted. They sat in silence for a while, both looking out over the crossroads until the buzzing of a yellow *ape* disturbed the silence as it arrived in the car park. They watched as a small man in overalls got out and walked into the bar and bought himself a bottled beer, and after giving them a nod, settled down to look up at the television streaming a game of football in the bar. "There's never any sound," Issac said and Nadia looked at him confused. "Television's in bars and restaurants. The volume is muted, so there's never any sound."

"I've never thought about that. It's something that's always been there. Would it be silent in Scotland?"

"Never, it'd be loud and everyone watching would get involved with the game. Football in Scottish bars is a very vocal affair."

"Do you like football?"

"I can take it or leave it." He must have noticed her forehead crinkle with confusion and added, "I'm not an ardent fan."

"You have so many phrases and words that are unusual to me."

"Would you prefer if we spoke in Italian?"

"Please. People tell me my English is good, but I don't know."

"It's probably on a par with my Italian."

"Par?" she asked, and as he explained, they both laughed and she realised the uncomfortable air had thawed.

"Tell me about Scotland," she asked him.

"It's cold compared to Abruzzo."

"As cold as our winters?"

"Colder. Especially in the highlands. But it's a beautiful country, very green with wide open spaces, and very rugged in places."

"I think I'd like to see that."

"Maybe I'll take you one day."

Nadia's heart stopped for a second. Had he meant to say that? Did he mean it?

"What about you?" his question unravelled her thoughts,

and she returned to the bar in Guarenna.

"Me?"

"Yes, what was it like growing up in Laroscia? It must have differed from my life in Scotland."

"I guess so. Growing up, everything was the same as other Italian families. School, church, looking after the land."

"Perhaps all that separates us is climate and culture and underneath it all, everyone is actually the same." Issac lifted his empty glass and Nadia nodded as he went back to the bar to fetch more drinks.

Are we basically all the same? She thought, *Was my life similar?* As she contemplated growing up, she looked over at Issac and wondered if she could open up to him.

He returned with the drinks and said he needed a loo break and watching him walk away gave her the opportunity to study him further.

He was about thirty centimetres taller than she was and he was broad; much wider across the shoulders than any Italian male. A carpet of sandy-coloured hair covered his powerfully built arms. Below his slim waist, wide hips balanced above equally muscled legs, and Nadia thought his temperament was contrary to his structure. But one thing she was certain of, was that she could trust him.

He returned to the table and asked about her thoughts. "You seemed to be in another world."

"I was thinking. We are as different to each other as we are similar."

"An oxymoron."

"Yes. I assume everyone growing up has the same wants and needs. Similar desires and emotions. It's just that life can deliver circumstances that change those things we all share."

He was looking at her more intently and she took a chance and said. "I thought I was the same as all my friends until I discovered I was different." She took a sip of her orange soda and said, "That difference is why I rarely drink alcohol."

"I had noticed that."

"I was around fourteen when I noticed my friends' parents differed from mine. My mother was sad and angry in equal measure, and my father was angry and detached."

She saw his smile loosen as his face straightened out. "You don't have to explain anything to me."

"I want to. If I don't say it now, I never will."

Issac listened as she told him about the constant tension of growing up in a home with a father who drank heavily and a mother that was growing to resent him.

"Eventually she walked away. She left us."

"Didn't she think about taking you with her?"

"She was too fragile to care for me. I was angry with her at first, but now I understand. We've talked it through and I accept her reasons."

"So, you still see your mother?"

"No, I haven't seen her for two-years, but we speak over the telephone. Please don't tell my father he doesn't know."

"Of course."

The conversation stalled, and she looked out of the window before she realised Issac hadn't spoken because he was waiting for her to speak.

"I'd come home from school and find him sleeping off his habit. I looked after the both of us and no matter how awful I felt, I couldn't bear the thought of walking away from him. After the accident and while my father was in hospital, I spent my days clearing out the bottles of grappa and whisky that were around the house. The amount I found was astounding. They were down the backs of chairs and in the kitchen, hidden in boxes of cereal. Drinking made him a complicated man, but he was my father, and I loved him."

She fell silent again, then said, "I still do."

***

"I'm sorry I cannot offer you anything stronger than coffee or chamomile tea," Salvatore said. "Since my return from hospital, we have had what the doctors term 'a dry house'."

"There's no need for apologies."

"I blame myself for the predicament I find myself in."

"You can't hold yourself responsible just because you bought a coffee. It sounds like what you have told me already, that the accident wasn't your fault."

Riccardo watched as Salvatore's eyes rolled up in their sockets. *He's remembering,* he thought. They both looked out at the new patio, making small talk about the work that Issac had completed when Salvatore said, "Cristina loved this garden."

"Your wife?"

"Yes. It was so important to her. She made it beautiful and because of me, it fell into ruin."

"Why do you think that?"

"Because I drove her away." He moved his wheelchair closer to Riccardo and said, "People in this village know all about the fights that went on almost daily between us."

"It takes two people to have an argument."

"Believe me when I was drinking, I could argue with my reflection."

"I loved her though…"

His voice trailed off again and Riccardo said softly, "I don't doubt it."

Salvatore snapped out of his apathy, straightened up and said, "Cristina supported me, gave me the space to chase my dream. She looked after the land while all I wanted to do was create beautiful things. I had a deep desire to develop a successful business that would support us all." He paused.

Reaching over, he lifted a small trinket box and passed it to Riccardo. "I made this. I made many things and at first sales were good. Of course, I celebrated my success and day by day my celebrations became more important to me than having my hands in clay."

Riccardo turned the porcelain box over in his hands. Decorated with small purple-pink flowers, it was exquisite.

"Cyclamen," Salvatore said.

"So what happened?"

"I had secured an order with two shops, one on the coast in Montesilvano, another in a souvenir shop down in San Salvo. Christina said it was a start and we should plan to expand into L'Aquila and beyond. But the drinking meant my first order was late and eventually the second business owner cancelled his too."

"Did you look for other buyers?"

"Cristina did. One day she bought a shop owner to my studio…" Riccardo noticed the tilt of Salvatore's head towards the building attached to his villa. "They came in hoping to see my wares, and what they found was a drunk lying on the floor surrounded by broken pottery. That was the start of the end… And do you know something? I don't blame her."

***

Issac enjoyed his time with Nadia, he found as she spoke, he gazed at her for a few seconds longer than was necessary. What was it about this Italian girl that entranced him? It was almost as if she had bewitched him. He pulled himself out of his temporary fugue and said, "Shall we go back? I think Riccardo will have finished speaking with your father."

"Okay," she said, "Excuse me for a moment. I'll just use the ladies' room."

Issac watched her as she crossed the room. He'd appreciated her honesty and a feeling of warmth spread through him, a feeling he'd never experienced before.

He picked up their glasses and returned them to the bar, where the barman thanked him and said, "I'm not sure it's a good idea for you to be out with Nadia."

Shocked by the barman's directness, Issac asked him why. "Her family has seen much trouble in the past. I'd be careful if I were you. Her father is not a man to lock horns with."

The facility door opened and Nadia walked towards the bar and Issac leant in and said, "I'll take my chances."

Twenty

Venti

Salvatore was sitting on the patio. The sky above him was forget-me-not blue and despite the sound of Issac's brush cutter slicing through the undergrowth, everything about the morning was pleasant. He was watching as Alina lined up pots of small lavender cuttings on the wall of the raised bed. "Luca at *Le Stelle* showed me last year how to make these from bigger plants." She told him, "I took these new cuttings from my nonna's lavender bush at the front of our house and now I have twenty new plants to bring for your garden." She pointed to where the patio ended. "Issac is going to make a path there and plant two rows on either side."

"Has anyone ever told you that you're a very kind girl?"

"Oh yes, all the time," laughed Alina, and Salvatore joined her.

"I'll fetch some drinks and you can tell me all about your garden."

Salvatore returned with three plastic tumblers and a bottle of cola and Alina poured the drinks as he called Issac over.

"Alina tells me you're extending a path from the patio."

"Yes," said Issac, "It will make it easier for you to get to the border, where the flower garden meets the olives and woodland beyond."

"I was telling signor Pasquini about the lavender edging."

"Please Alina, call me Sal."

Alina smiled; she liked it when adults treated her like a grownup.

"What will happen to the roses?"

"I've checked over the area I'm cutting back and marked off where they are. I want to clear the weeds before I attempt to move the roses, I think I can save."

"Where will you move them to?" Salvatore asked, and Issac removed a folded sheet of paper from his overalls. He spread it out on the patio table and showed Alina and Salvatore his initial design for the garden.

Issac pointed out the layout he'd come up with, explaining it could change as the work progressed. "I'm looking to make a feature of the old press, maybe create a ruin and repurpose the millstone for elsewhere."

"Surely that will be too much work for one person?"

"I've a pair of builders who are going to help me. Two brothers."

"What's this?" Alina said, pointing to a red X marked at the end of the path.

"I'm not sure yet," Issac said. "See here," he pointed to an L shaped bed by the proposed ruin, "Here I want to build another raised bed with a seating area."

While they studied Issac's drawing, Salvatore glanced across at Alina. She was looking at Issac with a sparkle in her eyes and he assumed she had a crush on the gardener.

Everyone looked up as Nadia appeared in the doorway, holding up a clear storage container. "Valentina has sent over some cake for you all. Cook made it yesterday, and she didn't want it to go to waste."

She exited into the kitchen, with Salvatore following her. "More charity," he said in a hushed tone, keeping his remark away from the people outside.

"It's not charity. Cook was going to throw it away and Valentina asked if Issac was working here and so sent it over for you to have after lunch."

Salvatore huffed; his face fixed with a scowl.

"*Papà*, you really need to stop being ungrateful."

"Ungrateful? I don't think I'm ungrateful."

"Maybe that's not the correct word. Suspicious is probably what I ought to have said."

"How can I not be? All of this attention lately has overwhelmed me."

"I get that *papà*, but honestly, people are just being kind."

"But why me?"

"Why not?" Nadia kissed the top of his head and after handing him some cake plates, she wheeled him back out to the others.

Later that afternoon, after Nadia had returned to the stables, Alina was sitting picking out weeds from an area Issac had already cleared for a pergola that would support the purple bougainvillaea that had grown into a rampant tangle beside the newly built raised bed.

"I wish I had your energy," Salvatore said to Alina.

"Nonna says I'm like a dervish. But I don't know what one of those is."

"I guess similar to a dynamo." He smiled when her brow creased with confusion.

"Nonna says I should never let my disability slow me down, so I don't."

"Yes, I've seen that. And I heard about how you rescued the horses from the fire at the stables."

"It wasn't easy. I was in hospital afterwards and I didn't like it very much."

"I was in hospital too after my accident and I didn't like it very much either."

"Nonna told me about the crash. Did it hurt?" Alina's face creased, and she shook her head. "What a silly question. Of course, it must have hurt."

"Actually, not as much as you'd think. The doctors told me I was in shock when I went to the emergency room in Lanciano." He noticed she was looking at where his leg had once been and knew she was forming a question.

"What is it like not having your leg?"

"It's strange and upsetting, and I don't think I've got used to it yet."

"It's the same leg as mine."

Alina stood up and brushed the dirt from her hands, and Salvatore listened as she told him about her condition. "The doctors' call it hemiatrophy. I'm used to it now. Sonny says it's what makes me, me. Makes me unique. Just like how being one-legged makes you, you." Salvatore smiled at her unfiltered remark and thought, *If only I felt that way.* "You'll see. It just might take some time." Alina smiled back and nodded her head to confirm her statement.

"What might take some time?" Issac said, joining them and putting a hand on Alina's shoulder before taking the bucket of weeds from her.

"We're just talking about the garden," Alina said, giving Salvatore a conspiratorial wink.

Issac walked away to drop the weeds on the bonfire he was building at the top of the garden and after thinking, *Alina, you're a clever girl*, Salvatore said, "I can see that you're good friends with Issac."

"I am. I like him. He's a talented gardener."

"It's good to have friends."

"Yes, but he's not my best friend. That's Santino Barone. Me and Sonny are BFFs."

"BFFs?" Salvatore asked, confused by her young parlance.

Alina giggled and said, "Best friends forever." Salvatore nodded his understanding.

"Well, it's obvious that Issac likes you, too."

"I guess so. But I think he likes Nadia more."

Salvatore was about to ask her to elaborate when Issac returned and said, "Come on Squirt, it's time I took you home."

"Who are you calling, squirt?" Alina said with her hands on her hips.

Issac told Salvatore he'd return in a day's time as he was

working at the vineyard the following day.

After loading his tools into the pickup, he climbed inside while Alina waved to Salvatore and shouted, "Don't forget to keep the lavender cuttings watered!"

Twenty-One

Ventuno

The month of May had brought with it warmer weather but also unexpected high winds, and when Riccardo came down to breakfast, he saw Issac was already working in the vineyard. He placed a hand on the Moka pot; it was still warm, and he poured himself a small cup of strong black coffee. He guessed he'd need it today. He was meeting with Salvatore's previous lawyer, Dante Zampieri. His research had told him that Avvocato Zampieri didn't always treat his clients professionally. Riccardo's previous legal partner, Vito, had warned him that the lawyer had a tendency to be lazy.

He stepped outside and called to Issac, "Coffee?"

"Please," Issac shouted back, and Riccardo retired back inside and refreshed the pot and placed over the gas.

The pot bubbled on the stove as Issac entered. "After the wind last night, I thought I ought to check the vine ties."

"Everything okay?"

"Yes, just a handful worked themselves loose."

Riccardo put two cups of coffee down on the table and opened the tin that contained their pastries, removing two. He tossed on across the room and Issac caught it and opened the cellophane, taking a bite of the buttery cornetto filled with apricot jam.

"Will you be okay on your own today? I have a meeting with Salvatore's previous lawyer. Something I'm not looking forward to, but it's a necessary evil."

"Do you think he has a good case?"

"It's difficult to say without the full facts. But from what he's told me so far, it looks good on paper."

"I hope it goes in his favour. He needs the financial security the compensation will give him and Nadia."

"He's got a tough road to drive down… no pun intended… before we get to court." Riccardo ate his cornetto and swallowed his second cup of coffee and before he picked up his briefcase he turned to Issac and said, "You're quite taken with Nadia Pasquini, aren't you?"

"I like her."

"Who do you like?" Gabby said, entering the kitchen.

"I was just asking Issac if he was smitten with Nadia."

"Oh yes. It's obvious," laughed Gabby, refilling the Moka pot.

Issac blushed to the roots of his red hair and made an excuse to slip back outside.

"We mustn't tease him," Riccardo said before he kissed Gabby and picked up his car keys. "I'll be back before lunch. I hope."

***

Riccardo had last visited the town of Casoli to meet Queenie and her husband Czeslaw months before, with news of their distant relatives who'd lost touch after the war. He thought if he had time after his meeting with Avvocato Zampieri, he'd drop by and say hello.

He drove up the hill, passing the police station, where he remembered he'd visited many times during his employment at the legal studio in Pescara. Riccardo parked his car in the car park near the Conad supermarket and pharmacy and after walking through the vico that led onto *Corso Vittorio Emanuele*; he paused and looked up at the castle that overlooked the town. *I can see why so many expats love this town,* he thought as he strolled through the streets. *It's the perfect image of the Italy travel brochures advertise. It's no wonder it was awarded the coveted 'I Borghi più belli d'Italia' in 2021.*

The temperature had risen and as he walked down the hill towards the town centre where Dante's office was, he mopped his brow with a handkerchief.

Riccardo found the small sign that advertised Zampieri's legal studio and rang the bell to no response. He rang again before he removed his phone and called the lawyer. A ringtone played on the warm air and looking along the road and spotted Dante sitting in a bar as he answered his phone.

He listened to the man's excuses, where he said he was wrapping up a meeting and Riccardo saw the embarrassment cross his face when he realised he was being watched.

Apologising, Dante slid his key into the lock and opened the door to allow his visitor to step inside. He followed up a dimly lit set of worn stone steps. "These are part of the original palazzo, now converted into commercial offices and residential apartments."

Zampieri's office was small, with a window overlooking *Vico 1 da Sole*, and although the *Pescheria* below had closed many months before, the walls held onto the aroma of fish.

"I understand you're taking over signor Pasquini's case," It was a statement rather than a question and Riccardo answered with a shrug as he removed his jacket and draped it over the only available chair opposite the lawyer's cluttered desk.

"Do you have the files I requested?"

Dante sat down and shuffled through papers on his desk before handing Riccardo a decidedly thin folder. "Is this everything?"

It was Dante's turn to shrug. "*Caso aperto e chiuso.*"

"An open and shut case. Why?"

"Pasquini will never win. The court will laugh out his claim."

"You can't make that assumption."

"Let's be honest, with his history, he has little chance of winning."

"Because of his drinking?"

"Exactly the man is a drunk. It's obvious he caused the accident."

Riccardo felt his hackles rising. "The medical evidence refutes that."

"Medical evidence isn't always accurate."

Riccardo opened the folder and scanned the pages inside before he removed one and held it out. "Here it says that both hospital and roadside tests showed his blood alcohol levels were well below the legal minimum."

"A clever legal team could argue, the phrase below the legal minimum doesn't rule out the results were one-hundred per cent clear."

"That would be a matter of conjecture presented as fact."

"What about the fact he has no recollection of the third car?" This revelation stopped Riccardo in his tracks and he watched as condescension travelled across Zampieri's face. "I see Pasquini has neglected to mention this." Riccardo flicked through the few sheets of paper he'd received and Dante nodded towards the folder and said, "You'll find the information in there."

Leaving Zampieri's office, Riccardo felt annoyed and sensed his temperament would not be conducive to visiting Queenie and Czeslaw. He made a mental note to ask Gabby to invite them over for lunch one day soon.

Driving back to Perano did little to calm his mood and when he arrived home, he waved to Issac who was working in the new parcel of land at the side of the villa. He dropped the folder on the kitchen table and was deciding between filling the Moka pot or opening a bottle of wine when Gabby entered.

"Good morning?"

"Not really." Her kiss soothed him slightly, and he reached over for the corkscrew. "I need a glass of this before

I boil over."

"That bad, eh?" Riccardo nodded. "I'll be finished in my office in half an hour, then I'll make a start on lunch. Why don't you unwind in the sitting room?"

"I'll make lunch. It might relax me."

Gabby kissed him again and as she returned to her office; he poured himself a large glass of Montepulciano.

Riccardo had enjoyed preparing lunch and, as he served up linguine with clams and lemon, Gabby placed the radicchio salad on the table and Issac uncorked a bottle of chilled Pecorino.

Eating their lunch, Issac talked about his morning, and Gabby recounted a conversation she'd had with Nolan about a new feature he wanted her to write. Riccardo, however, kept his own counsel.

Issac cleared away the dishes and Gabby slid the polenta cake across the table, asking him to fetch the sweetened mascarpone from the fridge.

Resting back in his chair, Issac patted his stomach. "I'm not sure I'll be fit for any work this afternoon."

"I'll come and give you a hand after I've read this." Riccardo placed his hand on top of the folder and Issac nodded his agreement.

The paperwork from Zampieri was brief. It was obvious he'd taken Pasquini's money and done the bare minimum of work. He read the account from the other driver involved and he was clearly saying that he had swerved because a third car had been travelling towards him at speed. Zampieri had made a few notes, but there was no suggestion that he'd tried to follow up these claims.

"Who do I speak to first?" Riccardo asked himself. "Pasquini or the other driver. Also, why doesn't the folder have any reports from the carabinieri officers who attended the scene?" He rubbed his eyes, stretched and, after changing his clothes, headed outside to help Issac. The fresh air would help to clear his head.

Twenty-Two

Ventidue

Issac was already working at the stables when Nadia rode her scooter into the driveway. He'd looked up and waved to her, but she hadn't noticed. An incident at home that morning occupied her thoughts, and so her attention was elsewhere. She removed her helmet and ran across the yard and into the villa, apologising for being late. "Slow down," Valentina said as Nadia gabbled the reason for her tardiness.

"My father spilled coffee down himself and I had to help him change before I could leave for work."

"Do you have to help dress your father?" Nadia noticed a look of concern cross Valentina's face. "It's not a job for a daughter."

"Oh, no. He can dress himself. I had to run upstairs to fetch him a clean shirt and trousers from his bedroom."

"Is he still sleeping downstairs?"

"Yes. He tried to use the crutches the hospital gave him to get up the stairs, but it's too painful for him. His back is still sore from the crash."

"Then we must sort something out for him. He'll never recuperate properly like this."

"Please, he says he'll be okay. I dare not bring the subject up again."

"Then I suggest someone else brings it up."

Nadia bit the inside of her cheek nervously. Lately her father's disposition had been buoyant, his dark moods had dissipated and when she peeked through the *salotto* doorway, he appeared to be less morose. She placed her helmet on the stand in the hallway and skipped off to attend to her duties.

On the first floor landing, she knocked on the door to Sonny's bedroom and announced herself.

"Come in Nadia," Sonny called and on entering, she found him at his desk, his laptop open and a textbook balanced on his knee. "Homework," he said, "boring, but if I get it done quickly, the more time I'll have for riding and exploring with Alina."

"I came to make up your bed, but it looks like it's already been made."

"I did it. You know I don't like untidiness."

"Is there anything you want, breakfast, a drink?"

"No thank you, I'm fine."

"I'm doing the laundry later, so I'll collect yours and leave you in peace." Nadia opened the linen basket and pulled out Sonny's discarded clothing.

"My riding kit is on the balcony," he said. "It's smelly. Yesterday I helped father move the straw in the new barn. I put it outside to air."

Nadia opened the door and as she collected his shirt and jodhpurs, she spotted Issac on the land at the rear of the property. Behind him, she saw Alina; she was leaning on a garden spade watching him dig. "I see Alina's with Issac."

"Yes, they're digging up some plants before the machinery comes in to lift the olives and laurels. Mother says the laurels are going to signor Pasquini's garden and a local farmer has purchased the olives."

Nadia stood watching for a few seconds longer, her eyes lingering over Issac, thinking to herself that he was easy on the eye. Sonny's voice burst her thought balloon, and she turned to see him smiling at her. "You like him, don't you?" She shook her head but Sonny continued, "Alina said you look at him with dreamy eyes."

She felt the blush starting in her neck and after she'd told him they were just friends, she scurried from the room, her arms filled with dirty washing.

In the laundry as she filled the washing machine, she

wondered if her feelings for the Scotsman were as obvious to others as they were to Alina. She hoped not; certain her father would have something to say about it.

***

Salvatore was sitting outside with the warm May sunshine warming the top of his head. Before she had left, Nadia had carried over the patio table and laid out a jug of lemonade and a cloche covered plate containing a slice of focaccia on which she had spread some nduja; Salvatore was keen on the spicy Calabrian salami paste. He looked around the garden; he was happy so far with the work in progress. Issac had made an excellent job of the patio and had already laid the foundations for the central path.

Yesterday two men; a tall, moustachioed one and short round one had arrived and they'd inspected the old *frantoio* with Issac. The constant arrival and departure of the gardener and Alina had given him no time to think, but sitting alone today enabled him to gather his thoughts.

'I think he likes Nadia', Alina had said, and now, thinking about it, he saw the hidden looks and half-smiles that had passed between his daughter and Issac.

Salvatore was the product of a tempestuous mother and an intolerant father. When they'd been alive, his parents had been old school, with traditional beliefs and standards, and some of their traits had become ingrained in his personality. Born towards the end of the Second World War, they had both grown up with a dislike of foreigners, and this had wormed its way into Salvatore's consciousness and now, when he thought about Nadia and Issac together this was all he could see, their countries of birth. He liked Issac, so why would this be an issue? Try as he might, he couldn't shift this, as he knew, irrational prejudice.

What if they get married? He thought, *and he takes her from Laroscia and me?* He removed the cloche from his sandwich and took a bite before he said aloud, "And there lies the problem."

A horn sounded out in the road and he replaced his sandwich as Issac appeared, coming through the gap in the fence that had opened up.

"Coffee or lemonade?" Salvatore shouted.

"Lemonade will be great, thanks."

Perched on the edge of the newly built raised bed, Issac explained that he'd brought over plants that he'd rescued from the land that was being cleared down at the stables. Salvatore asked about the plans and, to the best of his knowledge, Issac told him about the proposed restaurant and bar. "They'll start removing the bigger plants this afternoon, so I thought I'd get out of their way."

"Have you seen Nadia today?"

"I saw her arrive, but I haven't spoken to her."

Salvatore listened as Issac told him what plants he'd rescued and where he was going to replant them. "Most are ground cover, so will work well beside the fruit trees to help keep competing weeds down."

Salvatore nodded, not really interested in the mechanics of planting. He wanted more information about Issac's intentions towards Nadia, so said; hoping it didn't sound out of place. "Do you have a girlfriend who shares your passion for gardens?"

"No, I'm single. I don't really have time for a girlfriend." Salvatore smiled. This was an answer he would have hoped for. "It's difficult to find a girlfriend when you're working every day."

"So, are you looking for one?"

"Not actively, but I wouldn't say no if one came along." He laughed, but Salvatore didn't join in.

"There are probably only a few English girls here."

"Or Scottish… Right, I'd better get on."

Issac placed his empty glass on the table and Salvatore watched him as he strode back to the patch of land he'd prepared in readiness for the rescued plants. His questioning had yielded no firm answers and so he made a conscious decision to watch the gardener whenever he was near his daughter.

***

The sun had begun its descent in the sky when Nadia arrived home to find Issac's pickup still outside. *He's working over too,* she thought. She'd stayed on to help Valentina set up the dining room for guests that evening, and after work had visited the supermarket in Selva to do some grocery shopping.

Coming through the door, the villa was silent; she peeked into the *salotto* and saw her father asleep in his chair and decided not to disturb him.

In the kitchen, she unpacked the shopping and put away the items she wouldn't need for their evening meal before making a cup of coffee and carrying it outside. Rather than go through where her father slept, she left through the front of the villa and walked around the side to the rear garden.

"Have you lost track of time?" she said.

Looking around Issac said, "I'm just heeling the last of the new plants in then I'll be off. What time is it?"

"After 6:00."

"I'd better shoot." He took the coffee she proffered, "Thanks. I should text Riccardo and Gabby to let them know I'm running late."

"Will they mind?"

"Probably not, but I don't know what they're planning for dinner. It pays to be courteous to your landlords." He gave her a smile followed by a chuckle, and she inhaled deeply and smiled back. "Your face seems to light up when you smile."

Nadia felt herself blushing and thanked him. "You've a smudge of dirt on your cheek." Her hand moved up and she went to wipe the dirt away and Issac took it by the wrist and they stopped and stared at each other for what must have been seconds but Nadia felt time standing still. The moment shattered, and he moved towards her and, without warning, his lips brushed against hers.

Nadia's eyes were still closed as Issac pulled away and began apologising. "Please forgive me," he said, "I'm so sorry I don't know what came over me."

Nadia said nothing. Standing still, she watched as he gathered his things together, dropped some of them, picked them up again and, with another apology, stumbled out of the garden.

Eventually, hearing his pickup drive away, she moved.

***

Issac clattered into the villa at Perano. He didn't hear or chose not to hear Gabby as she shouted, "Hello," from the sitting room. In his room, he stripped out of his gardening clothes, grabbed a towel and walked into the bathroom, where he stood beneath the shower as it washed his day away.

"Was that Issac?" Riccardo asked from the kitchen.

"Yes," Gabby replied. "He seemed in a hurry to hit the shower." She removed some onions and carrots from the bowl of fresh vegetables on the counter and began chopping.

"Do you need any help?"

"You can peel me some potatoes, please. The butcher minced me some lamb earlier, so I'm making a good old British shepherd's pie."

"How did the butcher feel about mincing lamb?"

"Thought I was bonkers until I explained what I needed it for. I wrote out the recipe for him and he promised to ask his wife if she fancied giving it a go."

Issac entered the kitchen and Riccardo stopped his

potato peeling to open a bottle of wine and pour three glasses. "Good day, Issac?"

"Yeah."

"Has Ennio started clearing his land?"

"Aha."

"When will the laurels be ready for Pasquini's garden?"

"Tomorrow." Issac picked up his glass and excused himself, "I need to make a phone call."

Riccardo watched him go outside, then said, "Is he okay?"

"He seems a bit preoccupied."

"Maybe he's tired."

"Shall I go check he's all right?"

Riccardo nodded, and Gabby picked up her glass and left the kitchen.

Outside, Issac was standing at the end of the parking area out front. The vines sloped away, affording him a view of Quadroni below. Shops were lit up and he watched as car headlights moved along *Via Nazionale*. The windows in the houses that were bunched together in the narrow streets appeared as brilliant orange rectangles and the streetlights illuminated the terracotta roof tiles, giving everywhere a warm appearance that belied the falling evening temperature.

Gabby startled him as her words cut through his thoughts, asking if he was okay.

"Yeah, I'm fine."

"You know, if there's something wrong, you can talk with Riccardo and me."

"Yeah." He nodded his head and returned to surveying the landscape.

"Dinner will be in an hour."

Gabby returned inside.

Twenty-Three

Ventitré

"Riccardo!" Gabby shouted out of the rear door of the villa that led off from the kitchen.

"Yes?" he appeared around the side of the winery.

"Is Issac with you?"

"No! He's headed off to Laroscia. Why?" Riccardo had joined her at the door.

"He's left his phone on the kitchen table."

"Right. He'll probably come back if he needs it."

"You're probably right. Have you had breakfast?" Riccardo shook his head and Gabby promised to make him something to eat.

Rubbing his hands down the front of his jeans, the aroma of frying bacon tempted Riccardo inside.

"I got some thin American style bacon from Eurospin yesterday. Would you like a sandwich?" Gabby said, "We need a breakfast break from sweet things now and then. What plans do you have for today?"

Riccardo kissed her on her forehead before he took a bottle of ketchup from the pantry and said, "I need to go into Pescara to buy more wine fining, also I want to price up stills."

"Stills, why?"

"I'm thinking maybe we can use the excess grape skins to make grappa."

Gabby placed his sandwich on the table and hugged his neck. "Sounds like a good idea. I'm off for a shower."

"Okay. I'll probably be gone when you've finished, so I'll see you just after lunch."

"Shall I make us something?"

"No need, I'll grab a something in town." She lowered herself in for a kiss, but Riccardo had another idea. He lifted a finger and smeared a blob of ketchup on the end of her nose. "See you later," he laughed as she wiped it away and smiled.

Coming down after her shower, Gabby had changed into grey flannel trousers and a cerise linen blouse. She picked up Issac's phone and dropped it inside her handbag and picking up a bottle of wine; she left the villa.

The roads were quiet. All she encountered was a three-wheeled *ape* and a shopper pulling into the supermarket car park. Approaching Piane d'Archi, a feeling of joy spread over her. She recalled the nights during the start of her relationship with Riccardo. Date night at Ghiottone's pizza restaurant and drinks at the bar on the junction. Parking her car, she looked along the road wistfully; it was the road leading to Bomba, where her Italian adventure had started. *I must visit Agata one day soon*, she thought.

Gabby paid a bill at the post office and thankfully the queue there was short; she often joked that a trip to an Italian post office should include a packed lunch. She purchased some slices of square pizza from the takeaway and set off for Laroscia.

Parking next to Issac's pickup, she noticed an attempt had been made to brighten up the front of the Pasquini house, but it needed more work.

She walked up to the front door and knocked. No one answered, and she knocked again before walking around the side of the villa. Seeing Issac in the garden, she waved and crossed the opening in the fence and saw Salvatore sitting on the patio.

Issac joined her and as he led her to the patio she said, "In your haste this morning you forgot your phone."

Issac thanked her and introduced her to Salvatore.

"*Piacere,*" he said, taking her outstretched hand, "So you're the lady that looks after Riccardo." Gabby bristled inwardly at this outdated way of thinking but smiled politely.

"Nice to meet you."

"I'll the coffee make. no?" He said attempting some English for her.

Salvatore retired inside and Issac showed Gabby the work had had done so far. "That is where the pergola will be," he said, pointing to the pile of wood he'd delivered that morning. "It was hard to convince Salvatore that it was wood left over from work at Perano and not charity."

"Is he a proud man?"

"Stubborn would be a better word."

Hearing his name being called, Issac went inside to collect the coffee tray as Salvatore wheeled himself down the ramp onto the patio.

"I've brought this for Issac's lunch. There's plenty for both of you." She placed the paper bag of pizza on the patio table and reached into her bag and removed the bottle of wine. "You can have it with a glass of this. It's from our winery."

"*Che cazzo!*" Gabby turned to see the scowl that had fixed itself across Salvatore's face. "What is this? A joke?" Issac appeared in the doorway, and before he could speak, Salvatore launched into a tirade. "So you choose to bring food, thinking I need charity, and then you insult me with wine. Go! Get off my land. I have had enough of damned foreigners."

Gabby looked at him, stunned. She glanced across at Issac, who looked equally shocked at the outburst. Before he could say anything, she turned and ran from the garden, climbed into her car and didn't start crying until she had arrived back in Perano.

***

Gabby had rushed from Pasquini's garden and, standing

rigid, Issac looked at the space she had occupied before Salvatore's outburst. The atmosphere in the garden became heavy as if the sky was pressing down and Issac remembered a story about a chicken who ran around telling the other farmyard animals that the sky was falling down.

The silence that followed Salvatore's ranting hurt his ears and slowly he collected his tools and, without a word, he left the garden and loaded his pickup and drove away.

Driving past the stables, he saw Nadia's scooter and pulled into the yard. He left his engine running as he walked towards the door and knocked.

Luck was on his side as Nadia answered. He told her about the incident with Gabby and watched as her smile dissolved and she rushed back inside to find Valentina.

***

Riccardo arrived home and before he unpacked his car, he went into the villa and found Gabby sitting at the kitchen table, her face streaked with tears.

"*Amore mio, cosa c'è che non va?*"

"What's wrong… what's wrong… that man." Gabby spat the words out, her tears fuelled by anger.

Riccardo pulled out a chair and sat down beside her. "What man?"

"Salvatore Pasquini." Riccardo listened as she told him about her meeting up at Laroscia. "Not only is he a sexist pig, but I also think he's a racist."

"Surely not," he shrugged, thinking he'd need to speak with his new client. Riccardo told Gabby about Salvatore's struggles with alcohol. "You weren't to know."

"That doesn't excuse the severity of his outburst."

They both looked up at the sound of Issac's pickup arriving in the drive. He came into the house carrying the bottle of wine and the bag of pizza squares. "I had to come back. I needed to see that you were okay. I'm so sorry

Gabby."

"You don't need to be sorry. It wasn't your fault."

"I didn't mention his addiction, because it wasn't my place to share it."

"Same here... client confidentiality," added Riccardo.

"I don't blame either of you. I was just shocked at how quickly he went from cordial to consumed with rage."

***

Back inside the *salotto*, Salvatore stared at the wall, thoughts rushing around his head like ants over a dead beetle. He felt wretched. There was no need for him to reprimand himself. He was still angry, but now it was with himself. *All I do is sit and think, wallowing in self-pity.* Hearing the door open, he pushed aside his thoughts and looked up to see his daughter. She rushed to his side. *"Papà?"* She was shaking her head, so nothing more needed to be said. *"Perché?"*

Salvatore shook his head, and looked at to the floor, his shame obvious.

Nadia went to him and tried to hug him, but he shook her off and she went out of the room. He heard her moving about in the kitchen and she returned with a cup of camomile tea. "This will calm you," she said, placing the cup down on the table. "Try to drink it."

"*Fallimento*," he whispered.

"*Scusi?*"

"*Sono un fallimento.*"

"Nonsense *papà*, you're not a failure."

"What do you know?" He shouted, then took a deep breath as she stepped back, her eyes wide with shock. He'd never raised his voice to Nadia before, and now this was another weight to add to his ever-increasing feelings of low esteem.

"I'm sorry, *cara*." His words came out sounding as

broken as he felt.

"What's wrong?" Nadia said, placing a hand on his shoulder. His hand covered hers and he apologised again before he picked up the tea and blew across the surface to cool the pale yellow liquid.

They sat in silence for a time; he looking out of the window and she looking at the empty hearth that still needed to be cleared of the ash from days ago.

Salvatore spoke first. "What is wrong with me?" Nadia opened her mouth, but a raised eyebrow kept her silent. "What kind of man am I? Why can't I be like other men?"

Nadia reached over and covered his hand with hers, and he looked into her eyes and apologised once more.

"Everything is new now. Your life has changed."

"It's not change that makes me the way I am... have always been."

He looked at Nadia, and he saw the years of uncertainty and anger she had witnessed and immediately felt ashamed of himself.

"Have you eaten?" She asked. He shook his head, remembering the pizza that Gabby had delivered. Her kindness met with spite. "I'll make you something. You'll feel better once you've eaten."

Will I? he thought as she left the room.

He ate alone, a simple bowl of pasta with a tomato sauce and later with a half-filled stomach he lay down on the sofa bed, the springs digging into his back - a penance he felt he deserved after the outburst until sleep came and took him.

Waking as the early hours brought light back to the world, he looked up at the ceiling. His eyes travelled along a thin crack in the plaster and more thoughts jostled like a jumble of people standing outside a post office; each person knowing their place in the line, allowing the others to come forward in the order he needed to hear them.

You are angry with yourself, a voice in his head said.

His voice.

And you directed that anger towards Gabby.
"I know," he said aloud, as he replied to his thoughts.
So what are you going to do about it?
"Nadia said everything is new and—" he stopped speaking and allowed a new thought to push the queue back. He knew what he needed to do.

Twenty-Four

Ventiquattro

"Thank you," Nadia said as she climbed into the driver's seat of her friend's car. "We'll be gone no longer than an hour."

"Take as long as you like. I wasn't going anywhere today."

Nadia drove back home and collected her father and together they set off for Perano.

***

Gabby looked inside the winery and said, "Rachel just called asking if I fancied another girls' day out."

"When?" Riccardo replied.

"Tomorrow."

"Will you go?"

"Yes. I've nothing on except a conference call with Nolan later today." He watched her turn her head as he heard a car arrive outside.

"Nadia's here... oh shit."

"What's wrong?"

"Salvatore is with her."

Riccardo left what he was doing and went outside. He watched Nadia get out of the car and walk around to the back.

"Hello Nadia," he said, joining her as she opened the boot to remove her father's wheelchair. "What brings you to Perano?" he looked up and saw the concern on Gabby's face.

"My father. He wants to apologise to Gabby."

"He upset her."

"He knows that."

"Wait here. I'll see if she wants to see him."

Nadia waited as Riccardo spoke with Gabby before he turned and nodded towards her. He walked over to help her remove the chair.

"I'll make some coffee," Gabby said, slipping away into the villa.

Riccardo watched as Salvatore heaved himself out of the car seat and into his wheelchair, noticing he'd shaved and was wearing a newly pressed shirt and trousers. "This way," he said, pointing towards the villa's front door.

"I'm sorry," Salvatore said. Riccardo didn't reply as he led the visitors inside.

Shocked to see to see Nadia and her father, Issac got up from the kitchen table saying he'd make himself scarce. "I'll go outside, leave you all in peace."

"Nadia, go with Issac. He can show you around outside," Salvatore said and Riccardo guessed what he wanted to say wasn't for his daughter's ears. Seeing Gabby's hands shake, he took over the coffee making, and she pulled a dining chair away from the table and sat down.

"Please forgive me," Salvatore said, his voice barely above a whisper. "I'm so sorry I don't know what came over me." Silence enveloped the room and after a few beats, he continued. "That's not strictly true. Of course I knew what had come over me." another long pause.

"My pride and my shame."

Gabby and Riccardo listened as the man in the wheelchair told them the sorry tale of his life. "When my dreams failed, instead of accepting the blame was mine, I found solace in a bottle."

His story had moved Gabby, and Riccardo saw her eyes fill with emerging tears. He passed her a handkerchief from his pocket and watched as she slid it across the table towards Salvatore.

"Thank you for coming and apologising," she said. "I'd rather we put it behind us and move forward."

"That's very gracious of you. Far more than I deserve."

"While Riccardo makes another coffee, why don't you tell me about your ceramics?" Had she said this to emphasise that her relationship with Riccardo was based on equality? Maybe.

***

Walking outside, the body language between Nadia and Issac was closed off and the conversation stilted. Issac pointed out areas of the vineyard and Nadia just nodded and vocalised without words. With their eyes cast downward, neither looked directly into the others. Issac rambled on about the recent work he'd undertaken, the tying in of stray canes and the mulching. "The mulch mustn't touch the stem as the vine can rot."

Nadia gave another 'aha'.

"This is an excellent site because there's a breeze that helps keep fungal disease at bay."

Taking control, Nadia said, "Is that all you can think of to talk about, fungus and mulch?"

They stopped walking and standing looking down the hill towards Quadroni, Issac said. "About the last time we were together."

"Yes?"

"I'm sorry if I overstepped the mark."

"What is 'overstepped the mark'?" Nadia asked. Even in Italian, she hadn't understood the idiom.

"It means to behave in an unacceptable way."

"Is that what happened?" Issac looked at her and saw she was wearing a smile. "I liked it."

"I'm not in the habit of kissing girls willy-nilly. I thought I might have offended you."

"No you didn't. I was a little sad when I opened my eyes

and you were leaving." Her eyes dipped to the ground again.

"I perhaps should have stayed to explain myself." Issac used a finger to lift her chin up and she said, "I thought you had instantly regretted it."

"Not at all. I had wanted to kiss you for so long."

Nadia's cheeks mottled with pink, "*Anch'io.*"

After she said, 'me too', Issac took her hand and led her away from the villa and away from the windows he took her in his arms and they shared their first intentional kiss. Breaking away, he said, "Will you go out with me one evening?"

"Yes."

"We must arrange a date."

In a heartbeat, Nadia said, "Tomorrow. And what is this, willy and nilly?"

Issac chuckled when Riccardo's calling interrupted their moment, and they slunk around the corner of the villa.

"Salvatore is ready to leave."

Nadia moved quickly to the car and opened the boot, ready to take the wheelchair as her father appeared in the doorway.

As the engine turned over, Gaby leant in to thank Salvatore for coming, and before Nadia put the car into gear, Riccardo told Salvatore he'd visit his house in the morning.

As the car vanished over the hill, Riccardo said to Issac, "So what did you and Nadia talk about?"

Flustered, Issac blurted out, "Mulch and fungus." He watched a confused expression drive across Riccardo's face and excused himself and went around the villa and congratulated himself on securing the date with Nadia.

Twenty-Five

Venticinque

"Sorry, were you going out?" Rachel said as Riccardo, dressed in his suit, opened the door. "We're earlier than arranged."

"No problem. I have an appointment this morning. Come in. Gabby's in her office. I'll let her know you're here." He slipped outside and crossed the yard before he returned and said she was just finishing up a conference call and would be over soon. "Make yourselves at home."

"You might regret saying that," Louise joked. "I might live like a pig."

Riccardo smiled and Rachel thought he didn't really understand Louise's humour.

"If you'll excuse me, ladies, I need to be somewhere." Obligatory air kisses preceded his leaving, with, "*A dopo*."

Seconds later, Gabby entered the kitchen and explained she'd been on a call with the magazine's editor and the features manager.

"How is Nolan?" asked Rachel.

"He's good. He's coming over soon." Gabby explained to Louise that Nolan was the editor at the magazine and how he'd allowed her to stay in Abruzzo for the summer last year.

"And you met Riccardo?"

"That's right."

"Maybe I should spend more time here and snare myself a delicious Italian man. It'll stop me being the odd one out."

Rachel laughed, "As if you'd ever swap Ben for another man."

"It would depend on his looks and size of his..." she

smiled provocatively, "... wallet."

"Coffee?" Gabby said, and both Rachel and Louise shook their heads. "Well, it's too early for wine, so I'll fetch the juicer."

As she fed apples and carrots into the machine, Rachel asked her about Riccardo's appointment.

"He has a meeting with a client in Laroscia."

"That'll explain the suit."

"Despite it being an informal meeting, he likes to dress the part, says it helps him transition from *contadino* to *avvocato* easily."

Louise looked at her glass of brownish liquid and grimaced. "Get it down your neck," Rachel said, "It'll do you good."

"What will do me good is a glass of chilled prosecco and a plate of calamari by the sea."

"Sounds good to me. Why don't we take a trip to the coast?"

"Where do you suggest?" Rachel said. She'd been looking forward to her day off and didn't appreciate the idea of travelling all the way back to Marina San Vito, close to the hotel.

"I hear a new restaurant has opened on the coast near Torino di Sangro."

"Okay, let's give it a try," Rachel said. "Come on, Louise, drink up and we'll head off."

Louise looked at her drink, placed it down and said, "I'd rather not. Me and healthy aren't good friends."

***

Issac was working at *Le Stelle* so when Riccardo arrived at the Pasquini villa he knew he'd be alone with Salvatore. They exchanged pleasantries and Salvatore tried to say sorry again with Riccardo waving his apology aside. They didn't go into the *salotto* this time, as Nadia was at the stables, and so they were in the kitchen. Riccardo declined the offer of coffee and placed his briefcase down and opened it with a click and removed a file.

"I met with Dante Zampieri."

"Oh yes, and what did he have to say for himself?"

"Very little, like the work he appears to have done on your behalf."

"I thought as much," Salvatore said. "So what happens now?"

"Now, we start from the beginning again." Riccardo heard the exasperated huff that came from Salvatore but ignored it. "I'd like to get the full facts and if it takes longer, at least I can promise to do my best."

"Pity I didn't know you before I hired that half-arsed lawyer from Casoli."

Riccardo said nothing. He wouldn't feel professional about maligning another lawyer, instead he placed a small recording device on the table and asked Salvatore to describe the accident from the start.

"I'd been told there could be jobs available at *Trigano* at Contrada Saletti… A fool's errand that turned out to be. I was coming home through Brecciaio—"

Riccardo stopped him. "Why did you come through Brecciaio? Surely you could have driven down the SP119 to Piane d'Archi and up to Laroscia from there?"

"At that hour, afternoon shoppers often make travelling down the road slow."

Riccardo couldn't ever recall the sleepy road ever being congested, but he let it slide and made a note to take a drive there one afternoon.

Salvatore continued on with his story, recalling needing the bathroom and stopping at the bar. When he'd finished telling the lawyer everything, Riccardo sat back in his seat and placed his pen on the table and said. "And there were no other cars involved in the crash?"

"No!" Salvatore said immediately, his voice sharp. "I've

already said."

"I had to ask."

"Why?"

"The notes I received from avvocato Zampieri suggest another car being involved."

"There was no other car." Salvatore's face became a fixture of annoyance and he said, "Are we finished?"

"If there's nothing more you can tell me, then yes, we can leave it there. For now."

What are you hiding? Riccardo thought as he packed his things away.

Before driving back to Perano, he checked his phone and saw a text from Gabby saying she was going out for lunch and he'd have to fend for himself when he got home. He then scrolled through his contacts and placed a quick call before pressing the ignition button and, seeing Salvatore watching him, he drove away.

***

Brezza Marina, a blue and white nautical themed restaurant, looked pristine, its façade still newly painted. A waiter wearing a crisp blue and white sailor type shirt approached them as they entered between two troughs of flowers. He welcomed them, enquiring where they'd like to sit. The restaurant was busy, and it looked like all the outside umbrella tables had been taken. Spotting the only vacant one, Louise pointed to it and they followed the waiter over.

He walked away to fetch menus, and Louise gave a low whistle. "He's a looker, isn't he?"

"Stop it," Rachel said with a smile.

"He's coming back… Oh my, look at the front of his trousers. Is he smuggling the bread rolls?"

Gabby and Rachel laughed, and the waiter gave them a quizzical look before he walked back inside. "He's not so bad from the back, either."

Once their laugher had subsided, they checked out the menu, looking up briefly when a waitress delivered three glasses of complimentary frizzante.

The waiter took their orders and as they waited, Rachel told them Penny had suggested a forthcoming girls' day out. "She said she has something different to show us."

"I wonder what it could be."

"All I know is it's in Palombaro."

"Palombaro?" Louise said.

"Yes, it's a hilltop town with a large population of Brits."

"I've heard of it, but I've never been," said Gabby.

"Wait till you see the road up to it. It's like driving up to the edge of the sky."

Their conversation halted as their first courses arrived. They'd all plumped for a *secondo* and *dolce*. Gabby looked down at her sea bass stuffed with almonds and lemon, while Rachel and Louise had both opted for fried calamari with courgette fritters. In the centre of the table sat a salad bowl of crimson radicchio and a plate of slim fries.

There followed a lull in the chat as they all ate their lunch, occasionally looking up to watch the people who headed onto the beach. "Foreigners and ex pats?" Louise asked. She remembered Luca talking about an Italian superstition about bathing in the sea before July.

Rachel nodded. "More than likely."

Dolce was the unusually titled *zuppa inglese*, meaning English soup, which, in fact, was a trifle with fresh cream and crème patisserie. Louise laughed as Gabby told her about Luca's reaction earlier in the year to tinned custard.

"He's never forgotten," Rachel said, "he still says he can't believe we Brits eat yellow soup."

The talk turned to Louise's wedding plans, to which she said she'd had very few ideas, which both Gabby and Rachel found hard to believe.

"I know a pleasant hotel where you could have the wedding," said Rachel.

"Oh, that's right, fill your rooms at the expense of my wedding guests," laughed Louise.

"I'd give you mates rates."

"And we'd do you a good deal on wine," said Gabby, joining in.

Their amusement changed as Gabby spoke about her run in with Salvatore. "He at least had the balls to come over the next day to apologise."

"I should think so," Louise said.

"It wasn't a simple thing to do. They had to borrow a car to accommodate his wheelchair. It took a lot of organising and courage. I told him we'd draw a line under it."

"You're more forgiving than I am."

"That's right," said Rachel. "Louise is half woman-half Doberman Pinscher."

Louise woofed and, once again, laughter surrounded their table, earning them more disapproving looks from the other diners.

Twenty-Six

Ventisei

The apartment belonging to Alfredo Petrini was on the second floor. From the street, it looked tidy. The balcony had two flower troughs attached to it, with green verdant plants spilling over the sides. On the wall was an awning and unlike his neighbours, it was rolled up to prevent the wind from ripping the fabric.

Riccardo pressed the buzzer and waited. A male voice enquired who the caller was and after he'd confirmed his identity, the electronic door opened with a click and he walked into the lobby. The block had only three floors, so had dispensed with fitting a lift. Riccardo took the stairs.

In the corridor he straightened his tie – he'd chosen to wear one today – and knocked at the door. It opened, and a bespectacled man dressed in overalls beckoned him inside.

"I can only spare an hour. I've taken time off work to meet with you."

Riccardo looked at the insignia on the overalls depicting the logo of the garage where signor Petrini worked. "Thank you for agreeing to see me."

"You'd think I'd have given up talking to lawyers who doubt my word."

"I can assure you signore Petrini, I come here with an open mind."

"That's what the other man said... what was his name? Oh yes, Zampieri. A useless piece of–" Petrini stopped before he ended his sentence and, not wanting to make a comment, Riccardo opened his briefcase on his knee. "So what do you want to know, signore?"

"Di Renzo. Riccardo. Just tell me what happened on the

day of the accident in Brecciaio. I'd like to hear it in your words." He set the recorder on the table and waited.

Petrini took a deep breath and began recounting his side of the story. It was pretty innocuous, a recollection of events that led up to his driving along the stick straight road through Brecciaio. "I saw the car leave the bar. It was on the correct side of the road, so it would be logical to assume we'd pass each other without incident." Petrini stopped speaking, took a handkerchief from his overall pocket and removed his spectacles and polished the lenses before he spoke again. "I saw the other car coming down the road behind signor Pasquini's car. The distance it travelled told me it was speeding. It changed lanes; I'm assuming to avoid a collision with Pasquini heading towards me and instinct told me to get out of the way. That was when the impact occurred."

There was another moment of silence before Riccardo said, "Did this other car stop?"

"No. And don't ask me the make and model, everything happened too quick to notice. All I remember is it was a silver saloon." He polished his spectacles again and Riccardo assumed this to be a habit or a safety mechanism. Petrini lifted his eyes to Riccardo's and said, "I'm not saying the collision wasn't down to my swerving, but I am adamant that there was another vehicle involved. I just don't understand why no one will believe me."

Riccardo felt Alfredo was speaking the truth. He'd already admitted liability, so what did he have to gain from fabricating the existence of a third car? He wrapped up the interview and told Petrini his next stop was the carabinieri offices in Lanciano, "I want to see every document relating to the incident. I'm sorry for taking you away from your work. I'll be in touch again."

Twenty-Seven

Ventisette

Issac was already waiting for Nadia as she pulled up outside of the Eurospin supermarket in Selva Piana; he'd decided after his conversation with the Guarenna barman to stop using their car park at the crossroads.

Nadia walked over to his pickup, opened the door and climbed in, placing her crash helmet on the floor between her feet before she ran her fingers through her hair that the helmet had flattened.

"Hi," Issac said, hearing the nervousness in his voice.

"Hi. Where are we going?"

"Not far, but somewhere away from prying eyes."

They rode in silence as his pickup navigated the steep hill up to Casoli; Issac breathed a sigh of relief that his was the only vehicle at the T junction and turning left; he drove over the small roundabout and parked up in the spaces overlooking the valley below. He jumped out and walked around the front to open Nadia's door, but she beat him to it and was already stepping down. She took his outstretched hand and together they walked up the slope onto *Corso Umberto*. He stood aside, allowing her to choose a table arranged on the pavement outside a bar, and went inside and ordered their drinks.

Nadia relaxed her rarely drinking alcohol rule and sipping their Aperol spritzers they watched as couples went about their *passagiatte*; some of whom occasionally stopped to gaze at the jewellery in the shop window opposite.

"This is very pleasant," Nadia said.

"It is," Issac replied, his conversational skills dulled

because of nerves.

He couldn't believe Nadia had agreed to a date and as the time had approached, he'd got himself worked up over silly things like, what will they talk about? Will she find him boring? His experience with the opposite sex was limited, mostly because of his shyness, but also in part to his nomadic lifestyle before he'd come back to Abruzzo.

"Do you miss working up in the Veneto?" Nadia asked.

"Not really. I prefer to be here."

"Isn't it more glamorous up north?"

"There's very little glamour in working in a national park."

"But Abruzzo is so boring, it's old-fashioned and lost in time."

He smiled. Her response was a statement from someone who'd never left the place where they'd grown up and its familiarity had rubbed off the shine.

She listened as he marvelled at the landscape, the mountains and the sea. "Here, community matters, and life may be slower, but believe me, the pace is far more pleasurable than that in an indifferent, hectic city."

Nadia shrugged, "I think I'd love the excitement of a city like Milano or Roma." Her eyes dipped to her drink as she sucked the orange-coloured liquid up into her straw.

Issac's brain went into overdrive. *I bet she's tempted by reels and videos on social media that peddle the delights of faraway places.* This thought unnerved him. This was just a first date, and he was getting ahead of himself, worrying about their future. *Calm down*, his mind told him.

"Before I went up north, I spent some time in Molise. Now there's a place more laid back than here. It has a great feeling, like no one is in a hurry. Maybe that's why they live so long." He let out a small laugh, his topics of conversation drying faster than a bedsheet in the midday sun.

"So," he said, "Tell me about growing up in Laroscia."

Nadia talked about her childhood, paying attention to her

memories of the garden her mother had loved.

Issac nodded to the waitress and Nadia paused as a fresh round of drinks arrived. "School was okay," she said, resuming her storytelling. "I had lots of good friends, and we spent many afternoons either lazing around in mother's garden or messing about down by the river."

Issac sensed her story was about to change. Her shoulders tensed and she plaited her fingers together. She stopped speaking, and he waited, but the subject suddenly changed. "Could you fetch my father's bed downstairs?"

"Sure. I'll do it next time I'm at the villa."

"Do you know how much it would cost to change the downstairs bathroom into a wet room?"

The questions threw Issac off guard before he realised what she was doing. Nadia had shut down the dialogue, removing the need to talk about something he was certain caused her pain.

"I ought to be getting back." She checked the time on her phone and finished her drink.

"I'll take you to collect your scooter," he said, and together they walked back down the slope to the pickup. This time, they didn't hold hands.

He watched as she rode out of the car park and up the lane that would take her home. The date he had dreamt of hadn't lived up to his expectations. His heart felt as heavy as the new moon that was taking up residence in the evening sky and, turning over the ignition, he drove away in the opposite direction.

***

Salvatore called out as Nadia placed her crash helmet on the kitchen table. "Is that you Nadia?"

"Yes, *Papà*."

"Did you have a good night with your friends from school?" He said as she looked around the doorjamb.

"Yes *Papà*. It was good to catch up with them. I'm tired, so I'm going to bed."

"*Buona notte mia cara.* I'll see you in the morning."

"*Buona notte Papà.*" Nadia closed the *salotto* door and as she walked up the stairs, she replayed her conversation with Issac and wished she had been brave enough to speak up. In the bathroom, she looked at herself. Hoping that the lie she had just told her father, and her secret, remained hidden behind her eyes.

Twenty-Eight

Ventotto

Still dressed in her pyjamas, and wrapped in a towelling dressing gown, Gabby stood outside the front of the villa cradling her morning coffee. She was looking across at a patch of late flowering poppies, their delicate red heads moving in the morning breeze when Rachel's car pulled into the driveway.

"You're early," she called. "I'm not dressed yet."

"We had to give these two reprobates a lift," Rachel shouted from her rolled-down window and Gabby watched as Luca and Ivan climbed out of the back seats.

"Any chance of a brew?" Ivan said.

"Sorry about him," Mole said, getting out of the car. "He'll be asking for hot buttered toast next."

"Oh, yes, if there's some on offer, I could go a slice or two."

"See what I mean. I hope you don't mind me tagging along?"

"Not at all," Gabby said. Everyone exchanged morning greetings and Riccardo popped his head outside the door, inviting them all inside. "I'll get the coffee on the stove."

"And some bread in the toaster," laughed Ivan.

Gabby excused herself and went upstairs to shower and get dressed. On the landing, she met Issac and asked him how his date had gone.

"Ugh," he replied.

"As well as that?"

"Worse." He disappeared into the bathroom and seconds later, she heard the shower running.

In her bedroom, she undressed and entered her en-suite

shower and, as warm water sloughed away the remnants of sleep, wondered what the day ahead held for her. Rachel had said they were meeting Penny, but that was as much as she knew.

Issac was already downstairs when she entered the kitchen. Everyone was sitting at the kitchen table, cups of coffee in front of them, while Ivan munched on toast. Issac was standing in the corner. He looked lost and Gabby decided she'd talk to him later that evening.

"How come you guys are here?"

"We're helping Issac up at the Pasquini garden today," Luca said.

"I need help to cut back a bougainvillea that's outgrown its space." Issac said. "And I want an opinion on my idea for the old *frantoio*."

"*Frantoio*?" Louise asked.

"Olive mill," said Luca.

"So what do you ladies have planned?" Riccardo asked.

"We're off to Palombaro to meet Penny. She has something interesting she wants to show us, then it'll be lunch somewhere—"

"And shopping, no doubt," interrupted Ivan.

"Of course," Louise said with a smile. "Are we ready then, girls?"

Gabby and Rachel said they were and after kisses and promises to not spend too much money, they were in Rachel's car and driving away.

"We must call in here one day," Rachel said, pointing to a bar with gold-coloured doors set against yellow walls. "*Lu Pennese*. They do the best porchetta for miles. I know people who travel from San Vito to come here."

The road twisted and Gabby flinched as a lorry come around the bend, its wheels crossing the centre of the road. A sharp bend later and they were on a wide flat road and she felt she could breathe again.

After yet another sharper bend, they were heading

upwards on a steep hill that looked like it was leading up into the clouds.

"This is high up," Louise said as they moved onto a narrow lane and pulled into the hilltop town. The road took them down past a church and they parked in a small car park that overlooked the valley below with the mountains opposite.

Penny was already waiting for them outside a bar opposite, and she waved and waited for them to join her. After a multitude of greetings, she led them down a street flanked on either side by houses until they stepped into a small piazza and she pointed ahead of her, "There," she said. The four women stood looking at the end of a three-storey building, all wearing a mask of puzzlement. "This is a holiday establishment, the likes you have never seen before. I jumped at the chance to promote it."

The group walked past a shop front on the ground floor that was filled with people and stopped at an aubergine coloured door with a huge brass knocker. A petite blonde opened the door and Penny introduced Hannah to the ladies.

"Come inside," Hannah said, opening the door wider to reveal a staircase with ornate iron baluster and handrail. The stairs led to a set of double doors which opened onto a wide room with corridors leading in opposite directions.

Hannah invited everyone into a sitting room with sumptuous sofas in bold colours that matched the artwork on the vaulted ceiling. "This place is fabulous," Mole said. "Is it all yours?"

"Yes. My husband and I bought the palazzo six years ago, when it was little more than a shell. It's taken a lot of work to complete it."

"Hannah opened it up as a holiday venue six months ago," added Penny.

"We specialise in retreats. No Wi-Fi, no screens." She pointed to the sofas and with everyone sitting, she opened a side door and stepped inside a galley kitchen and retrieved a jug of freshly squeezed fruit juice. "I can do coffee if anyone fancies one, and I have prosecco for later." Gabby noticed Louise's face loosen as Hannah mentioned the wine.

Hannah told them how she had put together the retreat for busy professionals who want to get away from the hurly-burly of corporate life and explore the real Italian *dolce vita*. "We direct our guests to explore the surrounding towns and get involved with local life. We have some farms and small businesses that will take people for a day or two to show them how life ticks along here."

"Sounds great," Rachel said, do you do day activities?

"Not presently, why?"

"I own a hotel and I wondered if any of my guests would like to get involved."

"It's something to think about," Hannah said. "Did you see the shop downstairs?" Heads nodded. "I opened it up for local people to congregate, and a woman from the town organises things like crafts and demonstrations there."

Gabby was seeing a feature opportunity for the magazine and she filed away everything she was hearing in her journalistic mental filing cabinet. "Do you do yoga and such?"

"Heavens no, this isn't a happy-clappy establishment." Hannah said with a smile that lit up her face, making her pale blue eyes shine brighter. "The idea here isn't a detox. It's all about stepping into another world without having to endure mung beans and tofu."

Hannah gave them a tour of the bedrooms; none of which looked like a hostel with their tasteful, soft furnishings and space. Most had an en suite with only a handful sharing a bathroom.

The communal room housed a vast honesty library and easels and paint for guests to borrow. A cupboard and table dedicated to crafts like knitting and cross stitch took up a corner of the room and opposite were a selection of comfy chairs that looked out towards the mountain with binoculars and a telescope placed beside them.

Hannah opened a door to a kitchen where four people were standing, watching as an elderly woman was showing them how to make pasta. "This is Monica. Her English is sparse, but the people who come to her classes don't seem to mind."

"*Piacere,*" Monica said.

"*Buon giorno, cosa preparate oggi?*" Rachel asked the woman what she was making.

"*Orecchiette.*"

"Ah, little ears."

"*Si. Perfetto con i broccoli.*"

"We share the meals they make between everyone who wants some, either guests or the people downstairs," Hannah said, giving Monica a smile, before she apologised for disturbing her lesson and closed the door.

"We have another room on this level that's vacant, but as yet, we can't decide what to do with it. My husband, Rex, thought about painting workshops, but I don't think I could put up with the inevitable mess. I'll show it to you. Maybe one of you will have an eureka moment I could steal." Hannah gave a modest shrug, which Gabby caught, and it made her like her more. After seeing the empty room with chairs and folding tables stacked in a corner, Hannah took them to see the roof terrace before they retired to her private sitting room, and the cork popped on a bottle of prosecco and the conversation flowed until it was time to enjoy the lunch Monica and her students had made.

***

Issac was hoping he'd be able to speak with Nadia but on arrival Salvatore had told him she'd gone out with friends to Pescara for the day. He introduced Luca and Ivan and before they could tackle the unruly bougainvillea; he led them to the *frantoio* and explained how he wanted to remove the crushing wheel and turn the building into an attractive ruin.

"What will you do with the wheel?" Luca asked him.

"I was thinking of making either a water feature or a large round table. What do you think?"

"I think you could do both. Leave it with me and I'll have a think about it."

Ivan asked about recycling the roof tiles and stone and Issac said he hoped to reuse as much as he could. "I have a friend who turns roof tiles into wall hangings."

"How?" Issac asked.

"She uses a mix of hand painting and decoupage. I'm sure she'd give you a good price for any leftover tiles."

"I'll give it some thought."

Issac walked them around the garden, outlining his plans until they'd trekked through the olive grove and woodland up to the lane that formed the property's border.

The three men opted to tackle the bougainvillea from the top down and, with Salvatore's permission, they climbed the stairs up to the bedrooms. Issac wondered which of the three bedrooms belonged to Nadia but had no compulsion to look inside. *That would just be creepy*, he thought.

All the bedroom doors were closed, making the landing dark and opening up Salvatore's room didn't allow in much more light as the balcony door's roller shutter was firmly closed. The room smelt musty, the unoccupied odour of desertion.

Luca opened the shutter, and it was clear to see that the flowering climber had taken over most of the balcony with its twisted stems blocking out much of the light from outside. *How long has this been like this?* Issac wondered. He opened the doors, pushing them against the plant, forcing its stems away from the villa's walls. "No one has opened these doors for a long time," he said. He stepped onto the balcony and saw that the job was going to be harder than he had first imagined and became thankful he had Ivan and Luca to help. Luca went down into the garden to direct the pruning from below, and Ivan and Issac began the thinning out from above.

Once they'd wrestled the flowering climber into submission and cleared away the unwanted branches to the ever-increasing bonfire stack, they relaxed at the patio table with cans of orange soda that Salvatore delivered from the fridge.

"I remember that bougainvillea when my wife first bought it home. It was little more than a twig," Salvatore said, looking up at the neatly trimmed plant. "Regardless of its lethal thorns, she loved the purple papery blooms."

The conversation focussed on the garden with Issac outlining his ideas while Salvatore described its previous layout. Luca occasionally made suggestions, but very few. Issac knew that as a gardener himself, Luca would know how protective other landscapers can be about their work.

The midday heat was fading and it no longer felt heavy when Issac mentioned Nadia had asked if they could bring Salvatore's bed downstairs for him.

"That won't be necessary. As soon as I'm fit again, I shall be able to use my bedroom once more."

Issac shuddered inwardly, thinking about the drab, unappealing room that needed an airing. "Once you're better, we can take it back upstairs for you."

"It seems a waste of energy."

"I hope you don't mind me saying," Ivan said, "but I do maintenance work for people with holiday homes. It includes painting and decorating, and I was wondering if you'd like me to redecorate your room for you?"

"Why would you do that?" Issac saw Salvatore toss a suspicious look towards Ivan.

"I just thought now there's more light coming in and once the bed is removed, it would be a unique opportunity to freshen up the space. Make your return there special."

"I don't need special."

Ivan and Issac watched as Luca lowered his voice and said something peppered with dialect that they had difficulty understanding.

"Very well." Salvatore said, "Luca has some paint back at the hotel that needs to be used up or thrown away. You can use that," he paused. "But no feminine colours."

Up in Salvatore's bedroom when they had unscrewed the bed ready to carry downstairs and reassemble, Luca said, "We have a tin of the duck egg blue paint left unopened from when we decorated the bedrooms at *Le Stelle*. I thought you could use it to brighten up the room. It looks like no one's touched it in years."

"Or cleaned properly," Ivan said, holding up an old newspaper so thick in dust it was impossible to read the masthead.

"What did you say to change his mind?" Issac asked.

"I just said he should let the Englishman paint the room for him. If the fool wants to give up his days for free, then he deserves the hardship of working in the summer heat."

"Sneaky," Ivan said, then did a double take and laughed as he said, "Fool?"

Twenty-Nine

Ventinove

Over breakfast, with Riccardo out of the villa, Gabby had an opportunity to speak with Issac. She asked him how he was feeling, saying she thought he'd looked down the past few days. He opened up and told her about his date with Nadia, asking her to promise to keep the information close to home. "I don't mind Riccardo knowing, but I think it's best we keep it from becoming common knowledge."

She listened as he told her everything was going okay until he'd asked her about growing up in Laroscia. "She seemed to close up, almost as if she was keeping her history a secret, hiding herself away. I think I've spoiled the opportunity to get to know her better."

"You never know. Take it from someone who knows what it was like to be closed off. Talk to her, let her know how you feel. It really can work wonders." She placed a supportive hand on his shoulder before she went to her office, leaving him to think about her words.

***

After spending his first night in a proper bed since leaving the hospital, Salvatore woke refreshed. He felt good; his sleep had been deep and undisturbed. The men who had removed the old sofa bed had taken it upstairs to store in the spare bedroom, which stood empty apart from some cardboard boxes stacked against a wall.

Before she'd left for work, Nadia had made him a pot of coffee and left it beside the bed along with two cornetti and he lay propped up by pillows gazing out over the garden.

The Golden Oriel returned and sat on a low branch singing, and this pleased Salvatore. It gave him a feeling of hope. Hope that today would bring him happiness. He unwrapped a cornetto and watched the bird as he dipped the pointed end of the pastry into his tiny cup of coffee. The natural world had always fascinated him, and this, along with the golden bird, gave him an idea.

He showered and then returned his breakfast tray to the kitchen and picked up his keys. Pulling the front door closed behind him, he made his way out to the front of the villa. The plants that Alina had donated were flowering, and this added to his good mood. He stopped for a while and sat looking over the empty street, wishing someone would pass by to say hello and pass the time of day. Being confined to his home and chair was a lonely existence.

Several weeks had passed since Salvatore had last opened his studio, and nothing had changed. Clay dust covered the work surfaces, tools lay undisturbed and ceramics in various stages of manufacture lay untouched. He collected a metal bucket and, with it perched on his feet, slotted between his knees, he started clearing the nearest surface to the door. Neglected clay pots left to dry for too long were no longer worth keeping and those along with balled up paper and dried pots of glazes and colour where dropped into the bucket. He took a hand brush and swept the surface clean, getting more of dust on himself than the floor.

When full, he took the bucket outside and wheeled himself across the tarmac to the *comune* waste bin and deposited the contents inside. He repeated this action several times until the workstations and his wheel were clear. He tested the tap at the sink and the water ran a dirty grey before running clear and once again he filled the bucket and, taking a cloth, he washed the potter's wheel until the rotating disc was once again pristine.

He left the blocked clay extruder until another day and avoided opening his kiln, keeping his attention on making the studio clear of dust and debris first.

As he almost completed bringing the main room to order, he heard his daughter's scooter arriving outside. He looked through the windows, glad he'd not cleaned them yet as the dirt gave him some cover. He saw Issac's pickup pull into the street and as the door closed with a clunk, Nadia walked towards it. Salvatore watched them talking. Initially, there was nothing suspicious in their conversation until he saw their hands creep towards each other and they joined before they broke apart and walked towards the side of the villa and disappeared from view.

Quickly, Salvatore opened the studio door and wheeled himself up the path and let himself inside his home; he'd worry about locking the studio later. For now, he didn't want Nadia to know he'd been inside. He moved over to the kitchen window and could only see the pickup and Nadia's scooter; he made his way into the *salotto* and saw them in the garden talking. Standing apart as Issac pointed to different parts of the garden. He moved back slightly as they looked over at the *porte-finestre*, and Nadia gave him a wave. He returned it and they made their way towards him. Salvatore fixed a smile on his face and opened the door. "*Ciao*," he said. "What are you two up to?"

"I saw Issac as I left work and he wanted to show me something in the garden," Nadia said.

Nothing has changed since you last saw it.

He didn't believe his daughter's response, but smiled, hoping it would hide his thoughts.

Issac made his excuses and left and Nadia came inside and went straight to the kitchen to make a start on dinner. Salvatore sat with thoughts brewing, his assumptions fermenting as he listened to his daughter humming as she prepared their evening meal.

Thirty

Trenta

"I received a text from Nolan last night." Gabby said as she rinsed the last of the breakfast dishes and placed them on the drainer. "He arrived in Monte Marcone yesterday. Spent the night with Nico and asked if we'd like to meet up for dinner tonight. He says he wants to talk to me about forthcoming features."

"Tonight is good for me," Riccardo said. "Today, I have to go over to see Ennio at the stables. I should be back before lunch. What are you up to?"

"I thought I'd give Hannah a call. Remember I met her with Penny a few days ago?"

Riccardo nodded, picked up his briefcase and kissed Gabby on the cheek and after he'd said, "Love you babe," He was out of the door and on his way to his meeting.

Gabby went to her office and fired up her desktop computer and downloaded her emails before sitting down. She scrolled through her mail, everything from missives from the magazine to sales pitches from writers who assumed she could get their work seen by the editor through a digital back door. There was nothing that needed her immediate attention and the piece she'd been working on just needed a final read through before she submitted it. She checked her schedule of forthcoming features and checked the numbers for the new season of creative writing classes that would resume at the end of the month, before she locked the door again and went outside.

The sky was blue and cloudless, a sure sign that the day would be warm. Standing with her hands on her hips, looking down the fields that sloped down to Quadroni, she could see a man walking through his olives, a large white Pastori dog at his side. She remembered being chased by one of the white beasts the year before, and she still shuddered at the thought of meeting one up close.

As she turned away, a lizard stopped still on a window ledge and looked up at her, ready to dart to safety if need be. She gazed at it as it soaked up the sun's rays before she took out her phone and dialled Hannah's number. As the call rang out Gabby thought about how lucky she was, how the brief pleasures like watching a lizard enriched her life.

"*Pronto*," a voice said.

"Hi, Hannah. It's Gabby. I've been thinking about what you said about searching for that eureka moment."

"Oh, Hi. Yes?"

"I wondered if we could meet up one day to discuss it?"

"Well, I'm free today if that suits you."

"I can't get away today. Riccardo has taken the car."

"I could come to you if you don't mind?"

Gabby gave Hannah directions and agreed to meet her in an hour's time. Until then, she'd take a walk and enjoy the morning.

***

Issac was already at the stables when Riccardo arrived. He was standing in the cleared olive grove amid the holes in the ground where the trees had once stood. In his hands he was holding a plastic tray with small plants that he must have spent the morning digging up.

"Cyclamen," Ennio said nodding towards Issac in the field, "He's been here digging them up to transfer them elsewhere."

"I came to see how the work was progressing and it looks like it's ahead of schedule."

"Yes, today the ground team is coming to level the land and mark out where the buildings and pipe work will go.

It's rather exciting to see our new project taking shape."

The men retired to the patio table and as Nadia brought out a tray of coffee; she told Riccardo that her father wanted to give him something. "I'll call on him when I've finished here," he said.

Over coffee, he and Ennio went over plans and documents that needed to be signed for the *comune* to allow construction to begin.

"When do you think you'll be up and running?"

"We're hoping. Italian builders permitting," Ennio had a cheeky smile as he spoke, "to be open for business around September."

"I think local people looking for work will appreciate you."

"Yes, Valentina is hoping to find a more permanent position for Nadia."

"That should keep Issac here."

"Really? Are they…?" Ennio didn't need to complete his sentence.

"It's still early days." Riccardo looked across at Issac working in the field. "Perhaps I shouldn't have said anything."

"I understand." Ennio made a locking gesture with a finger and thumb in front of his mouth and mimed throwing away a key.

"Alina's nonna has been over discussing menu options with Valentina."

"It looks like your family has settled into the community favourably."

"I think we have."

Riccardo shuffled the paperwork on the table into a neat pile and placed it back inside his briefcase and stood up. "Thanks for the coffee. Give my regards to Valentina. Now I need to pay Signor Pasquini a visit." As he drove away, he saw Ennio in his rear-view mirror waving, before he slid around a bend and headed to the top of the village.

Riccardo thought the Pasquini villa was looking better with every visit.

Someone had trimmed back the borders and new bedding was in place to complement the plant pots that were now blooming. The weeds in the gravel driveway were no longer there, and it looked like someone had raked it level. Getting out of his car, he noticed the chain to the studio next door was loose, the padlock open and hanging from a link. Salvatore opened the door before Riccardo had reached it and welcomed him. "Nadia said you wanted to see me?"

"Yes, come in." Salvatore wheeled his chair backwards to allow Riccardo to step inside.

In the kitchen, Riccardo declined another coffee and told Salvatore that he had nothing new to report about his case. "There is something I wanted to ask you."

"Yes?"

"It's about Issac."

"What about him? Are you unhappy with his work?"

Salvatore shook his head and said, "It's delicate. I think he is becoming over-friendly with Nadia."

"Over-friendly?" Riccardo asked.

"Yes. I've seen them whispering in corners and holding hands."

"And this concerns you?"

"Yes. I think she's too young to become involved with a man." Riccardo felt Salvatore was keeping something more to himself.

"Maybe it will be brief. A young and simple romance."

"I don't want her to have a romance with a—" he stopped speaking abruptly.

Riccardo thought it was what he'd not said that spoke volumes before he replied. "Would you like me to speak with him?" Salvatore opened his mouth to speak, but Riccardo's upheld hand stopped him. "Although I don't see it as my place to speak with Issac, I will. But I cannot and will not advise him in any way. All I will do is explain that you have your reservations. But I will advise you to speak frankly with your daughter."

"*Grazie, Avvocato.*" Salvatore smiled and then moved across the room and picked up a vase and passed it to Riccardo. "I've been clearing out my studio, and this is one of the last pieces I made. I'd very much like to gift it to Gabby… Unless you have any objections?"

"No, none. I think she'll be more than happy to receive it. Thank you, Salvatore."

***

Carrying a posy of wildflowers, Gabby emerged from the trees at the rear of the villa as a powder-blue Citroen DS21 pulled into the drive. She paused, watching the fusiform shaped classic park up, and Hannah climb out of the left-hand side. "That's some car," she said, making her way over to her guest. "How old is it?"

"It a 1967 model. Used to belong to my father's neighbour in France."

"It's a real beauty. But how do you get around the narrow streets of Palombaro in this? Look at the length of the bonnet."

"It would be problematic. And probably wouldn't make it up the hill." She gave a small laugh. "I have a friend with a lockup in Piano Aventino. I keep it there and during the week, I use my little Yaris."

The women embraced with air kisses and Hannah followed Gabby inside. She stood looking around the kitchen and said, "This is a lovely room. I love that big wooden table and the drying rack above it covered in pots and pans. Looks the image of perfect Italian rural living."

"Thanks." Gabby held up the Moka pot and Hannah nodded, spooning in coffee she said, "The table belonged to Riccardo's family. This was his family home."

Hannah ran a hand over the wooden dresser against the

wall and commented on the array of plates in various styles and patterns. "Family china?"

"I collected them when I lived in London from charity shops and second-hand markets."

"I miss the markets in France."

"Where you there long?"

"I didn't live there. My parents live near Limoges and I visit them as often as I can. It was their move that inspired me to make the move to Italy."

Gabby placed the coffee on the table alongside some cups and reached over and brought a tin of biscuits to the table. "What drew you to Abruzzo and Palombaro?"

"An accident." Gabby's eyebrows raised curiously. "I had my heart set on a house in Lazio when a friend who was here on a skiing holiday fell and broke her wrist. I came to see her and one day she introduced me to the owner of our palazzo and as soon as I stepped inside, I fell in love with it."

"Love at first sight?"

"You could say so. The owner joked, asking me if I'd like to buy it, and without thinking, I said yes. My mother rolled out the adage, 'buy in haste, repent at leisure.' It needed a lot of work; the electrics were lethal and the plumbing had to be condemned, but I've never regretted it."

The conversation centred around each of their journeys to Abruzzo and although they were historically worlds apart, Gabby felt they were alike in many other ways. Both determined. Both driven and independent.

Gabby gave Hannah a tour of the vineyard, telling her its history, choosing to leave out the darker parts of the family's past and, as it ended in her office, she told Hannah about her idea.

Riccardo arrived as Hannah was leaving. Gabby introduced him and he made a point of commenting on her car and as it moved down the drive like a slender torpedo, his gaze followed it.

Riccardo reached into his car and retrieved the vase and handed it to Gabby. "It's one of Salvatore's. He asked me to give it to you."

"Did he make this?"

"Yes. He said it's one of the last ones he made."

"It's beautiful," Gabby said, looking at the finely tapered sides with stems of lilac-coloured borage that were so well painted they could almost be photographs. Gabby ran a finger over the small painted flower and spotted a painted honeybee in the vase's mouth, tiny, but with exquisite detail.

Thirty-One

Trentuno

The restaurant Nolan had chosen had an unpretentious, modern look. Tables made from what looked like repurposed wood with scrubbed surfaces had orange chairs that worked well with the multitude of golden globes of light that were suspended from the ceiling. The bar had a more industrial look, with what looked like scaffold poles supporting the distressed boards that made up the countertop. Shining down were more glass globes, each one was illuminating the glass inserts set into wood. The waiters were suitably attired in crisp white shirts beneath fashionably faded and torn denim dungarees. "This place looks amazing," Gabby said as they were directed to a table facing the door. A bucket containing chilled prosecco was already waiting for them and, as the waiter removed the cork, Gabby noticed Nolan and Nico in the doorway.

Nolan had always had a penchant for tall, muscular men, and Nico wasn't how Gabby had imagined him to be. Nolan wasn't tall, but neither was Nico. He was shorter than Nolan by around two inches and had a slim physique that matched his long, slender face. His dark and wavy hair was shoulder length, giving him the look of an American rockstar. She imagined he wouldn't look out of place as a guitarist in Jon Bon Jovi's backing band. The illusion shattered when he spoke, his voice heavy with an Italian accent thickened with his English pronunciations.

After the niceties of polite introductions, they all took their seats and the waiter hovered beside them as they looked at the menu. He sauntered away with the orders, his mincing gait at odds with the uniform.

"I am happy at meeting you," Nico said, and Gabby smiled. "My English is not good, sorry."

"I think it'll be much better than Nolan's Italian," she said and saw her boss toss her a scowl.

"So, tell me, what is it you do, Nico?" Riccardo asked him in Italian.

"*Sono un dentista.*"

For the first time Gabby noticed Nico's perfect white smile and thought, *that makes sense*.

The dinner arrived and as they tucked into their *primo corso*, Nolan enquired about how things were going with the vineyard. Riccardo answered his questions while Gabby chatted quietly with Nico.

With the plates cleared, Nolan asked Gabby how she'd been getting on with a current project for the magazine.

"It's almost finished."

"Good. I'm taking a trip with Nico to see a castle in Tuscany that does retreats for amateur painters."

"I didn't think you were interested in painting," Riccardo said.

"Oh heaven, no, I'm not. Paint under the fingernails isn't something I'd embrace. Our features department is thinking of doing a monthly feature on hobby based places to stay in Europe. Last week, I visited a hotel in the Cotswolds that runs a course for people who want to communicate with their departed family members."

"Did you speak to anyone who'd passed over from your family?"

"Come on Gabby, what do you think? I can hardly bring myself to communicate with those that are still living, let alone them that have sashayed away, as Mama Ru would say."

"Well, if you're looking for somewhere out of the norm, I may have found a place. It's a palazzo in Palombaro."

"Tell me later. Here comes the second course."

"Ah, I adore *coniglio selvatico*," said Nico. "Have you

had this before Gabby?" She shook her head and Nico told her how his nonna used to make the wild rabbit stew. "My family is originally from the island of Ischia, where this is a very popular dish."

The evening continued with cordial conversation. Gabby noticed that being with Nico, Nolan seemed to rein in his usual caustic wit and was more involved rather than dominating the conversation. After digestivi, they all said goodnight and Nolan and Nico declined an offer to drive them home, choosing to walk as the evening air still held on to its warmth.

"Do you think Hannah will be open to showing Nolan around her place?" asked Riccardo as the tree canopy in the lane up to their villa plunged them into darkness.

Before she replied, Gabby felt the car slow. They'd often encounter wild boar or deer in the lane at this time of night. "I've already spoken to her about some ideas I have for her retreat, and I think a magazine feature could boost her occupancy. But she'll have to square the idea with Penny first."

They stopped outside their villa and as the cooling engine ticked, the front door opened, flooding the drive with golden light. "I heard you arrive," Issac said. "Good evening?"

"Yes, it was really nice," Riccardo said.

"Nico was a surprise," Gabby said.

"In what way?"

"Open a bottle of red and I'll tell you. If he was six inches taller, he wouldn't look out of place in a line-up of male strippers."

***

The following morning, Gabby called Hannah to tell her about the conversation with Nolan the night before.

"I've been thinking about what you said about using the

vacant room as a writing retreat." Hannah said. "Are you sure you could spare the time to run it?"

"Absolutely. Your suggestion of two fourteen-day sessions twice a year should cover it."

"Magic. Let's give it some thought and talk about it again at a later date."

"Okay, I'll put together a proposed timetable of activities."

Gabby put her phone down and walked outside and stood looking out over the valley, as she did most days. "I could never get bored with this view," she said to herself softly as she thought about her own creative writing workshops. They were less formal than her proposed idea of writers who were aiming towards publication. Her group was mostly doing it for fun and for the social side of things. Issac had been her only published pupil, writing naturalistic and gardening articles for the freelance market.

Thinking about Issac, she wondered if he'd smoothed things out with Nadia.

Thirty-Two

Trentadue

Both Nadia and Issac were working at *Le Stelle* for the day. They'd undertaken their usual arrangement where she left her scooter in the Eurospin car park, and he'd driven them both to Sant'Andrea. "I'm glad we're friends again," she'd said as the pickup moved along the coast road.

"Just friends?"

"You know what I mean," he'd placed his hand on hers and for a moment their fingers entwined until he returned his to the wheel.

"I'm helping Luca plant tomatoes today," he said. "We've cleared a space twice the size of the hotel's orto to grow them this year. I can't believe how many Tiziana and the kitchen get through."

"I can," laughed Nadia, "this is Italy, after all."

Outside the entrance, Nadia skipped across the gravel and entered the hotel via the reception area. Silvana had said she thought it was proper that staff came into work through the rear of the building. "I don't think it matters," Rachel had said, much to Silvana's annoyance.

Nadia went to put on her apron and went upstairs to assist with the room changes. While she worked, she glanced out of the window to see Issac with his sleeves rolled up; he was digging the holes that Luca dropped the tomato plants into. It was Nadia's last day at the hotel and she felt a little sad; she'd enjoyed working for Rachel, but she also wondered if her sadness was because she'd no longer share the journey to Sant'Andrea with Issac.

There was a break mid-morning and Nadia spotted Issac leaning against the outbuilding in the orto; Luca had gone inside to find Rachel. She ambled over, looking back over her shoulder, hoping Silvana didn't spot her. "Busy?" she asked him, coming around the ramshackle building that was used as a tool store.

"I'm enjoying the shade. It's getting hot today."

Nadia reached out for his hand, and they clasped them together. Standing opposite, they looked into the other's eyes. "We have to be careful. I don't want to upset Silvana."

"Best not. She's a dragon when angered." Issac laughed.

"She's not that bad. Just a stickler for rules. It could be worse."

"How?"

"It could be my father finding out about us."

"Do you really think he'd be upset?"

"I'm not sure, but I dare not risk it."

Issac cupped her chin in his hand and gently lowered his lips onto hers, before he said, "Would you like me to talk to him?"

"No. Maybe I will bring the subject up later." She rested her head on his chest, wondering if speaking with her father was a good idea. *At least I'll know how he feels,* she thought as she listened to Issac's steady heartbeat.

Walking past, Louise disrupted their moment of togetherness and they broke apart quickly, a slight reddening flushing Nadia's cheeks.

"Your secret's safe with me," Louise said, causing Nadia's blush to redden further.

"I'd better get back," Nadia whispered to Issac, she gave Louise a smile and with rushed back to the hotel.

"Sorry, did I spoil things?"

"No, we were just having a moment alone." Issac said.

"So, how is it going with you two?"

"Could be better." Issac saw the question cross Louise's mind before she asked it and said, "It's her father. We don't think he'd approve."

"After everything you've done for him, you'd think he'd

be happy for his daughter to meet someone so caring."

"I don't think it's as simple as that."

"You never know," Louise said. "You may have misjudged him."

***

Alina carried a tray of sunflower seedlings as she walked alongside her nonna, who was carrying a cake she'd made the day before. "I hope signor Pasquini likes polenta cake."

"Everyone likes your polenta cake," Alina said as she spotted Salvatore outside the front of his villa. She introduced her nonna, who held up the cake and then said, "Where are your window boxes?"

"I've painted them. I was just about to put them back in place."

"Sonny is coming over to help me plant these in the border behind the raised bed, so we can do that for you."

"That's good of you. Well then, why don't we all go inside and I'll make coffee and we can enjoy a slice of cake."

Salvatore and Nonna were sitting under an umbrella on the patio chatting as they looked over to where Sonny and Alina had planted the sunflowers. "They will make a cheerful backdrop to the herb garden Issac built for me."

"Yes, they will," Nonna said. "He's such a kind young man. He tidied up some of our land and pruned the olives."

"Do you think he'll stay here in Abruzzo?"

"I'm not sure. He seems to be happy here."

"But if his gardening business doesn't work out, he'd maybe be tempted to go back home."

"Maybe. But I think he'll make a success of it. He's certainly not afraid of hard work. Valentina, at the stables, speaks highly of him."

Sonny and Alina interrupted and said they'd fixed the newly painted window boxes in place and this ended the conversation about Issac as everyone went out front to look at them.

***

Nadia said goodbye to Issac and climbed aboard her scooter to head back to Laroscia. All afternoon she'd been mulling over what she'd say to her father. Several times she had dismissed the idea, but it kept rotating in her head and she realised that if she didn't broach the subject, she'd never know his opinion, *What if I'm worrying about nothing*, she thought as she turned the ignition key and pulled out of the car park.

She smiled when she saw the neatened up entrance to the villa. Ever since Alina had planted the flowers, the Pasquini villa had become more welcoming. The hot weather had warmed the geraniums, and their scarlet and pink heads were a riot of colour alongside the orange marigolds in the terracotta pots. Alina had sown zinnia seeds along one border and the plants were reaching upward, their young buds promising vibrant flowers.

She parked her scooter in the shade and checked the cassetta for mail, then went inside the house, where the shaded rooms were a cool and welcoming respite from the sun.

Salvatore was in the kitchen when Nadia entered, and on the table under a net cloche were two pork steaks and a bowl of salad. "Have you had any dinner?"

"Yes, Tiziana served us all a bowl of pasta." Nadia returned the steaks to the fridge and set the Moka pot on the stove. She felt her heart thumping as she told her father she wanted to talk to him over a coffee.

Salvatore had settled himself into the armchair that looked out over the garden and Nadia placed the tray of coffees beside his chair and on a plate, she'd placed two apricot crostatini.

"The garden is looking better."

"Yes, it is," Salvatore replied. "Issac is doing a good job."

"*Papà*. What do you think of Issac?"

"He's a good-hearted young man. I admire his work ethic."

"But do you like him?"

"Why do you ask? Is something going on between the two of you?"

"No!" Nadia realised she'd answered too quickly. "No *Papà*, we are just friends."

"Good. I hope it stays that way."

"Why *Papà?*"

"Because I want you to find a nice local boy. You should be with your own kind."

"Own kind... Italian?"

"Abruzzese. I wouldn't be happy if my daughter got involved with an Englishman."

"But, Issac's not English, *Papà*."

"Don't be insolent! You know what I mean."

Her father's response was enough for Nadia to shut down the conversation. He'd not raised his voice to her for a good while, and she didn't want to go back to the days where he harboured internal anger. *It's best Issac and I keep our relationship secret;* she thought as she picked up her fruit pie and bit into it. The conversation was closed and no longer up for discussion, but Nadia wondered why her father was vehemently against the idea of her being with Issac.

Thirty-Three

Trentatré

Salvatore left the villa and opened up his studio and once inside, he locked the door behind himself, shutting out the conversation with his daughter.

The discussion with Nadia had brought self-imprisoned memories to the surface. Recollections he'd pushed down inside himself. Locked away by alcohol fuelled evenings, he'd secured them in a place he never dared to go to – now they were back at the forefront of his consciousness.

It was the week before Cristina had finally left him; the memory played as vividly as if he was watching it on a screen. They were standing opposite each other with faces etched with anger. He was hurling accusations at her, a volley of allegations that she had grown tired of defending. It didn't matter how many times she told him the Englishman was just a co-worker from the office where she worked. The more she denied it, the more he doubted her. The drink fed his paranoia, making him more unreasonable as the argument progressed.

Seven nights later, as he lay comatose on the sofa, she'd gone.

Salvatore thought of the wardrobe filled with the clothes she didn't pack. Had she hated living with him so much she took no reminders, or was she escaping in fear? A question that had tormented him constantly.

He shook the memory away and wheeled himself around the studio; it was looking better now he'd began the cleanup. He'd laid out utensils in an orderly fashion and decorated pots and vases; pieces he was proud of stood on a shelf across the room.

It was time he cleaned his kiln and, opening the door, he peered inside. It was empty apart from the solitary bottle he'd hidden there long ago.

He looked over his shoulder as if expecting someone to be there, but he was alone. He reached in and took out the unopened bottle of clear spirit. The grappa spoke to him, almost like a friend from his past. His head told him to pour it away, and he moved towards the sink and broke the seal, but a gnawing in his body, something tugging at his insides stopped him and he screwed the lid tight again and stood it on the countertop and went back to the kiln. He swept out the dust, constantly looking back over at the bottle that seemed to whisper his name.

Thirty-Four

Trentaquattro

Earthmovers and workmen had moved onto the land belonging to the stables the day before with shouting workers and rumbling machinery that was at odds with the normally serene countryside. Ennio had stabled the thoroughbreds with a neighbour, only the trekking, less nervous horses remained, including Sonny's horse, Ferro. Because of this, Sonny took less time over the morning checks. The paddock was off limits and Sonny knew his rust-coloured horse missed its morning exercise in the rectangular area of grass.

Alina had arrived and helped Sonny to tack up his horse and a grey mare she was fond of riding, and as the generators started grumbling behind the stable block, the two horses trotted out onto the lane.

With the sound of construction fading, Alina asked Sonny how long the work would take. "Nonna said yesterday that it disturbed her afternoon nap."

"Father says two or three days, then the cement lorries will pour in the foundations, but I think the noise will carry on for a while."

"I'll have to find Nonna some cotton wool to stuff in her ears then," laughed Alina.

"Where shall we go this morning?" Sonny said, "The river or up towards Cotti?"

"Let's go to Verratti. We haven't ridden there for a while."

A thin layer of cloud shielded the sun, making the morning pleasant and not too warm. It was the perfect morning for a ride.

Coming into the piazza leading to the Verratti road.

Alina pointed out the front of the Pasquini villa, with its new window boxes and planters in full bloom.

"That looks much better now," Sonny said. "How is the garden coming along?"

"You must come and see the planting around the new seating."

"What about the horses?"

"We can tie them up to the fence at the fence for a few minutes. They should be fine; they'll still be able to see us."

Alina led Sonny into the garden and was pointing out the changes that Issac had made, making a point of talking about the parts of the patio beside the ruin where she'd worked. "Come look at the raised beds," she said.

On the patio Alina became so absorbed as she talked about the flowers she'd planted, and the ones she'd sown herself, that she didn't notice that Sonny wasn't listening to her. She turned around to see him with his nose pressed up against the glass of the *porte-finestre*. "Alina, come look."

"What is it?"

"Signor Pasquini. He looks strange."

Alina joined him, and shielding her eyes, she peered through the glass into the *salotto*. "He looks asleep."

"I'm not sure. I don't think he looks well."

Alina pressed her face closer and said, "You're right, what's that down his shirt front?"

"I don't know, but I think we should wake him and check he's okay."

Alina called Salvatore's name while two pairs of small fists banged against the glass. "He's not moving. He can't hear us."

Sonny tried the door. "It's locked." Their banging fists became more intense until Sonny said. "We'll have to go back and tell Nadia. She's working this morning."

Panic gave their feet speed and Alina, knowing her disability would slow them down, told Sonny to race back and she'd meet him there.

Being urged on, Ferro cantered down the lane and turned swiftly into the stable yard. Sonny dismounted and ran inside the villa, calling out for Nadia.

Coming back outside as Alina's grey mare came into the yard, he shouted, "She's not here."

"What's going on?" Issac said coming from behind the stable block, "What's all this commotion?"

"Where's Nadia?"

"She's gone out with your mother. Why?"

Alina was gabbling. Words tumbling out of her mouth with urgency. "It's Salvatore… the Pasquini villa…"

"He looks dead," Sonny shouted. "We banged on the glass."

"Slow down," Issac said. "Slowly, tell me what's the matter here."

Alina took a deep breath and recounted what they'd seen looking through the glass of the *porte-finestre*.

"It was locked," added Sonny. "We tried it."

"Wait here." Issac brushed compost off his hands, ran to his pickup and, with a squeal, it reversed and left the yard, leaving Alina and Sonny looking after it, concern written on their faces.

***

Leaving the pickup door open, Issac raced to the door of Pasquini's villa and banged his fists against it. Getting no response, he remembered Nadia telling him she kept a spare key hidden under the plant pot beneath the mailbox. He lifted the pot and removed the key and, calling Salvatore's name, he opened the front door.

The hall was dim. Slanted stabs of light came from the gaps in the shutters and Issac opened one to allow the daylight to spill inside.

He walked to the *salotto* door and pushed it open and the fetid stench of vomit and alcoholic spirt assaulted his nostrils. Instantly, he knew what had happened here.

Issac closed the door behind himself and walked over to the bed and pressed his fingers to Salvatore's neck. A relieved breath escaped Issac's lips; he was alive.

Glad to see the key in the door, he opened the *porte-finestre*, allowing fresh air inside. Turning back, he looked at Salvatore; he had passed out on the bed with vomit painting a vile trail down his shirt front. A pillow supported him, and with his head elevated, Issac thought that his position had saved him from choking on his vomit and, thus, saving his life.

Issac tried his best to rouse the man. "Salvatore?" he murmured.

A phlegmy cough rattled in his throat, and stale vomit dribbled from his mouth. He grumbled as he woke, his eyes glassy and unfocussed until they closed again. Issac slid his arms beneath Salvatore's armpits and lifted his body, shuffling him into a sitting position at the edge of the bed. He tried lifting him, but the vomit caused him to slide. Although he was much slighter than the Scotsman; he was a dead weight and lifting him upright was like wrestling with a human rag doll.

"Wait," he said, and resting Salvatore against the bedhead, he went into the shower room, opened the cubicle, and turned on the water. Returning to the *salotto*, he undressed Salvatore and then lifted him like a sleeping child and carried him into the shower room and under the flowing water. Together they stood there, one man fully clothed, the other naked until the remnants of his soiling washed away. After doing his best with shampoo and body wash, Issac returned Salvatore to his bedroom and, after wrapping him in a towel, placed him in his wheelchair while he went upstairs.

His wet shoes squelched, and he was afraid of slipping on the tiled floor. In the bedroom, he found a shirt, clean underwear and trousers and went back to dress him.

Leaving Salvatore to come around properly, he stripped the bed; the sheets were stained and wet, another nasty odour to add to the first. The washing machine in the shower room filled with water and began washing away the mess from the bed and Issac removed his own clothes and pushed them inside a supermarket carrier bag that had held a carton of laundry powder. He pulled on Salvatore's dressing gown; it was far too small and barely covered his modesty, but without a thought, he dragged the mattress from the bed and lay it outside in the sun before he went upstairs to fetch clean bedding. He cleaned the shower room before going back to check on Salvatore, who had opened his eyes and in silence watched the gardener take care of everything.

In the kitchen, Issac filled a glass with water. "Drink this," he said, handing it to Salvatore, who opened his mouth to speak. Issac shook his head, "We can talk when you're sober." A tear slid down Salvatore's cheek, but Issac ignored it. He wanted everything to be put back straight before Nadia came home. He couldn't let her see this.

After an hour, he sprayed the mattress with fabric freshener and although it hadn't dried fully; he flipped it over and remade the bed. Throughout the time it took for the room to be put back in order and the bedsheets to be pegged out on the washing line, Salvatore had said nothing, his eyes following the young Scotsman about as he rectified the Italian's fall from grace.

Thirty-Five

Trentacinque

Louise was having breakfast in the hotel's dining room when Rosa joined her at the table. "*Qui. Perché?*" She only had a limited knowledge of Italian but had picked up enough to understand what the old woman had asked her.

"Why here?" Louise said. "Because I am too lazy to make my own." She folded a slice of salami in half and popped it into her mouth as a waiter delivered two warmed *cornetti* to the table. Rosa's understanding of English was zero and so she just shrugged and pulled a corner off one of Louise's pastries and popped it into her mouth just as the waiter delivered her a coffee – something that happened regularly to the old woman from down the lane.

"*Buongiorno Rosa*," Rachel said, coming into the dining room; she acknowledged the waiter who enquired if she'd like a coffee too and took a seat at the table. "What time is Ben arriving?" she asked Louise.

"Ben?" Rosa said, her eyes lighting up. "*Mi piace Ben. Sta venendo qui.*"

"We know you like Ben, and yes, he's coming today."

"*Perché?*"

"We're having a small party for him and Louise to celebrate their engagement."

Hearing the word 'Party,' Rosa's eyes lit up again, and she asked if it was to be a grand affair and if so, what should she wear?

Louise's eyes questioned Rachel: she often felt left out of their Italian conversations, not because she thought things were being said about her, but because she was, in her own words, 'a nosy bitch.'

"Rosa was asking what she should wear to your party?"

"Tell her it's going to be on the beach. She could come in a bikini if she wants to."

Rachel translated for the old woman and she scowled and said something in dialect that neither of them understood, then her chair scraped on the floor as she stood up, swallowed her coffee in one mouthful and said, "*Bikini? Vado subito a sceglierne uno.*" They could hear her laughter as she left the dining room and walked through the reception area, and Louise shuddered as Rachel told her Rosa was off to choose one to wear.

"To answer your question earlier," Louise said. "He called me and said he was having a stopover in Ancona, so should be here just before midday."

"You'll no doubt want to talk about wedding plans."

"Oh no, we'll be too busy doing the horizontal shuffle in your spare bedroom."

"Too much information," Rachel laughed.

Ben arrived at the time he had promised, and after unloading his car with English supplies for Rachel and Gabby, he showered and joined Louise in the garden. She was waiting for him inside the gazebo. Mirella had delivered an ice bucket and chilled bottle of prosecco and, seeing Louise, he broke into a wide, toothy smile. "I thought you'd be waiting for me in the apartment," he said, leaning down to kiss her.

"I was tempted. But thought it would be more romantic this way." She removed the bottle and poured two flutes of fizzing wine. Taking one each, they chinked their glasses together, and he took the seat opposite.

They remained sitting in silence for a few moments, sipping their drinks and letting the relaxed atmosphere take over. The lilies planted beside the gazebo were opening early, releasing their heady scent into the still air. The sky had been cloudless all day, and the heat had become stifling. Looking eastward, dark clouds were gathering, swirling about like water travelling down a plughole. "Luca thinks there'll be a thunderstorm today," said Louise. "He said we need a storm to cool everything down. Rachel told me she thought it was hotter this year."

"That'll be global warming," Ben said. "Interferes with nocturnal nookie."

Louise gave him a playful slap on the arm. "Nothing should interfere with bedtime cuddling."

"Isn't that the truth?" He pulled her close and his lips were on hers in an instant.

After they'd broken apart, Louise raised her hand to allow her engagement ring to sparkle in the sunshine.

"Happy?" Ben asked

"Yes. I am." They kissed again, gently and less fervently, savouring their moment.

Picking his glass up, Ben said, "Do you think Rachel would be up for letting us get married here? The setting is perfect."

"I'm not sure. We joked about it, but I would hate for her to think we were looking for her to do it at mate's rates."

"I'll talk to her, let her know we'll pay the going rate."

Holding hands and both with smiles that could be seen from space, they put down their drinks and walked down to the boundary fence and looked out over the olive groves below.

Louise gave a contented sigh and, looking at her closely, Ben said, "You really like it here, don't you?"

"I do. But I don't think I'd be brave enough to up sticks and move here like Rachel did."

"Her situation was different."

Changing the subject, Louise pulled him close and kissed him again and then said, "Come on, it's getting hotter out here. Let's grab our swimming gear and go down to the beach."

Ben left Louise in reception talking to Rachel and Rosa; the old woman who hadn't been shy of letting them know she'd taken a shine to Ben told them if she was younger, she'd beat Louise to the altar.

"You wouldn't say that if you lived with him," Louise laughed, "He's so messy. I often think he needs a mother, not a wife."

"I'd soon shake that nonsense out of him," cackled Rosa.

"I'm certain you would."

Ben arrived with Louise's beach bag as the three women laughed loudly and Rachel wished them both a happy afternoon at the beach and added that she'd asked Tiziana to prepare something special for dinner that night.

Thirty-Six

Trentasei

Salvatore looked out of the kitchen window and watched as two men left the Fiat that had pulled up outside his home. He knew the taller man with the huge moustache that hid his mouth, but didn't know the smaller, rotund man with him. He opened the front door and invited them both inside.

"This is my brother, Cosmo," Massimo, the taller of the men, said. He introduced Salvatore to Cosmo and after lots of hand shaking, he asked if there was coffee to be had.

"I'll make it," Nadia said, coming down the stairs. More introductions followed before she placed the Moka pot over the flame.

"Massimo and Cosmo are here to help Issac dismantle the *frantoio*," Salvatore told his daughter as she delivered the tray of coffees to the *salotto* where they were all seated.

"What time is he arriving?" asked Massimo.

The rumble of a small yellow excavator caught their attention as it appeared to push its way through the trees at the rear of the garden and Salvatore said, "Looks like he's just arrived."

Issac jumped down and strode towards the house as Nadia opened the *porte-finestre* and asked if he'd like a coffee. He declined and after morning pleasantries, Massimo and Cosmo followed Issac to the old olive mill, where they began dismantling one wall and stacking the stones for recycling at a later stage.

After a couple of hours, they had turned the *frantoio* into an artistically designed three-sided ruin. The large milling stone was now revealed, looking heavier and larger than it had inside the building.

"Lunch," Nadia called as she delivered a large bowl of

pasta alla Norma to the table on the patio.

Salvatore opened a carton of fruit juice and was pouring it into tumblers when the men arrived at his side. He spotted Issac looking at his hand as he poured and became conscious of the tremor.

"It's cooler today," Nadia said as she placed a basket of bread down.

"Perfect for working outside," Cosmo said, lowering himself into a seat.

"Will you be moving the millstone this afternoon?"

"Yes," said Issac, "by the end of today it should be in place over there." He pointed to a small square wall that he'd previously built. "There's a tank below for water."

"Good job you've brought along the excavator," said Massimo, "we'd never be able to move it ourselves."

"It must have taken many men to lift it into the trough when they built the mill." Nadia said.

"I imagine most of the men from the village and a couple of overworked mules," added Salvatore.

The conversation over lunch was about the garden and Issac's designs and as Nadia cleared the table Massimo turned to Salvatore and said, "Do you still make ceramics?"

"Not any longer," Salvatore said.

"*Pap*à still has his studio," Nadia said.

Salvatore glanced across at Issac, fearing he'd mention the grappa he'd found in the kiln, but Issac kept the incident to himself as Massimo told everyone how beautiful Salvatore's pottery had been. "You should take it up again."

"I'm not sure."

"Why not *Papà*?"

"What would I do with the things I made?"

"Sell them."

Salvatore shook his head. He'd been here before and it hadn't ended well. He was afraid to revisit that part of his life.

"Some of the gift shops on the coast could be interested

in stocking your ceramics again. Especially for the tourist trade," said Massimo. "I remember the seller had been pleased with the sales your pottery made for his Montesilvano shop. Why did you stop?"

Salvatore's eyes lowered to the floor, and he muttered, "It was just one of those things. The business didn't fit into our lives at the time." He thought this was the easiest answer he could give without going into detail.

"You could always set up an online shop. I'd help you." Nadia said.

"I've probably lost the skill by now."

"Nonsense." Nadia interjected.

Issac must have sensed that Salvatore was losing patience with the conversation, because he stood up and rallied everyone together to resume their work. He looked at Salvatore and gave him a discrete nod when he mouthed a thank you.

It took a lot of effort and swearing to move the millstone into place and standing back, everyone agreed it looked impressive.

"So that was the red X in your design that Alina pointed out?" Salvatore said.

"Yes. It will be a gentle water feature rather than a fountain," Issac said, and the wheel is wide enough for people to use it as a stone table.

"Alina will love it."

"It'll be so nice to eat here on sunny days with the water bubbling up through the centre." Nadia said, and Salvatore noticed how her eyes shone when she spoke to Issac about it. *Maybe he wouldn't be an awful choice for my daughter*, he thought, thankful for Issac's discretion. *Have his actions spurned a change in my opinion?*

"I'd better return the excavator to the builder down at the stables." Issac said and, climbing aboard, it trundled back through the trees as Massimo and Cosmo said their goodbyes.

After dinner, Nadia was in the sitting room when Salvatore appeared at the door and told her he was going next door to the studio. She looked up from the book she was reading and said, "I meant what I said earlier *Papà*. I could help you set up a shop online."

"We'll see," he replied, then he paused and said, "Are you going out with Issac tonight?" She looked shocked before she smiled and shook her head. "I'll be next door if you need me."

The strip lights above the studio ticked as they flickered into life. The room appeared larger in the evening, with every sound echoing around the space. Salvatore stopped at the pile of plastic bags containing the clay he'd abandoned years ago; it would be useless now and he'd need to throw it out, but he made a note to buy fresh clay. Maybe taking up his hobby again would help him deal with the boredom of being at home all day.

He picked up an unglazed bowl. The rough surface felt familiar to his fingertips. He moved across to his workbench and picked up a pencil and started drawing from memory. He was out of practice, and after his evening of drinking, his hand was shaky, but he was happy with the design he'd created. "With time, I'll get better," he said as the door opened and framed Nadia in the doorway. He beckoned her inside and held out the bowl for her to see.

"Have you drawn this tonight?"

"Yes. They're zinnia's. The flowers Alina has sown in the front border." Nadia leant down and kissed the top of her father's head and he looked up at her and said, "I'm going to give this another try."

"Bravo *Papà*."

Thirty-Seven

Trentasette

Riccardo had returned home after another ineffective meeting with Salvatore. He had explained that Alfredo, the other driver in the case, was still adamant that there had been a third car involved. No matter how hard Riccardo presented this argument, Salvatore was as equally unwavering as signor Petrini.

He opened his briefcase and removed the documents he'd received from both the police and the insurance companies and began poring over them one more time. He was shuffling through witness statements. One from a bar owner who stated he'd seen a third car and one from a pedestrian who had failed to spot a third car, but said she'd turned around only as she'd heard the accident happen.

"I must be missing something," Riccardo said aloud as Issac entered the kitchen.

"Problems?"

"Something just doesn't add up."

"Anything a fresh pair of ears might help with?"

Riccardo explained the dilemma to Issac; he wasn't telling him anything that could jeopardise the case; he was trying to explain the conundrum he was dealing with.

"Sounds to me like someone is mistaken or telling lies."

"But why lie? Neither party has anything to gain from it. All it's doing is delaying the outcome. And with this supposed third car hanging over the case, Petrini's insurance company won't pay out and Pasquini's claim will end up failing."

"Sorry I can't help." Issac shrugged his shoulders and said he was going outside to do some weeding among the vines and left Riccardo scratching his head at the kitchen table.

He was still reading the files when Gabby appeared. "Are you still going over those statements?"

"Yes, I must be missing something."

"Take a break from it, clear your mind, and come back to it with fresh eyes."

"I think I'll do that. What are you up to?"

"I'm planning the first workshop of the season for the writing group. I needed some notes I made earlier."

"I'll get changed and help Issac in the vineyard."

Later, Gabby placed a tray of sandwiches and coffee on the table outside and returned to her office, leaving Issac and Riccardo to their lunch.

"It's done me good to have a break. I needed to clear my head."

"What will you do if you can't get a resolution?"

"I'm not sure. Maybe I need to speak with the witnesses myself. But for now, I'm happy to spend my time pulling up weeds."

They sat in companionable silence for a while before Riccardo asked Issac how things were going with him and Nadia. "Okay. She told me her father had come around to the idea. He's mellowed, she said."

"Really. Salvatore doesn't strike me as the mellowing kind."

"He's so closed off sometimes that I think it takes time for him to relax with people."

"So, when are you seeing Nadia again?"

"Tomorrow. We've had an invitation to Louise and Ben's beach party."

"In that case, why don't we all go in one car?"

The sound of a car horn swallowed Issac's reply and the two men saw Nolan and Nico pull into the driveway.

The introductions over, Issac offered to make coffee and Riccardo went to fetch Gabby from her office.

"This is very English. Coffee and biscuits in the sitting room," Nolan said as Issac delivered the tray. "I thought you Italians always entertained in the kitchen."

"Nico is the only Italian here." Gabby said.

"What about Riccardo?" Nolan said.

"I'm a mongrel," he laughed. *"Metà e metà."*

"Don't lump me alongside all of you. I'm not English." Issac's statement confused Nico, and he explained he was Scottish.

"Right, with our heritage explained, what can we do for you, Nolan?"

"I've been thinking about what you told me about this woman who has the retreat in Palombaro. Do you think you could arrange a meeting with her?"

"Sure. Why?"

"I'd like to see if there'd be any mileage in a magazine feature."

"Fair enough. I'll call her."

As Gabby left the room, Nolan asked the others if they were going to the beach party the following day.

"I didn't know you knew Louise and Ben."

"I don't. Rachel invited me along and Nico's working, so it'll save me from being alone all day."

Gabby returned and told Nolan she'd made the arrangements for him to meet Hannah and he rose from the sofa. "Fabulous. Nico's taking me out for the afternoon, so we've got to run. I'll see you all tomorrow. Text me what time you'll pick me up." Riccardo opened his mouth to speak but Nolan cut him off with a broadcast of air kisses and a loud, *"Ciao a tutti."*

"Mamma mia," exclaimed Issac in Nolan's wake. "He's effusive, isn't he?"

"Isn't he just," laughed Gabby.

"I think I need to lie down."

Thirty-Eight

Trentotto

The thunderstorm a few days before had temporarily cleared the air, but now the first day of June arrived with a cloudless sky and the promise of a hot day.

The high sun made the sand look white as Riccardo and Gabby made their way down the steps to join the party of people erecting beach umbrellas and sunbeds. Gabby chuckled as she saw Luca struggling with a huge vinyl flamingo that seemed to resist all of his attempts to tame it.

Rachel held out a unicorn inflatable which Sprog took and ran with into the surf.

Ben opened two cool boxes and Louise wasted no time in popping a prosecco cork. "Get your fizz here!" she shouted, and Mole appeared at her side, holding out a plastic tumbler.

Beside the rocks under a portable gazebo was a picnic table with paper plates and forks beside another two cool boxes filled with food prepared by Tiziana in the hotel's kitchen.

Riccardo put down the beach chairs he was carrying as Gabby went to say hello to her friends and grab herself a drink of the prosecco before the sunshine warmed it. Penny called for the assistance of a 'big strong man' and Gabby pointed out Issac, who was in the middle of erecting an umbrella. Looking up, Isaac saw the woman at the top of the steps and went to help her, carrying all manner of beach paraphernalia while Penny held onto her sunhat and a clinking carrier bag of bottles.

Nadia sat watching as everyone sorted themselves into groups for their day at the beach. She'd been nervous about coming, because she didn't know many of the people socially and, having worked for Rachel, she thought she would feel awkward. Luckily, everyone had welcomed her and her anxiousness dissipated. Issac had told her the event was to celebrate Louise and Ben's engagement and she felt honoured to be a part of their celebrations. *Life is certainly different being with Issac*, she thought as he returned and handed her a glass of prosecco, his smile as wide as the horizon where the sea and sky met.

Ben produced a football and, being a typical Italian male, Luca was on his feet in an instant with Riccardo as the men began a kick about.

Nadia stood by the shore watching as Ivan swept Sprog up into his arms. He held her above his head, threatening to drop into the water next to Mole, who was floating on the inflatable flamingo. Sprog let out a scream of joy as her father dropped her and she sank under water, coming up spluttering and laughing at the same time.

Rachel joined Nadia and topped up her glass, asking her if she was enjoying herself.

"Yes, I'm happy to be invited."

"I'm sorry that I couldn't offer you any more shifts at the hotel, but if you're still interested, I can let you know when something becomes available."

"Thank you, that's very kind."

"Come, let me introduce you to Penny."

"Have we met before?" the woman in the oversized sunglasses and sunhat asked.

"I think I saw you some weeks ago at the Barone stables. You were talking to Valentina," said Nadia.

"Of course. That's where I've seen you before," Penny said, lowering the sunglasses to make eye contact over the frame, "It's lovely to meet you. Have you come to give us a hand with the buffet?"

"I have," Rachel interjected quickly, removing the film wrap from a bowl of salad.

"Can I help too?" Nadia said.

"Sure," Penny said, "But let's take our time." She gave a small laugh and reached over for an open bottle of prosecco, topped up Rachel and Nadia's glasses and added soda to make spritzers as she said, "No need to rush, is there?" The three of them set up the table, with Penny topping up glasses again as Nadia removed covered bowls and plates from the cool boxes.

Rachel covered a plate of tuna carpaccio with a cloche, the red flesh already turning darker with the lemon juice Tiziana had added to it, while Nadia removed a plate of baked mussels with a fragrant herb crust.

The football ended when Issac kicked the ball too hard and it flew into the bamboo at the edge of the beach and along with Ivan; he went to retrieve it as Ben asked if it was time to eat. Nadia chuckled when she heard Louise shout at him, "Can't you wait?"

"Kicking a ball about makes me hungry."

"Everything makes you hungry. No wonder you're spreading out around the middle." Everyone laughed when Ben feigned offence, his hand held against his forehead in a rather fey way, and Louise warned him he needed to lose weight if he wanted to be featured in *her* forthcoming wedding photographs.

"They're funny, aren't they?" Nadia said.

"They play fight all the time, but they adore each other."

"I can see that. Louise is very forthright, isn't she?"

"That's possibly one of the most polite things anyone has ever said about Louise's personality." Rachel smiled and then added. "She's been my best friend for years. I don't think I could have recovered when Marco died without her help."

Nadia didn't feel the need to make a comment. Issac had already told her about Rachel's history and knowing sadness herself, she didn't want to bring down the mood, so said, "Have Louise and Ben set a date for their wedding?"

"Not yet. Knowing my friend, they'll probably run away to Gretna Green and do it there."

"What is this… Gretna, that is green?"

"Issac can explain. It's a place over the Scottish border where people run away to, to get married in secret." Rachel looked up as Rosa called her name from the top of the steps and excused herself to help the old woman down to the beach.

At the table, Rosa removed the lid from a casserole dish and Nadia breathed in the aroma of a simple tomato sauce flavoured with anchovies and capers that Rosa had added to cooked pasta.

At a flat rock, Luca set up a portable gas ring and heated olive oil as he cleaned prawns and softened pieces of fresh calamari in milk.

The sea air and sunshine had given everyone an appetite and with glasses refilled and the football retrieved, everyone fell onto the buffet. And with Rachel and Penny serving while Luca handed out plates of hot fried squid and prawns, it didn't take long before the party was sitting beneath umbrellas with plates of food in their laps.

Everyone made a fuss of Rosa. Ben offered her his inflatable armchair, and she sank into it with a happy sigh. Nadia laughed as the old woman called Issac over to sit beside her and patted his cheek as he lowered himself onto the beach blanket. Sprog appeared at her side and handed Rosa a plate laden with delicacies from the buffet while Rachel brought over a glass of red wine.

Used to a frugal existence, the vast array of food and drink at the party appeared quite decadent to Nadia, and she thought she could get used to living like this. *Is this what it's like to be a foreigner in a new land?* She wondered, *These people must have had splendid opportunities in England to have enough money to live here like this.*

"Enjoying yourself?" Louise asked her as she refilled her glass again.

"Yes, thank you for inviting me."

"You're welcome. Why don't you join us over by the rocks? Looks like Rosa is keeping Issac entertained."

Despite being younger, when Nadia joined Rachel, Gabby and their friends, she felt she was a proper part of the group. The conversations in English went over her head, and even with the offers of translation, some of the content didn't convert well, but this didn't affect her enjoyment. Nadia was experiencing something new, something she'd never shared with her friends, Flavia and Pina.

The food slowed everyone down and except for Ivan and Sprog, who were back in the sea, the others relaxed and conversation became the king of activities. The men were in a group of their own, and this pleased Nadia. She enjoyed hearing about Louise's life back in England and Penny's ribald tales about holidaymakers. Nolan joined the women, saying the men's chat was too alpha, and the conversation changed to his favourite topic – men. Pretty soon, between top ups of wine and prosecco, Nadia was blushing at the stories Nolan was sharing.

As the temperature dipped in the late afternoon, Nadia rose to rejoin Issac. He saw her stagger towards him and got to his feet and went to steady her. As she crossed the beach, she swayed and giggled and he thought, *she's had too much wine. This is so unlike her.* He took the tumbler from her and tipped its contents onto the sand. "I think you've had enough," he said.

"I'm just…" she paused and giggled again. "As you British say, letting down my hair."

He helped her to sit down and fetched her a bottle of water. After unscrewing the lid, he passed it to her. She took a sip and spat it out. "Ugh, it's warm."

"I'll see if there's a colder one."

She grabbed his hand to stop him from going, "No, tell me about Gretna Green." Issac looked at her confused and she recounted the conversation earlier with Rachel.

"There's a famous blacksmith's shop where people used to run away to, to get married in secret."

"Why?"

"Because maybe their family was against them getting married or thought they were too young. It's not possible now, though."

"Oh, what a shame. Why not?"

"People have to apply about thirty days in advance and other kinds of rules apply."

"So we can't run away in secret, then?" She laughed again; this time louder and Issac looked to see some of the party guests had glanced over at them. "We like secrets, don't we?"

"We?"

"Yes, humans. We keep secrets all the time. I know all about your secret." Nadia reached out for a bottle of beer standing in the sand and he moved it away. Seeing his face, she thought he looked puzzled. "My father told me about the grappa and how you helped him. He said you kept it secret to protect him."

"I see."

"The clean bedding on the washing line was a giveaway." Issac shook his head gently with the realisation he should have brought it inside before he'd left the villa. "I'm glad you protected *papà*. It tells me you are a man to be trusted."

"I hope so."

Nadia's eyelids felt heavy. She was falling asleep, and he laid her back, making sure the umbrella shaded her face. As Issac went to move away, she opened her eyes, placed a finger against her lips and said, "Shh, I have a secret too."

"Try to have a nap. You'll feel better."

She murmured and whispered, "Issac?"

"Yes Nadia," he whispered back.

"I know who was driving the car."

"Which car?"

"It was Luciano." Her eyes closed again and barely audible as sleep took her, she mumbled, "shh, it's a secret."

Thirty-Nine

Trentanove

"Thank you. I look forward to hearing from you," Issac said as he entered the kitchen. He ended his phone call and punched the air with an enthusiastic, "Yes!"

"Someone's happy," Riccardo said as he knotted the tie around his neck.

"Ivan has sold the roof tiles. The buyer is going to come over to collect them. Salvatore will be happy with the extra cash for his garden."

"I'm guessing he won't be so happy if Nadia wakes up this morning with a hangover from hell?"

"What was that about Nadia?" Gabby said, coming in from outside. Riccardo recounted their conversation, and she said, "She did drink rather a lot."

"The poor girl was wasted." Riccardo said, "I'm grateful she wasn't sick in the car."

"I think Louise thought she could keep up with everyone and kept topping up her glass."

"She could have said no.".

"Come on Issac. She's young, who at her age hasn't got drunk at a party? Cut her some slack."

"I just thought with her father, she'd–"

"Life doesn't work like that," interjected Gabby. "Let's just hope she'll have learned from it."

"I'm glad you could get her up to bed without her father seeing her," Issac said.

Riccardo picked up his suit jacket, and as he slid his arms inside the sleeves he added, "Yes, it was a bit of luck to find he was working in his studio."

"I didn't realise you were working today," Gabby said.

"I'm off to talk to the Pasquini/Petrini witnesses."

"Good luck."

"I need it. This case is baffling." He picked up his briefcase. "There has to be a definitive answer. I just can't find it."

Issac turned away; he remembered what Nadia had told him at the beach, and as he unscrewed the lid from the Moka pot, he recalled her words, "It's a secret."

Riccardo's car left the villa, and Gabby asked Issac what his plans for the day were. "I was taking the day off, but I'll go over to see Salvatore to tell him about the tile sale."

"Just keep Nadia's foolishness to yourself. He may not know."

"I will," he checked his pockets for the pickup keys and thought as he walked through the door, *I've had enough secrets to contend with already.*

As he passed the stables in Laroscia, Issac spotted Nadia's scooter in the yard and he felt a weight lift. At least he wouldn't have to face her this morning. Driving into the small piazza, he saw Alina and Sonny outside Salvatore's villa. Salvatore was in his chair, watching as the teenagers planted annuals in decorated pots.

"Issac," Alina called as he got out of his pickup.

"Hi, what are you up to?"

"Alina had these plants on her potting table and she thought we could plant them in Sal's pots," said Sonny.

Sal, thought Issac, hearing he was on first-name terms with Sonny.

"I found the pots in my studio and thought they'd look nice outside." Salvatore said.

"These plants are a little long and leggy, but it saves throwing them on the compost," added Alina.

"Exactly. Give them a trim and they'll look okay in a couple of weeks."

"So, what brings you here today?" Salvatore asked.

"I have good news."

"Good news is always welcome. I'll make coffee… would you two like a soda?"

"Yes, please," chorused Alina and Sonny as Salvatore disappeared inside his house.

Issac couldn't detect anything amiss in Salvatore's demeanour and took that as a good sign. He picked up a calendula seedling and, after pinching out the orange buds, handed it to Sonny, who had already dug a hole for it. "This will look lovely when it's in flower."

"I've mixed some red… I think Alina called them, impatiens, in with the marigolds, to make a hot display. Alina said they would blend with the zinnias and geraniums."

"She's right. Proper little garden designer she's becoming." She chuckled as he ruffled her hair when Salvatore called them all inside for a drink.

"It's cooler in the kitchen," he said as the four of them gathered around the dining table. Alina spotted the crisps he'd tipped into a bowl and reached over to take one.

"So, what's the good news?"

"Ivan's friend has agreed to buy the *frantoio* tiles. She's coming over with a van later to collect them."

"That is good news."

"And she'll pay in cash."

"Better news." Salvatore replied. "What will you spend it on?"

"That'll be up to you. It's your money and your garden."

"I know, a rambling rose over the *frantoio* walls."

"Good idea, Alina. That will make it look like it's been a ruin for years," said Salvatore.

"Looks like you'll be my advisor soon," chuckled Issac.

***

Riccardo wasn't getting very far with his questioning. He'd spoken with the owner of the bar, who was insistent that what he'd said in his original statement hadn't changed. "I heard a car in the distance and looked up."

"What made you look up?"

"It was loud. Obviously speeding."

"Can you describe the car?"

"It's all in my statement." The barman said, obviously unhappy having to go over it all again. "I'm busy, so if you don't mind."

"Not at all," Riccardo said as the door to the bar closed, leaving him standing alone outside.

He fared better with the pedestrian, signora Tazini. After he'd listened to the minutiae of her morning, she pushed a cup of coffee in his direction and got to the matter in hand. "I had been visiting a friend, Olga. She'd been unwell the previous few days. I walked home as usual. My apartment is just a short walk away. I had just put my key in the door when I heard what sounded like a car roaring loudly. I didn't look around as often people drive too fast through Brecciaio; maybe because it's a long straight road. An almighty crash sounded, and I looked around and saw the two cars crumpled, one with its front wheels on the pavement."

"What did you do next?"

"I put my key back inside my pocket and went back to Olga's house to tell her what I'd seen. I buzzed her doorbell and she let me in straight away saying she'd heard the noise."

Riccardo sighed. There had been nothing new in signora Tazini's statement. He was putting his notebook back inside his briefcase when she offered him another coffee. He declined and was leaving her apartment when she said, "Olga knew I had come back to tell her what had happened."

"How did she know?"

"She saw me on the little camera in her doorbell."

***

When Alina and Sonny had finished planting up the pots and Salvatore had asked them to make sure they'd washed their hands, he settled down in the *salotto* with Issac who told him about some ideas he had that he could utilise the tile money for. "I'll leave it to whatever you decide," Salvatore said. "I trust your judgement."

"Thank you."

"Talking about trust. I wanted to thank you for not saying anything about what occurred last week. Trust is something that people have to earn, and I'm not sure I deserved yours, but I was grateful for it. But there is no need to worry about Nadia knowing about my weakness when faced with a bottle of grappa. I've told her–"

Issac's eyelids lowered as he thought, *that's two secrets surrounding alcohol I've had to keep.*

"And judging by your reaction, she's already told you."

Issac nodded his head and gave Salvatore a weak smile to show him everything was okay. "Your secret would always have been safe with me."

"There is a problem with secrets that I have discovered throughout my life. They have a habit of coming back to catch you out. A secret can weaken a relationship, it can force people apart. It can cause harm when all the keeper is trying to do is protect the other person. I've grown to realise that honesty is the best way to move forward, even if it can create conflict."

Is Salvatore saying that he already knows about Nadia getting drunk? Should I say something? Issac's thoughts shut down when the door opened and Nadia stepped into the room.

"I saw your pickup parked outside."

"Yes, Issac came to tell me we've sold the roof tiles."

"That's great news *Papà*."

"Issac was also telling me what new garden projects he can do with the money."

"Oh, what projects?"

Issac smiled and rose from his seat and quickly said he needed to be going, "I've some things to collect from the supermarket for Gabby."

He hoped his lie had sounded sincere as he drove back to Perano.

Walking through the front door, Issac could hear the softer sound of a wine cork being removed from a bottle rather than the loud popping of a prosecco cork. In the sitting room, Riccardo was holding a bottle of his own red wine and turning, he said, "You're just in time for a drink."

"I take it you had a result today?" said Issac joining him and Gabby.

"I have had a breakthrough, yes."

Gabby and Issac listened as Riccardo told them about signora Tazini and her friend Olga. "She has a doorbell camera and didn't know how to delete the footage, so it was still there on her hard drive."

"And is this good news?" Gabby asked as he poured three glasses of wine.

"Her daughter had set it up on an old laptop for her. I found it and the date and time stamp are intact on the footage, so I've transferred it to a flash drive. It proves that there was a third car."

Forty

Quaranta

Nolan was standing at the counter as he drank his early morning shot of coffee. He'd learned a long time ago that it was customary to stand, not to sit down. "Sitting is for tourists," Nico had told him when he'd once offered to reserve them a table. Nolan had also learned that tradition dictated that you never order a cappuccino in Italy after 11am. He may have been observing convention, but he stood out from the crowd, dressed in a pair of pastel blue shorts and a floral shirt. Gabby was about to approach him when he picked up a trilby that matched his shorts. There followed a chorus of 'ciao' and 'arrivederci' as Nolan said goodbye to the men dressed in work overalls and adjusting his hat at a jaunty angle he slipped on his sunglasses and moved away from the counter.

"Look at you mixing with the locals," Gabby said after the customary air kisses.

"Just doing my best to fit in." Nolan said.

"You're certainly doing that." Gabby's shoulders gave a small rise and fall as she chuckled to herself as they left the bar.

Climbing into Gabby's car, Nolan said, "This place we're going to see. Do you think it'll be worth a feature?"

"I think it could make an interesting story. It would fit into the business section as a young entrepreneur feature, or a travel piece. Either way, it won't hurt to check it out."

Gabby pulled away from the kerb and, fearing it would blow away; Nolan removed his hat. Gabby loved driving with the top down; it made travelling through the countryside more enjoyable and she smiled, knowing when they arrived he'd spend time faffing about with his hair before he'd let her introduce him to Hannah, but for now they both appreciated the view.

"Cripes," Nolan said as the car came around a bend and he saw the steep hill in front of them, "That's scary."

"Wait until later, when we have to come down," she laughed.

"I hope there's a bar. I'll need a stiff drink before we leave."

She took the narrow turning onto *Corso Umberto* and passed the small church before she parked the car.

"Wow!" Nolan said, looking down over the valley. "This is amazing." Gabby allowed Nolan several minutes to take in the view. To their right was the town, its houses stacked one on top of the other. To the left were the mountains, speckled with purples and ochres and below a valley blanketed in every shade of green possible and in the distance, hills covered with a patchwork of cultivated fields and olive groves. "This is so different from Nico's place in Monte Marcone."

Outside Hannah's palazzo, Gabby pointed out the building that took up half of the narrow street. "As you can see, it's huge."

"It will be impossible to photograph the entire building."

"I think that adds to its mystery." Gabby said as she lifted the large brass knocker in the centre of the aubergine coloured front door.

From inside, they could hear footsteps on the stairs, and Nolan's face lit up as the door opened and a tall man with dark hair and soft brown eyes greeted them. He stepped forward and introduced himself as Hannah's husband and Nolan's smile faded with disappointment.

"Pleased to meet you Rex," Gabby said, taking his offered hand and shaking it. "Look at us being so British," he laughed and, leaning forward, he gave her the more continental greeting of air kisses.

Hannah's head appeared over the bannister and she said with humour, "When Rex has finished manhandling you, come up."

Rex showed them into the private sitting room and after introductions, he offered drinks. "Tea, coffee, wine, beer?"

"Beer for me," Nolan said, watching Rex's rear as it left the room.

"Put your tongue away," whispered Gabby.

Hannah breezed into the room, her long floral dress moving like a mistral around her ankles. "Sorry I wasn't here to meet you. One of our guests froze on the roof terrace."

"Froze? In this heat?"

"Not literally. She has a morbid fear of heights."

"So why go up there?" Nolan said.

Hannah shrugged. "Your guess is as good as mine."

Rex brought in their drinks and Nolan listened as they told him the story of how they came to buy the palazzo.

"Originally, we were going to open it as a traditional bed-and-breakfast, but Hannah had the idea for the retreat."

"I couldn't see myself cooking breakfasts and smiling politely on the stairs," Hannah said. "I wanted to give people more than just a basic holiday experience while giving something back to the town."

Gabby explained to Nolan about the community room in the old shop.

"Yes, it's a space where local people can meet up and get involved with some of our activities. Monica, who teaches Italian cuisine, was one of our local ladies who used to visit a few days a week."

Rex offered to show Nolan around, and Hannah fetched a bottle of wine from the galley kitchen.

"Just a small one for me," Gabby said. "I have to navigate that hill on the way home."

"You could always go out of town the other way."

"And spoil the enjoyment I'll get from scaring Nolan?"

laughed Gabby. "I'm glad we're alone. I have given some thought to the idea of running a writers' workshop here."

Hannah poured the wine as Gabby said she could commit to two two-week sessions a year. "Any more will dilute the bookings."

"I think you're right. How many people do you envisage?"

"Well, that all depends on profitability. What numbers work for you?" Gabby took a sip of her wine as Hannah paused, thinking.

"I think if we can slot the courses into weeks where we have quieter pursuits taking place, then maybe eight to ten people would work."

"A maximum of ten would work for me. Being hands on that will allow everyone an equal share of one-to-one coaching. I'd like them to take up a cooking lesson and a tour of local villages, too, as I can incorporate it into their writing."

"Let me do the numbers and I'll get back to you." Hannah looked up as the door opened and Nolan and Rex returned. "Monica is preparing us lunch. I'll just check how she's getting on."

They ate lunch on the roof terrace, and when Nolan wasn't talking about his second favourite subject - himself, he was taking photographs on his phone.

After lunch, Hannah took them downstairs to look at the community room. Three women who were chatting as they crocheted looked up and said hello to Hannah, showing her their handiwork.

"This is Ottavia," she introduced a small round woman with eyes as black and shiny as buttons. "She teaches lace making to our guests."

"Is there nothing you don't do here?"

"We'd like to find a man for our nude, life drawing classes, but we've had no offers from the men in the town. Do you fancy giving it a go, Nolan?"

Gabby laughed, "I think that's the first time I've ever seen you blush."

"I'm not blushing. It's warm in here." Nolan fanned himself and went outside, leaving Hannah to join in with the laughter.

Forty-One

Quarantuno

Salvatore recognised the moustachioed man who lumbered through the rear garden. "What's Massimo doing here?" he asked himself. "Issac didn't say he was working today." Massimo waved, and Salvatore opened the French windows and called out a friendly hello. "*Caffè?*"

"*Si, grazie.*"

As Salvatore filled the Moka pot, Massimo entered the villa and made himself at home on the sofa.

"*Zucchero?*" called Salvatore from the kitchen as he lifted a jar of sugar.

"*Non per me.*"

Salvatore had become quite adept at manoeuvring his chair while balancing a tray and re-entered the *salotto*, handing Massimo his drink. "What brings you here today?"

Massimo stirred his small cup of coffee and placed the spoon in the saucer. If he'd been alone, he'd have licked the crema from the spoon, but in company, this was never done. "Remember the last time I was here, and we talked about your ceramics?"

"Sure."

"I was thinking about the store in Montesilvano that used to stock your pots."

"What about it?"

"The uncle of a friend is the leaseholder. He rented it to a man from Ravenna, who went back up north. The new tenant runs a sports store."

"This is interesting, but how does it affect me?"

"I remembered the man from Ravenna left the shop filled with stock. I asked my friend's uncle what happened to it and he told me he put it into a lock-up." Salvatore felt his forehead crease as his friend said, "Your stock is just sitting there unsold."

"I see, and what does the uncle want, rent?"

"No. He said he tried to contact you about it but never received a reply."

I can believe that, Salvatore thought.

"I thought, if you collected your stock, it could help to re-start your old business."

"I don't think so."

"What have you got to lose?"

"I have already lost everything."

"*Amico mio…* Forgive my being straightforward, but you're getting your life back on track. You are becoming a new man. So the second time around could be a success. All you have to do is–"

"Not drink. I know," Salvatore said butting in. "Come with me." He spun his chair around, grabbed his keys, and led Massimo out to his studio.

The air was heavy with the odour of fresh pigments and glazes and overhead the fluorescent tubes buzzed and flickered as the builder scrolled through the sketch pad looking at the new designs that his old friend had been working on. Salvatore moved towards the open door of the kiln and reached inside and removed a cobalt blue vase decorated with ox-eye daisies. "This is a new design."

Massimo put down the sketchbook and took the vase and turned it around in his hands, letting the light illuminate the shiny surface. "You've always been able to draw and paint flowers that look alive."

"To be honest, I've been coming here most days. I never thought I'd be able to reignite my passion, but I feel reinvigorated."

"I'm happy to hear that."

"Maybe I will think about taking it up again."

"Looks like you already have." Massimo placed a hand

on his friend's shoulder and gave it a squeeze. "I'm proud of you Salvatore."

After Massimo had left, Salvatore took his sketchbook outside onto the patio, and as his friend's parting words ran around inside his head, he sketched the bougainvillaea, holding fast the smile they had brought to his lips.

***

Issac paid for their lunch at the pizzeria beside the beach at Le Morge and as they walked on the sand to choose a place to sit, he was telling Nadia about his work in various parts of Italy. "Before I went to the Veneto, I worked in Molise and Calabria," he said. "The heat in Calabria was fierce."

"Hotter than here in August?" Nadia asked.

"As hot as hell."

He placed the wrapped slices of pizza down and unfurled towels for them both to sit on, and Nadia asked, "What was Molise like? I've always wondered, but I've never been over the border."

"I liked it. I was in the countryside, so never went into the capital," he replied. "Maybe I can take you and we can spend a day there exploring."

"That would be lovely."

They ate as they watched the sea as it almost silently swept in and out from shore. The sea at Le Morge is shallow, making it popular with families with small children, and Nadia smiled as she watched two toddlers digging in the sand.

Issac stood up and removed his shirt, dropping it onto his towel as he said he was off to wash his hands in the sea. Nadia found it difficult not to look at his body. A fine coating of red hair covered his chest, thinning as it travelled down to disappear into his shorts. His pale skin had a slight colouring from his days working in the sun, but she knew he could easily burn. Taking a bottle of sun cream from her bag, she said, "Come here; let me put some protection on your shoulders." As her hands smoothed the lotion into his skin, she thought, *he needs protection from me more than the sun*; touching him made her as hot as the sand beneath her feet.

Issac returned from the sea and knitted his fingers with hers and sitting so close, they talked in whispers and stole kisses from each other until Nadia could bear it no more. She felt her pulse race. She was a feeling something she had not experienced before. Strange, but strange in a good way, and she knew she had to cool off. She pushed her lips hard against Issacs, then stood up quickly and said, "Catch me if you can," as she ran towards the sea.

They spent the rest of the afternoon relaxing on the beach, parting only briefly when Issac walked back to the pizzeria to buy gelati. Nadia watched his back as he walked, and her heart sailed up into her throat.

Later, when they were the only people on the beach, as dusk fell, he stepped away to make a telephone call and Nadia wondered who he was calling, but it didn't worry her; she was happier than she had been in months. At a distance Issac's red hair stood out, a colour she wasn't used to seeing in Abruzzo where most of the men had hair the colour of bitumen. She thought it was more Venetian blond than red, very much like that of an angel she'd once seen in a Caravaggio painting.

Issac returned and held up her blouse for her to slip her arms inside; he nuzzled her neck and said, "I have a surprise for you tomorrow."

Forty-Two

Quarantadue

Issac had arrived early that morning to collect Nadia. Riccardo had kindly loaned him his car, saying the pickup would be too uncomfortable for a two-hour journey, and especially for a date with a pretty girl. As they headed southwards, the terrain swapped rural villages for the autostrada at Val di Sangro and the journey became a monotonous grey road with blurred patches of green that moved past at speed. Nearing San Salvo, Issac caught a glimpse of the sea and left the motorway and took the SS650 where the landscape was more appealing. Driving parallel to the border, low hills and great swathes of green fields replaced the peaks of Abruzzo's Appenine Mountains. Roads stretched onwards with just the odd rendered, orange roofed house to break up the scene. They crossed the border and after Issac had navigated a series of terror inducing hairpin bends; the villages appeared and gave way to the outskirts of Campobasso.

"I've planned the day for us," Issac said as they selected a table outside a bar. Nadia sat facing the piazza so she could watch people going about their day as Issac went inside to order drinks. Placing two glasses of limonata on the table Issac continued, "I thought we could be tourists today."

"We are tourists," Nadia laughed.

"We'll start at the castle," he said.

"Let's record our day," Nadia said, taking out her phone. She held it up above their heads and they smiled for a selfie, before she checked it, pressed a few buttons and uploaded it to her Instagram account.

They first visited Castello Monforte; Issac was aware Nadia would already have seen many castles; Italy's history meant the country had over 20,000 of them dotted from north to south, but she told him she thought the view was spectacular. Issac smiled as Nadia embraced the 'being a tourist' element of their day and gazed down over the town's rooftops and over to the surrounding countryside.

"Stand here," she said, pointing to a wall with a verdant landscape behind it. "I'll take your photo." After checking the image, she said, "I like how all the houses below look like a model village. It's as if you could just pick them up."

Leaving the castle, Nadia turned to take one more photograph. "Unlike our Majella stone castles, this one is a drab grey-white colour, but it looks majestic against the blue sky." Issac agreed with her before she asked, "Where are you taking me next?"

Her phone never left her hand and as they wandered through the medieval streets, she snapped away at sites that Issac assumed would look similar to her. She took quite a few shots of the peach coloured façade of the Palazzo San Giorgio with its arcaded colonnade and seemed very pleased with the images.

Issac thought back to trips he had taken back home in Scotland, and how when he visited places the architecture looked familiar, but it was the newness of the experience that delivered the urge to record digital memories.

They sauntered through a narrow vico where no sunlight could penetrate and Nadia stopped walking and pulled him into her and kissed him in the shadows before, hand in hand, they made their way to a trattoria for a late lunch.

The day was perfect, just the two of them experiencing something new together. Issac found he couldn't stop looking across at Nadia as they walked side by side. Her dark hair sailed in the lazy breeze, and occasionally when she screwed her eyes up because of the sun, she had crinkles each side of her nose that made his heart skip. He couldn't help himself; despite their young ages, he knew he was in love with her.

He had planned to take her to one of the town's many museums. But plans often change when the heart takes hold of the reins. They spent the rest of the day holding hands and window shopping, eating gelato and buying postcards they'd never send. For the day was all about the two of them and being strangers in a new town.

Forty-Three

Quarantatré

"Looks like you had a good day yesterday," Gabby said as she poured herself a coffee. "Don't look so confused. I saw the photographs on Nadia's social media."

Issac nodded. With Louise's advice, he had set up accounts for his gardening business, but the social media revolution had passed him by. "Yes, it was a good day. We didn't get to see everything I had planned, but we had a great time."

"Are you seeing Nadia today?"

"She's working at the stables. Later we're going out for a pizza in Piane d'Archi."

"Riccardo and I used to go there on dates when we first met, then end up at the bar in Bomba at the end of the night."

"We could do that in reverse," Issac said, the idea forming in his mind. "Why don't you and Riccardo join us?"

"You don't want us intruding."

"Well, give it some thought. I'm sure Nadia won't mind."

Issac picked up his cap and headed outside to carry on with his work in the vineyard.

With Gabby busy in her office, and Riccardo away for the morning, memories of their day in Campobasso invaded his thoughts, reminding him how his feelings for Nadia had changed. *Ironic for a gardener*, he thought. *I grow plants for a living and didn't see my love for her growing until it was in full bloom.* As he worked between the rows of vines, he wondered if he should tell her. *Is it too soon to make a declaration of love?*

Thinking he'd maybe talk it over with Gabby later, he put it to the back of his mind and continued cutting off the tops of the young weeds that had appeared following the thunderstorm.

***

Riccardo's meeting with the carabinieri hadn't gone well, and he was still angry when he returned home. He slammed the car door and stalked across the driveway. The encounter he'd come from had spoilt his day, and now all he wanted to do was open a bottle of wine and sink into its red comfort. Ignoring Issac, who had called to him, he disappeared down the side of the villa and into the cantina. He heard Gabby outside asking if Riccardo had come home and taking a bottle from the rack of wines; he looked up as she appeared in the doorway, blocking out the light, making the wine cellar as dark as his mood.

"How did your meeting go?"

"Not good. I'll tell you about it once I've had a drink and calmed down."

Gabby stepped aside and Riccardo walked past her and into the villa. "Face like thunder," she said to Issac pulling an angry face.

"I'll stay here until the coast is clear," he said with good humour, as Gabby went to join Riccardo inside.

With his tie loosened at the neck, and his jacket draped over the sofa, Riccardo opened the wine and poured himself a glass. He held up the bottle, offering a drink to Gabby, who shook her head. "Have you eaten?" She asked him.

"Nothing since breakfast."

"I'll put something together."

Gabby walked into the kitchen, leaving him in the sitting room, from where he called, "I'm not especially hungry."

"I'll just prepare some nibbles. You take off your shoes

and relax."

Placing a prepared platter on the kitchen table, Gabby popped her head into the sitting room. Seeing Riccardo had almost finished the entire bottle, she said. "Looks like you'll need a something to soak up all of that wine."

Riccardo looked at the large oval plate furnished with slices of salami and prosciutto, hunks of several cheeses, including a young lemon flavoured ricotta that one of their neighbours had dropped in the day before. "There's some of Agata's sun-dried tomatoes under oil in the cupboard if you'd like some?"

"This will do fine. Thank you." Riccardo put the bottle and his glass down and slid an arm around Gabby's shoulder and kissed her gently on the cheek.

Gabby cut him a slice of crusty bread and smothered it with the ricotta and watched as his face relaxed when the zesty flavour touched his tongue. "Better?"

"Yes, thanks."

They ate in silence. Gabby watched as his body loosened like his tie and he sighed as he swallowed another mouthful of soft cheese draped with a wafer thin slice of ham.

Issac entered the kitchen and as he washed his hands at the sink, Gabby invited him to join them at the table, "Just grab a plate from the drainer," she said.

"This looks nice," he said, looking at the grazing board and helping himself to some salami and cheese. "The grapes are coming along nicely. Hopefully, if we get some more rain this month, we could have a good harvest this year."

"Fingers crossed," Riccardo said, pouring Issac a glass of wine.

"How was your meeting today?"

"Not good," Riccardo said as he shook his head. "It would be fair to say my bubble was burst."

"Why, what's happened?" Gabby asked.

"I thought you'd solved the mystery of the third car." Issac added.

"So did I, but it appears I had got my hopes up."

"Were the carabinieri pleased with your discovery?"

Riccardo picked up an olive and chewed the flesh from the stone as Gabby and Issac waited for his response.

"I thought now there was footage I could put the question of a third party to bed. You can clearly see the speeding car, but the carabiniere I spoke to said it proves nothing as the car's registration isn't visible and it's impossible to determine who is driving."

"So what happens now?" Gabby said.

"Looks like I'm no further on than I was before."

Gabby's phone rang, and she picked it up, looked at the screen and said, "Nolan," before she answered the call.

Issac rose from the table, swallowed his glass of wine in one mouthful and said it was time he returned to his work outside.

"Work?" Riccardo asked Gabby as she ended the call.

"Yes, but nothing important. Listen, Issac said he's going out for pizza with Nadia tonight. He's asked if we'd like to join them."

"I've had too much wine to drive."

"I can drive." Gabby placed a hand on his shoulder.

Riccardo placed a hand on top of hers. "If Issac is going to be out tonight, I'd rather have an evening alone with you all to myself." He squeezed her hand, and she leant down and kissed his cheek.

"That'll be perfect."

***

Issac watched as Riccardo, now changed into overalls, busied himself working on the vines they had planted earlier in the year. He replayed their lunchtime conversation over in his head, wondering if it could be connected to Nadia's secret. *Should I ask her about it tonight?* He mulled it over, deciding that because she had been drunk, she might not remember what she had told him.

That evening when Issac had showered and changed for his date, he came downstairs and saw Riccardo sitting at the kitchen table, the files and folders belonging to Salvatore's case in front of him. "You're not going through them again, are you?"

"I have to. There could be something obvious that I'm missing."

Issac pulled out the chair opposite, lowered himself into it and in a serious tone said, "I'm not sure if this bears any relevance to your case."

"What?"

"It's something Nadia said the day we were all at the beach. She was drunk, and it's more than likely something and nothing. It was just a passing comment."

He coughed, suddenly feeling uncomfortable and wishing he'd not said anything. "I didn't think it was important, but when she said it was a secret, I couldn't stop thinking about it."

"What did she say?"

"We were talking about secrets and she said, 'I know who was driving the car.' I asked her what car, and she said, 'it was Luciano,' and then she fell asleep. We've not spoken about it since."

"Who is Luciano?"

"I don't know, a friend, I'm guessing." Issac rose from the table, "Look, it might be nothing." He shrugged his shoulders as Gabby entered and lifted the mood in the room. "You look very smart."

"Thanks." Issac gave Gabby a fragile smile and left the room.

***

"Prosecco?" asked Gabby, holding up a bottle. Riccardo nodded, and she removed the foil and cage. "Issac looked a little subdued. You'd think he'd look happier to be going on a date with Nadia."

"Maybe he has something on his mind."

Gabby gave a little laugh. The cork popped loudly, and she said, "No doubt we'll see how the night is going."

"How?"

"On Nadia's socials, she's always posting photos. I bet we'll see which pizza she's ordered before the night is out."

Riccardo stood up, his chair squealing on the tiled floor. "Gabby!" he threw his arms in the air then pulled her into him. "You're a genius."

"Am I?"

Forty-Four

Quarantaquattro

Riccardo opened his laptop and saw Gabby's Instagram account was still open. Last night, they'd looked through Nadia's photographs together. Like most young women, she seemed to spend a lot of time posting images about every aspect of her life. Meals she'd eaten, places she'd visited and friends she'd been with. Looking at the dates, she had stopped posting regularly in January, only becoming more active again in late April when she became friendly with Issac and now, she was uploading two or three images a day. "This is pointless," Riccardo said to himself after an hour of checking the likes and comments on Nadia's photos. There has to be an easier way of finding her followers. He opened another window and logged into his Facebook account; he'd set one up for the vineyard, but like the one he'd had at the legal practice, he rarely interacted with it. After a simple search, he found Nadia's page, but it was private. All it displayed publicly was her profile image and name. Riccardo clicked on his own friends list and selected Issac. He too was friends with Nadia, but apart from the images she'd tagged him in, he couldn't find any other people on her list.

He went to make himself a coffee and remembered the previous night when Gabby had logged into her Instagram account to show him the photos of Issac and Nadia in Campobasso. "What if she uses the same password?" he said aloud. He returned the laptop and called up Gabby's Facebook account. It asked for the password and he entered three digits and stopped. "This is wrong," he said, "an abuse of trust. I'll wait until she's home."

Working outside took his mind off the search. He knew it would probably be easier to ask Nadia, but he feared without something concrete to back up his query it could damage her relationship with his friend, and Issac had seemed reticent enough when he'd made it known what she had told him in confidence.

***

"I don't remember there being so many boxes," Salvatore said as Issac and Nadia began unloading the pickup. "Maybe the owner sold none of my pots."

"I'm sure he did *Papà*."

"The shop owner said to give you this." Issac handed Salvatore an envelope. "It's a cheque the seller left with him for what he sold."

"Can a cheque go out of date?" Salvatore said, opening the envelope.

"I'm not sure. I'll take it to the bank for you," Nadia said as she struggled with a plastic crate filled with bowls.

The pickup was unloaded and as Nadia and Issac stacked everything inside the studio, Salvatore went inside to fetch them cold drinks.

When he returned, Salvatore saw Issac holding up a large platter decorated with peonies. He remembered painting the dish, and it felt like a lifetime ago. He had a vague recollection of the flowers being in a vase inside the *salotto*; Cristina had bought them inside from the garden.

"Everything is very dusty." Nadia's voice cut through his memories. "I'll wash everything when I check it over."

"Do you like it?" he said to Issac.

"Yes, the flowers look so lifelike."

"Take it. Call it payment for collecting everything from Montesilvano."

"If you're sure. Thank you." Issac placed the platter to one side and went back to helping Nadia unpack the boxes and stack everything on the workbench Salvatore had cleared in readiness.

After emptying the boxes and crates, and discarding a handful of cracked and chipped pieces, they looked at the collection of bowls and vases. "Can I have this one for my bedroom *Papà*?" Nadia held up a small round posy bowl with roses decorated around the sides.

"Of course, darling."

"When I've cleaned everything, I can begin taking photos ready to sell online."

Salvatore felt a rush of love flood his chest. As she sorted through the pottery, his daughter looked happier than she had in many months. Her eyes had reclaimed the shine they had lost since his accident. Was it the changes at home or her finding Issac? Whatever it was, it warmed his heart.

***

Rachel's car pulled into the driveway, and Riccardo looked up to see Gabby waving to him. "Good day?" he called.

"Yes. You?"

"I've got some work done finally…" A smile took over his face. "Without having you here to disturb me."

"Is he always this cheeky?" joked Rachel.

"Always."

"Why don't you ladies sit in the shade and I'll fetch a bottle of wine from the cantina?"

"Not for me," Rachel said. "I have to drive home. A sparkling water will be good, though."

Rachel and Gabby were talking about their shopping trip to Lanciano and Riccardo tried not to look disappointed as Issac arrived home. He had been hoping to resume the Facebook search and couldn't do it with Issac in the villa.

"What have you got there?" Rachel asked.

"It's one of Salvatore's," Issac said, handing her the china platter.

"This is gorgeous. Where did he get it from?"

"He made it."

"Made it?" Rachel's eyes widened. "This is remarkable. He's obviously very talented."

"We went today to collect all of his old stock from a shop that has closed." Issac said, before he explained that there were plans to sell it online. "He's finally got back into making again."

"One of these would be perfect for an engagement gift for Louise and Ben. Do you think he'd let me buy one?"

"I don't see why not. But it's best you go over and look, he's lots of other things."

"I'm heading back there once I've had a shower. I'll ask him for you."

"You going out with Nadia tonight?" Riccardo asked.

"Yes, we're going to the cinema."

This time, Riccardo tried not to look happy as Issac made his way inside and Rachel said she ought to get going too.

After dinner, Riccardo poured two glasses of wine as Gabby logged into her Facebook account. He watched as her fingers danced over the keys and she turned the laptop around to face him. "Here's Nadia's friends list, luckily she's not made it private."

He put down his glass and began scrolling through the list, looking at the photos until he found two images that had the name Luciano beside them. "So one of these boys could be our driver."

"You don't know that for sure. I really think you should clarify exactly what Nadia told Issac."

"I will, but first I'll do a little digging. I don't want to upset things unnecessarily." He took a screenshot, checked it before he closed the laptop and took a sip of his wine.

Forty-Five

Quarantacinque

Rosa was in the reception, chatting to a couple from London. Rachel felt that over time the old woman had become a vital part of the hotel's team, bringing a little bit of the real Italy to her guests. No one seemed to mind her chatter. A bright laugh came from the Londoners and Rachel watched as the husband took out his phone and snapped a photograph of his wife with Rosa. In fact, Luca had commented that she had become the most photographed part of *Le Stelle* of late.

Rachel had checked the hotel emails; another enquiry had arrived overnight with an update to a confirmation from Penny for a party of four later in the month. Business was better than she had imagined, with bookings up on the previous year. Briefly she thought about Marco, how he would have loved being here, the ruler of his own empire.

Thoughts of her husband no longer caused her sorrow; she still missed him, but the crushing feeling of loss had waned, and with Louise staying at the hotel, it gave her a chance to talk about him with someone who also knew him. Tiziana interrupted her thoughts and handed her a copy of the menus for the coming week. "I am going to ask the fish seller to deliver today. I plan to make *langoustines alla busara* for tonight's second course."

"Sounds delicious. Can you order extra and put four portions aside for us too?"

"Of course." Tiziana gave her one of her customary wide smiles and went back towards her kitchen.

"Morning," Louise said, coming down the stairs. "Can we have a chat later?"

"Sure. I have a few things to attend to first. How about I meet you in the apartment in an hour?"

"Great. Ben's gone for a swim, down at the beach, so he won't disturb us. I'll grab a coffee and see you later." Rachel watched as Louise sashayed across the reception area, kissed Rosa on the cheek and asked Mirella if she'd fetch her a coffee.

As Rachel opened the door to her apartment on the third floor, the sound of a prosecco cork popping met her.

"It's almost lunchtime, so I thought we could get away with some fizz," Louise said.

"Just one for me. I have to go back to work." Rachel dropped onto the sofa and watched as Louise poured the wine into flute glasses. "So, what is it you want to talk about?"

"The wedding." Louise handed her a glass and chinked the rims before sitting down next to her friend. "I was wondering if we could get married here at the hotel?" she quickly added, "I'm not hankering after a discount we'll pay the going rate." She took a large gulp of fizz and started coughing.

"Slow down," Rachel said. "Tell me your thoughts."

"Well, we've been talking. Ben and I, and we thought it would be great to get married here. We've seen the place evolve from a ruin into the business it is now and we've enjoyed being a part of your journey. We're not looking for a massive affair, just some family and friends… all of whom will pay full price for their rooms."

"I should hope so," Rachel gave Louise a friendly smile.

"And of course, so would we."

"Nonsense. If we agree on a date, your ceremony and accommodation will be a gift from Luca and myself." Louise went to speak, but Rachel held up a hand. "It's not up for debate. I would be honoured if you held your special day here."

"And of course you'd be my chief bridesmaid."

"Goes without saying." They laughed and chinked their glasses one more time. "Okay, put some potential dates together for me."

Louise let out a high-pitched girlish squeal, hugged her friend and said, "I love you."

That evening over dinner, after all four of them had complimented Tiziana on the meal, Louise told Ben and Luca the news that Rachel had agreed to let them get married at *Le Stelle*.

"Can I ask a question?" Ben said and everyone looked at him, expecting something important. "Do you think we could have those langoustines at the wedding breakfast?"

There was a mix of laughter and groaning, and Luca asked Mirella to bring over a bottle of grappa. Rachel grinned and winked at him as Ben blanched at the thought of the fiery shots.

Forty-Six

Quarantasei

Salvatore placed the last of the rinsed plates in the rack and, after drying his hands, he went outside. The sky was cloudy, and the day felt fresher without the sun beating down as he wheeled himself down the lane.

Six months had slipped by since he'd last been in this part of the village. His mind reminded him that the last time he'd voluntarily travelled this route alone was on the day of his accident.

A neighbour he didn't know waved to him from her garden; he returned the greeting and smiled, knowing she'd probably have ignored him months ago. Alina had told him that many of the villagers had asked about him, and he assumed she'd told them his foul temper had lessened.

He knew Alina's house before he saw her; not because it was opposite the stables, but because of the neatly tended borders filled with flowers and clipped shrubs.

"Sal!" he looked over and saw Sonny coming out of the stable's entrance and thought, *how comfortable young Santino looks in the saddle.* "I'm taking Ferro for some exercise."

A dappled mare appeared, with Alina astride it and as they came alongside Sonny, Alina said, "Nonna's made another polenta cake; she's waiting for you with Signora Barone." Salvatore wheeled himself into the stable courtyard and after a brief conversation, the teenager's on their horses trotted off up the lane.

"Salvatore," Valentina said, coming outside to meet him. "It's quite temperate today, so I thought we could take our lunch in the new seating area at the rear."

"Sounds perfect." He allowed himself to be shown the way and rolled to a stop beside a table already set for dining.

Nadia appeared briefly to say hello and Nonna followed her, carrying a jug of juice; she set it down and said, "*Succo di pera.*"

Valentina asked Nadia to let the cook know her guests had arrived and, in a few seconds, a woman bustled out with a pot of coffee and cups on a tray. "It's too early for lunch, but a coffee and a slice of polenta cake won't spoil us, I don't think."

Nonna cut three generous slices of her cake while Valentina poured the coffee and Salvatore talked about how his garden was shaping up.

"Has Issac given you a date it will be finished?" Valentina asked.

"He said he was hoping for the start of July."

"That should be lovely," said Nonna. "Perfect for sitting outside and enjoying the summer."

The conversation was buoyant. Valentina gave them an update on the progress of the restaurant and Nonna talked about how Alina's pumpkin border was taking over the orto. "I think we'll have far too many for the two of us, so there'll be a few donations made around the village."

"I'm sure we could take some. Our cook makes splendid *tortelli di zucca.*"

"Do you think Alina will take up gardening as a career when she leaves school?" Salvatore said.

"Oh definitely. She's still has some years left at high school but is already looking at special college courses for when she leaves."

"And what about Santino?" – Salvatore was careful to use his given name when speaking to Valentina.

"He wants to work with horses, maybe train to be a jockey, but I fear he's left it too late. Ennio says we should let him decide on his future. I just want him to be secure in whatever he chooses. There's so much uncertainty in the world."

"I agree. I think he'll make the right choice when the time comes."

They were interrupted by Nadia, who had been sent out to clear the tray. "Would anyone like a cold drink?"

Valentina asked if anyone would like a white wine spritzer and suddenly remembered herself and said, "I think we're all okay."

"Please, don't stop yourself enjoying a one because of me. I think it's time I got used to people drinking around me." He turned to Nadia and said, "I'll have a sparkling water if possible, to add to this pear juice and please bring the ladies a spritzer."

With fresh drinks delivered to the table, Salvatore told the others about Nadia and Issac, "I think they're becoming quite close."

"How do you feel about that?" Nonna asked.

"I'm settled with it now. My initial fear of her leaving me and moving away clouded my judgement, and it became entangled with the recollection of my parents' attitude to foreigners."

"I think he's a lovely man, and they make an attractive couple," Valentina said, before she stood up and went to let cook know they were ready for lunch.

When they were alone, Salvatore leaned in and said, "Six months ago I never thought I'd be sitting here making conversation with my neighbours."

"Just as the seasons change, so do people."

"I'm very grateful for the friendship people have shown me."

"Kindness makes the world turn smoothly," Nonna said. "No one wants a bumpy ride, me in particular as the approaching end of June brings another year of my life to a close."

"You have a birthday coming soon?"

"It's just another day, Salvatore. Just another day."

Forty-Seven

Quarantasette

Armed with a photo and their full names, Riccardo headed off in search of the two Lucianos from Nadia's Facebook friends list. The first was easy to find. According to his online profile, he lived in a tiny hamlet of just five houses. A quick ask around and Riccardo discovered that the youth had been away at university for the past two years, studying medicine in Bologna. The second Luciano was harder to track down, he lived in the town of Sant'Eusanio del Sangro, not a large town but the area spread out over a handful of neighbouring villages.

He began his search in the main town, asking in bars and showing the photograph he'd printed off from Luciano's Facebook page. After a couple of false starts, he was told the lad lived outside the town on *Via della Fonte*, but he hung out at *Bar Cielo* near the church on *Corso Margherita* most days. The bar was easy to find and as he approached it, Riccardo recognised the person he was looking for.

He ordered himself an orange soda and took a seat in the corner, watching as the group of three youths laughed and joked together. There was nothing out of the ordinary about them. Like many of their age, they were loud and self-assured and sometimes a little cocksure.

The boy he was looking at split away from the group and headed for the bathroom, and this gave Riccardo a chance to speak with him without alerting his companions. He took up position outside the door and as it opened, he said, "Are you Luciano Villani?"

The boy stopped in his tracks and looked at Riccardo and said, "Yes, sir. Why?"

Riccardo handed him a business card. Luciano looked at

it and said, "What can I do for you, Avvocato di Renzo?"

"Can we talk outside?"

Luciano didn't look concerned as he nodded and walked ahead of Riccardo.

Luciano leant against a wall. He looked relaxed and unruffled, making Riccardo wonder if this quest would lead to another dead end. He looked around, checking for privacy before he spoke. "I understand you know Nadia Pasquini?"

"I do. Why?"

Riccardo couldn't detect any concern or surliness in Luciano's response and continued with, "You must have heard what happened to her father in January, on the road through Brecciaio?"

"Yes. Terrible thing."

"Do you know anything about the accident?"

"No, should I?"

"I've reason to believe that Nadia knows more than she's letting on."

"How does that affect me?" Riccardo shrugged. "I can't tell you anything about the accident."

"You didn't witness it then?"

"I wasn't there… Was I?"

"I don't know, you tell me."

"I said, I wasn't there." Luciano delivered his response in an instant and Riccardo sensed he was becoming anxious. "If that's everything, I have to be somewhere."

"That's all for now." Riccardo watched as the youth walked away without looking back. He had denied knowing anything about the accident, but Riccardo didn't believe him.

***

Rachel was standing beside the studio sink chatting with Nadia as she rinsed the dust from the ceramics stacked on a worktop. "This is beautiful," she said, picking up an oval platter decorated with red and pink anemones.

"There's a matching salad bowl, too."

Nadia walked over to the worktop and picked it up. "We bought everything back from Montesilvano. *Papà* made them a while back, but the shop closed before selling them."

"The design is very cheerful." Rachel took the bowl from Nadia. "I think they would be perfect for an engagement gift for Ben and Louise." Rachel held the bowl up against the platter to show Gabby. "What do you think?"

"Perfect," Gabby replied.

"Before I forget," she turned back to Nadia. "We have a special function happening at the hotel in a week's time; a lunch party, and we'll need some extra help. Would you be interested? It's only an afternoon's work, I'm afraid."

A musical ringtone sounded, and Nadia picked up her phone and, after asking to be excused, stepped away from the sink. "*Ciao, Luciano*." The conversation started off cordially, but seconds later, she raised her voice and stepped outside. Gabby was across the studio talking with Salvatore, who had been showing her some designs he had been working on. Rachel could hear the argument Nadia was having outside. Suddenly the call appeared to end abruptly and red-faced Nadia looked inside the studio and said, "I have to go out." Turning without saying goodbye to Gabby and Rachel, she left the studio, and seconds later, her scooter started up.

Rachel was still holding the bowl and platter when Salvatore came over and said, "I have some tissue on my desk. Let me wrap those for you."

***

Riccardo had arrived home and was recording his meeting with Luciano in his notebook when he heard Nadia's scooter arrive. He glanced out of the window and saw Issac who had been sitting outside, enjoying a break from his work in the vineyard stand up and walk towards his girlfriend. He wasn't snooping, but Riccardo didn't turn away; he sensed something was awry with the couple's body language. They were too far away for him to hear what was being said, but he noticed the Scotsman's shoulders suddenly tense up as Nadia's voice became shrill as she shouted at him. He watched as Issac shook his head and raised both of his hands in submission. The argument became louder and Riccardo caught the tail end of Nadia's wrath as she shouted, "I never want to see you again."

Riccardo observed as Nadia, who had remained sitting on her scooter throughout their exchange, reversed and rode away. Only when the squeal of the engine had faded into the distance did Issac turn around and walk towards the villa.

"I shouldn't have said anything."

Riccardo explained where he'd been that morning and the details of his conversation with Luciano.

"So, you're telling me he's denied knowing anything about it?"

"Yes, but I feel he's lying."

"I'm sorry, Riccardo, but your feelings are not proof. I wish I hadn't told you now."

"I'm sure after a day or two, Nadia will calm down."

Issac opened his mouth as if about to speak but he chose not to and with a brief shake of his head, he walked outside, leaving Riccardo to watch through the window as the pickup drove away.

Forty-Eight

Quarantotto

"Have you seen Issac this morning?" Gabby asked as she made coffee.

"No. I don't think he came home last night," replied Riccardo.

"He'll soon see that you had no choice but to act on the information he gave you."

"I just hope he can make it up with Nadia."

"Rachel thought she was extremely rude yesterday. She had just offered her some work before she went outside with her phone, then came back inside and just left without saying goodbye."

"It must have been that call that sparked her anger and sent her here to break up with Issac."

"Possibly. The call came from someone named Luciano and Rachel said she heard them arguing and the name Gianni was mentioned."

"No prizes for guessing which Luciano it was. I'd put money on it being Villani."

The sound of a vehicle outside disturbed the conversation, and they both watched as Issac walked inside and, without a word, stalked upstairs to his room.

Gabby lowered her voice and asked Riccardo if he'd be all right when she went out. He nodded and she picked up her keys and, with a kiss, went to meet Valentina.

With everyone at work, the mid-morning drive to the stables was quiet. Gabby barely passed another car on the roads. Her mind focussed on Issac's relationship breakdown and she hoped Nadia would be at the stables so she'd be able to talk to her.

Valentina, dressed in her riding gear which showed off her slender figure, left the tack room as Gabby pulled into the drive. She removed her riding helmet and shook her hair loose and Gabby let her eyes travel up Valentina's jodhpur clad legs that seemed to reach from her heels to her armpits; It was obvious why Ennio loved his wife; she was the epitome of Italian elegance. "Come inside. I'll just change and join you in the sitting room."

After customary air kisses, Gabby followed her into the villa and took a seat opposite a window as Valentina took her leave. Looking outside, Gabby could see that the construction had moved at a pace. The children's play area was complete, apart from a safety surface that was due to be laid, and the restaurant now had four walls and a roof.

A sound caught her attention, and she spotted Nadia crossing the hall. She called out to her and Nadia turned, looked at Gabby and saying nothing, carried on walking. The moment passed quickly as Valentina appeared in the doorway dressed in wide legged linen trousers, the lilac and purple stripes teamed with a cream half sleeve blouse. "I'm so glad you could come. Cook is making our lunch. It's something special that I hope you'll enjoy."

"I'm sure I will," said Gabby.

"Nadia will lay the table on the patio for us when it's ready. Until then, would you care for a drink?" Valentina pointed to a tray where fruit juices rested in readiness.

"That would be lovely." Gabby watched as Valentina poured a generous measure of *succo di menta* into a glass, added ice and topped it up with lemonade.

"How is Nadia?" Gabby asked as she took the offered glass. "She seemed distracted a moment ago."

"I don't know. She came into work last night and there was an angry vibe about her, and today, it's like she's retreated into herself, and not said more than two words."

Gabby kept her counsel. She didn't want to share Nadia's situation with her employer.

"So," Valentina said with an expressive wave towards the door, "shall we take our drinks outside? I can show you how the work is progressing."

Outside, the day was temperate and the fragrance of roses and lilies sailed on the light breeze under a denim blue sky painted with lazy wisps of cloud. It was a perfect day for dining outside. Valentina was pointing to the play area. Swings and slides covered with a protective cladding waited for a safety surface to be laid before installation. A small picket fence, painted in primary colours surrounded the area and a separate fenced off area was alongside with some small shelters. "We'll be housing a children's petting zoo here. Pigmy goats, some lambs, and maybe a pair of foals."

Out of the corner of her eye, Gabby could see Nadia across the yard laying their table for lunch. "This will be a great place for families," she said, thinking how miserable Nadia looked.

"Ennio has said we must make this a free resource for the community. He thinks while children play, their parents will spend money in the restaurant."

"Sounds like a plan to me."

"Let me show you inside." Gabby followed Valentina into the new building. "The wiring and plumbing are already in place and the fittings are being installed."

One wall of the bar housed a long counter with enough room for a large coffee machine and beer pumps, and mirrored shelves, which Gabby assumed would hold bottled spirits. Valentina pointed out where she imagined the tables would be and, pointing to the large window on the far wall, she said, "Imagine an afternoon over drinks with that view. Tourists will love it." The window framed the Maiella mountains perfectly, with the olive groves rumpled like a regal green and silver fabric beneath them.

The kitchen had been partially fitted with new stainless steel units and the equipment sat unboxed in the corner.

"This looks the business," Gabby said. "I can't wait to

bring Riccardo here for a meal."

"You must come as our guests on the opening night."

Gabby said they'd love to be invited as Valentina opened double doors onto a large expanse of flattened, empty earth.

"This will be an outdoor dining area, with chairs and tables. Ennio is going to ask Issac to design it and plant it up for us."

"I'm sure he'll be happy to accept the contract. We're all looking forward to seeing the garden he has created up at Nadia's father's villa."

"I hope to see it, too. Nadia has told me so much about it."

Valentina ushered Gabby outside and together they strolled around the perimeter of the new building and back into the main yard. Sonny was coming in through the main gate on his horse when he spotted them and called to Gabby.

"*Ciao Sonny. Come stai?*"

"I'm very well, thank you. I've just taken Ferro for a ride up to Cotti, Alina is joining me on a ride there tomorrow."

"She'll enjoy that."

As they took their places at the table Valentina said, "We've asked Alina if she'd like to have a stall on the open day we're having. She's been growing some plants to sell."

"What a good idea." Gabby stopped speaking when Nadia, her eyes lowered, delivered their lunch before she walked away. *Poor girl, her shoulders are sagging. She's obviously unhappy*, thought Gabby.

"The open day is the reason I invited you today. To pick your brains, so to speak. But first, let's enjoy our lunch."

Nadia had delivered the *primo*, a small bowl of ditali pasta with sardines flavoured with sultanas and fennel. Gabby tasted it and her face lit up as the sweet aniseed flavour mixed with the oily fish coated her tongue with mouthfuls of pleasure.

"You like?"

"Very much. If you'd have told me it was sultanas and

sardines, I'd have grimaced inside, but this is gorgeous."

"I'll be sure to tell cook."

Over the first course, their conversation centred on themselves. Gabby talked about her work and the meeting she'd had with Hannah in Palombaro, while Valentina told her about a horse show she'd attended with Ennio in Turin.

Their second course arrived, a delicate poached turbot garnished with orange and saffron clams. "I thought something light would be nice on a warm day," Valentina said as Nadia cleared the used bowls.

This is paradise, Gabby thought as she sat in the warm Abruzzese air eating her delicately fragrant meal. *I could never have dreamed of this while I was living in London.*

"You look lost in thought," Valentina said.

"I was thinking about how my life changed over one Italian summer."

"For the better?"

"Definitely."

"Sometimes it's the simple pleasures that are the most perfect."

Although there's nothing simple about this meal, Gabby thought, smiling at her host.

With the table cleared, they sat relaxing with white wine spritzers and Valentina brought up the proposed open day again. "I thought we could have some stalls for people to browse."

"Like jams and chutneys?"

"Probably not. Being Italy, everyone makes their own."

"Of course. Coals to Newcastle." Valentina looked confused and Gabby explained it was an English idiom describing a pointless activity. "Like supplying a product to a place that already has plenty."

"I see," nodded Valentina.

"I can speak to Hannah," Gabby said. "She hosts a ladies' handicraft group. They could be interested."

Valentina topped up Gabby's glass as another idea came

to mind. "What about Salvatore Pasquini?"

"What about him?"

"He makes ceramics. Some of the most exquisite pieces of pottery I've ever seen. Maybe he could have a stall."

"Do you think he'd be interested?"

"I can ask him. The worst he could do is say no."

"Very well, I'll leave that to you and I'll speak with the *comune* about hosting the sales tables."

As she was leaving, Gabby was beside her car when she spotted Nadia standing outside the kitchen and it looked like she was crying. "I'll call in on signor Pasquini before I go home. Thank you for a lovely lunch."

The two friends embraced and swapped air kisses and before getting into her car, Gabby noticed Nadia had gone.

Parking outside the Pasquini villa, Gabby saw that the studio door was open and the lights were on. She knocked on the door and stepped inside and saw Salvatore at his bench, a paintbrush in his hand. Not wanting to distract him, she stood still as the bristles swept across the surface of the pot he was working on. Without looking up, he said, "Come in Gabby." She walked over to him slowly as he continued to paint. He put the paintbrush down and turned the pot towards her and said, "What do you think?"

"It's lovely, but a strange colour for a flower."

Salvatore laughed. "The colour will change with heat from the kiln."

He listened as Gabby explained the purpose of her visit, and he told her didn't think he was interested in the open day at the stables.

"It will be an opportunity for you to show everyone what you can do."

"It seems a lot of effort to come away with nothing."

"You won't know if you don't try." Gabby realised he might think his reputation might influence people's attitude, but she was becoming exasperated with his negativity.

"I'd need Nadia with me."

"I think I can arrange that."

"I doubt it. Valentina will need her to work for her on a busy day like she's proposing."

Gabby sighed inwardly and said, "I'll be there. I'd be happy to help you if you needed me." Salvatore shrugged and Gabby knew she'd beaten his negativity into a corner. "Just give it some thought. I'll ask you again in a few days."

"Very well." He picked up the paintbrush again as Gabby said goodbye and she walked away, but reaching the door, she turned back. "Can I ask, how is Nadia?"

Salvatore stopped painting and, without turning around, he asked why she was concerned.

"Are you aware she's ended her friendship with Issac?"

Salvatore turned towards her and putting the paintbrush down, said, "I thought something must have happened. She's been sullen and withdrawn."

Gabby explained Riccardo was following up a lead for Salvatore's claim. "I could just be hearsay; however, I think Nadia was angry that Issac had told us."

"Where does Issac come into this and how is Nadia involved?"

"Nadia told Issac something in confidence and he told Riccardo."

"Secrets again."

Gabby was confused.

"There's so much unsaid that is festering like an untreated wound."

"What do you mean, Salvatore?"

"Ignore me. I'm rambling. I will give some thought to Valentina's proposal. Until then, I need to get back to work."

He picked up the brush and dipped it into the coloured glaze. The conversation was over.

Forty-Nine

Quarantanove

"There's something I need to tell you," Gabby said to Riccardo over dinner. "I spoke with Salvatore today."

"I know. He called me."

"And you're not angry?"

"Why should I be? He was bound to find out."

"I hope Issac doesn't think I was interfering."

"Things might get a little worse before they get better."

"Why?"

Riccardo reached over to the end of the table and pulled the laptop towards him. Opening it, he said, "I was looking through Luciano's friends list; luckily his profile is public and I think I've found Gianni."

"Are you sure?"

"I think so. There's only one on his list and they have lots of photos of them hanging out together. I'm going to look for him tomorrow."

They both looked up as Issac entered and just as he had that morning, without speaking to either of them, he went straight up to his room.

***

The following morning, looking out from the kitchen, Riccardo knotted his tie as he drank coffee. Clouds covered the sky and the air coming through the open window felt damp and he hoped for a day of rain to give his vines some relief from the above average temperatures they'd experienced recently.

Issac was supposed to working at Perano today but he

came into the kitchen and walked straight outside, climbed into his pickup and drove away. "I must speak to him later," Riccardo said to himself. "After all, he's supposed to be working here."

"Morning," Gabby said, coming into the kitchen. She walked over and kissed Riccardo on the cheek before lifting the Moka pot and pouring herself a coffee. "Was that Issac?"

"Yes. I was just thinking I need to speak to him. His silence won't solve his issues."

"It's plain ignorance," Gabby said, leaving Riccardo thinking she was being a little too harsh.

"He's been hurt. He told me something in confidence."

"That is beside the point. We're giving him bed and board. The least he can do is to be polite."

Riccardo looked at his watch, and Gabby pointed to his tie and shook her head.

"Too formal?"

"Yes." He removed the tie, draped it over the back of a chair, and left the villa.

Riccardo found Gianni at the same bar he'd found Luciano. The youth looked much younger than his eighteen years. He walked over to the youth, and assuming Luciano had described him, he saw a flicker of instinctive recognition flash in his eyes.

"Can I speak to you?" Riccardo said as Gianni made to leave the bar through the fire exit.

"Sure."

Riccardo signalled towards a table outside, and the two of them took a seat. "I think Luciano will have already spoken to you?"

"Yes, he has." Gianni spoke softly, lacking his friend's bravado.

"So you know why I'm here?" the boy nodded. "You understand this is a serious matter?"

"I said we should we tell someone, but Luciano was

frightened. He said if his father knew, he'd be furious."

"So you were both in the car that caused the collision in Brecciaio?"

Gianni nodded; his eyes lowered beneath heavy lids. "Luciano was driving. I don't have a car."

"Does Luciano have a car?"

"No, it was his brother's." Gianni swallowed loudly, then quickly said, "He knew we had it. That afternoon, he had given Luciano permission to drive it. He told him not to drive like a dick."

"And he did–"

"Drive like a dick… yes."

The conversation remained calm and Riccardo noted down details about the accident from Gianni, who appeared to be relieved that the secret was out in the open. Riccardo noted the names of all the car's occupants and Gianni gave up their addresses before he said, "Everyone will know now that I'm a grass."

"It's not about being a grass." Riccardo closed his notebook and looked at the insipient tears in Gianni's eyes. "It's about doing the right thing and I think you can help to resolve this matter."

"How?"

"Look," Riccardo gave Gianni an empathetic smile, "I'll give you some time to speak with Luciano and…" he checked his notebook, "… Flavia and Pina. My suggestion is you all meet up with Nadia and decide how you will resolve the issue."

Riccardo rose from his seat, offered his hand. This shocked Gianni, who shook it before he said, "Will we go to prison?"

"I shouldn't think so. Don't worry about that. Look towards putting everything right."

Driving home, spots of rain dotted the windscreen, turning into fat blobs of water as he neared Perano.

Pulling into the drive, Riccardo smiled. It looked like

everything was falling into place, both for his vines and for Salvatore.

Getting out of his car, he spotted Issac working around the side of the villa and decided that it was time he spoke with him.

Fifty

Cinquanta

Rachel opened the bedroom shutters and smiled. After a few days of grey skies and rain, she was happy that the weather had returned to normal. The morning of the hotel's function arrived with a flax blue sky and a high yellow sun. "Looks like our plans to eat outside will come to fruition," she said to Luca, who was still slumbering beneath the bedsheets.

"That means I'll be setting up the tables and chairs," he groaned, half-asleep.

"Ben can give you a hand." Rachel grabbed a robe, and wrapping it around herself, she left the room.

Louise was already in the open-plan kitchen when she entered, she'd made a large jug of coffee and was pouring a tall mug when Rachel slid an empty one across the table towards her.

"I'll just take this into Ben and then make you one," Louise said, picking up the mug and disappearing to her bedroom. "I said I'd get that," she said on her return, seeing Rachel cradling her morning coffee.

"Can Ben give Luca a hand to set up for the lunch this morning?"

"Sure. Anything I can do?"

"If Nadia doesn't turn up, I might need you to wait on."

"Is she still in a strop?"

"Probably. Gabby said Issac is still not speaking to her and Riccardo."

***

The phone on the table vibrated loudly. Nadia picked it up and stepped outside. She had seen Luciano's name on the screen and listened without speaking.

"You need to come to Sant'Eusanio del Sangro at lunchtime," he said. "We need to talk."

"That's not possible. I'm working today and need to be in Sant'Andrea at 11:00." The phone went dead, and she imagined Luciano spitting with annoyance.

"A problem?" Salvatore said as she came back inside.

"No *Papà*. One of those annoying marketing calls." Hiding the blushing, she collected her keys and jacket and headed out for work.

The sea air caressed Nadia's face as she travelled along the coast road. Her scooter wasn't the only one. Girls with their arms around boys; young couples riding to the beaches like her skirted through Marina San Vito with its tourists seeking seafood and gelati. When the road became wider and faster moving, she took a detour onto the smaller tracks that ran parallel with the beaches until she reached Sant'Andrea.

In the staffroom, Nadia changed into her blouse and apron and joined the other girls, who were being given instructions about the menu by the sous chef. He paid particular attention to directing them to deliver the portions of lobster risotto swiftly and to pay attention to the wine for each course. "Any problems, speak to Mirella, who, as you know, is our sommelier." He handed the waiting staff copies of the menu to study, and they shuffled away to read them.

Nadia went outside and, standing beside the hedge separating the kitchens from the pool area, she looked over at the tables set out for lunch. They reminded her of the Easter dinner when Ben and Louise had got engaged. The memory gave her a stab of heartache as she recalled Issac sitting at the table as she'd served him.

"Action stations," hissed a kitchen porter, "the guests are here."

The staff assembled beside the pass and Mirella checked them over, asking one to fasten her blouse buttons and another to give her shoes a wipe over.

Rachel appeared and wished everyone well, telling them all that Tiziana will save them some of the lunch for when their shift ends. "Nadia, any chance you can help Mirella today?"

Nadia stood with Mirella in the gazebo as the guests took their places. Men dressed formally, but in linen suits and their companions attired in floaty floral dresses. Luca and Ben had covered the tables with sails that shaded them from the intense summer sun. An industrial fan at a distance away supplied a constant stream of cool air as it blew air over baskets of ice.

A man wearing a sash in the Italian tricolour welcomed the guests and as he made a handful of acknowledgements, Mirella said to Nadia, "Remember to serve the mayor and his companion before anyone else at the table."

Nadia filled glasses with a white frizzante from a cantina in Casalbordino, a wine the mayor himself had requested, and the waiters delivered Tiziana's delicate lobster risotto.

The lunch was a success, the main course being a whole porchetta carved at the table by the sous chef, guests clamouring for the crackling in fear there'd be none left by the time he got to serve them.

The dolce plates were being collected and Mirella and Nadia placed quarter litre bottles of limoncello, grappa and ratafia at intervals so the diners could serve themselves.

"You can get off now. I'll manage the digestivi," Mirella said and Nadia walked into the kitchen to see the waiting staff already carrying plates of food out into the staffroom.

"What would you like?" the porter asked her.

"Just a cold drink." He nudged a can of cola in her direction and served the boy behind her with a bread roll filled with leftover porchetta.

Rachel came in to congratulate everyone and told all who were old enough there was a glass of frizzante for each of them.

Turning to Nadia, she asked how she was and seeing the tears pricking at her eyes asked her to come outside for a chat. Sitting at a patio table, she explained she had heard that her relationship with Issac had ended and enquired about how she was coping.

"It's much harder than I thought it would be." Nadia accepted the tissue offered to her. "I thought because I ended it, I'd be okay."

"And you're not?"

"No. I guess I liked him more than I thought I did."

"Can't you speak to him? Maybe make things better?"

"No. He betrayed my trust."

"Was it really so serious?" There was no reply as Nadia nodded and more tears flowed, accompanied by heaving sobs. Rachel patted her hand and waited for the upset to fade out and asked, "What will you do now?"

"I'm going to concentrate on my father's business. I want to sell his ceramics for him."

"Good idea. It will occupy your mind." Rachel spotted Louise walking across the lawn and an idea came to her. "Louise?"

Louise said hello to Nadia and asked Rachel why she'd called her over.

"Nadia is setting up an online business, selling her father's ceramics. Do you think you could give her some tips on how to go about it?"

"Sure, if you fetch me a large gin and tonic."

Nadia sat listening to Louise, happy to have her mind taken away from thoughts of Issac, she was absorbing what she was being told when out of the corner of her eye she saw Flavia and Pina across from the pool. Her heart plummeted, and she stalled Louise, saying she needed to use the bathroom.

She skirted around the pool and coming out from behind the pool house, she saw Gianni with Luciano. Beckoning them over, she asked them through gritted teeth, "Why are you here?"

"We need to talk," Luciano hissed.

"Not here. I'm working."

"Looks like it, sitting cosy with a drink chatting by the pool."

"You know nothing." Nadia was getting annoyed and hadn't checked her volume and several guests glanced over.

"I know you're a grass."

"Yes," Flavia said, "Why couldn't you keep your mouth shut?"

Gianni held up his hands and told everyone to calm down.

"Why did you tell that lawyer Luciano was driving?" Pina said.

"I didn't. He found out from someone else."

"So!" Luciano spat out loudly, "Who else have you told?"

"No one apart from –"

"What's going on here?" Silvana said, a look of disapproval on her face. "Shouldn't you be working?" she said to Nadia.

"Beat it, old woman. This is none of your business," Luciano sneered.

Nadia swallowed hard. She knew Luciano would regret those words. "None of my business?" she leant in close to Luciano and Nadia saw his bravado slip as he leant back. "Little boys like you should learn some manners." She grabbed him and pulled him closer and, spitting out the words, said, "I have eaten bigger scraps of meat for dinner than you. Now take this advice…" she let him go as Luca and Ben appeared.

"Everything all right Silvana?"

"Just dealing with this child."

Luciano won't enjoy being called a child, thought Nadia.

With Ben and Luca now at her side, Luciano lost all of his swagger. Silvana pointed out, "This is a hotel, not a kindergarten. A place for grown-ups, so I suggest you take your playmates and leave before my friends here throw you out."

"Come on," Gianni said.

"Later," Luciano said, pointing at Nadia and with Flavia and Pina giggling, the group slunk away.

Turning to Nadia, Silvana said, "I'll give you three-minutes to compose yourself then come to reception with an explanation."

Fifty-One

Cinquantuno

Nadia had woken up feeling wretched, and the feeling had lasted all day. Yesterday had started out being a good day. She had enjoyed working alongside Mirella until Luciano and the others had spoiled everything. She wondered if she'd ever be free from the effects they had on her life. Since the accident, she had distanced herself from them, even giving up her friendship with both Flavia and Pina. Silvana, though annoyed rather than angry, said she had to tell Rachel everything, which she was embarrassed to have to do. During their conversation, Rachel had promised she would help her whatever way she could, and Nadia believed her, but was unsure how she could. However, strangely, it had made her feel relieved to have told someone about the incident involving her father. It had felt like a cloak had lifted from her shoulders, leaving her free to move her arms again.

Before she left for work, her phone rang and Riccardo told her about a conversation he'd had the previous evening with Rachel. At the start of the call, she became annoyed, but pretty quickly, Riccardo had put her mind at rest. He said he was calling in to see her father that afternoon and if she wanted him to, he'd call into the stables to speak with her.

"Don't worry," he said, "the contents of your conversation with Rachel are safe with me until you instruct me otherwise."

The call disconnected, and she felt she could breathe again. It was like she was reconnecting with her old life.

"You look happier today," Salvatore said as she placed a coffee in front of him.

"It's a lovely morning *papà*, not a day for a long face."

"The light has been good these past days. Maybe I'll do my painting in the sun this morning."

"As long as you wear your hat and don't forget the sun cream." She kissed him and wished him a good day before leaving for the stables.

***

Sitting in the bar in Sant'Eusanio del Sangro, Riccardo was going over his morning. He was pleased with the progress he'd made, now all he needed to do now was wait.

The day had grown warm without so much as a breath of air to bring any respite. This didn't stop the few tourists from ambling through the street, taking photographs of the church opposite and the views of the countryside that appeared between the houses. He was mulling over what Rachel had told him when he spotted two figures in the distance. "Ha! I knew they'd turn up. Creatures of habit the youth of today." Watching as Luciano and Gianni sauntered towards the bar, Riccardo thought about what he was going to say to them. It was Gianni who saw him first, and he froze, with Luciano behind cannoning into him. "Hello boys." Luciano looked around him and Riccardo said, "No point thinking of running away. I know where you both live. So I suggest you take a seat." Using his foot, Riccardo pushed a chair towards them. Luciano dropped sulkily into it while Gianni pulled out another and sat down.

"I hear you went to the hotel in Sant'Andrea yesterday."

"It's a free country," shrugged Luciano.

"Is it?"

"We wanted to speak to Nadia," said Gianni.

"At her place of work. That could have been a foolish mistake."

Luciano gave a chin flick, gesturing he didn't care and said, "You're boring me now."

Riccardo leant forward and softly, with a touch of intended menace, said, "If I were you, I'd lose the attitude." He sat back and continued, "if you know what's good for you."

"Are you threatening me?"

Obviously rattled, Gianni said, "Luciano, shut up."

"I think you should listen to your friend." Riccardo opened a folder from the table and held up two envelopes. "This morning, I went to see Flavia and Pina and in the presence of their parents, they have signed statements about the incident that you and they were involved in."

"I told you; I don't know what you're talking about."

"Let's not play games. I'm here to tell you I shall file these statements with the carabinieri tomorrow. So think on about your next move." He pushed his business card across the table. "I'll finish by saying this." Luciano and Gianni's eyes left the card on the table and looked at Riccardo, who pulled his sunglasses forward to look over the frames. "If you approach Nadia Pasquini again before I've registered these documents, I promise you will both feel the full force of the law." Riccardo pushed his sunglasses back onto the bridge of his nose and walked away.

Driving the short distance to Laroscia, Riccardo was certain the meeting would have the effect he required to sew up Salvatore's claim. Now he just needed to tell Nadia he didn't think they'd bother her again.

Arriving at the stables, there were so many vehicles in the driveway that Riccardo had to park on the side of the road. "Sorry, there's so much commotion," Valentina said, "we're getting ready for the open day at the weekend."

The sounds of hammering and power tools filled the air as workers added the final touches to the play area and erected stalls next to the tack room.

"I just popped in, wondering if I could have a chat with Nadia," Riccardo said.

Valentina ushered him into the villa. "I'll fetch her," she

said. "Better to talk in here, less noisy."

Nadia looked sheepish when she arrived, and Riccardo hoped his smile would put her at ease. He told her about his meetings with Flavia and Pina that morning and that he'd told Luciano to keep his distance. "Can I suggest you talk to your father?"

"I can't. He'll know it was my fault."

"How was this your fault?" Nadia gulped loudly, a prequel to the sobbing that followed, and Riccardo didn't push the question. Although he felt sad for her, he knew she had become trapped by a secret of her own making. "I'll leave you to your thoughts, but I have to say, now that I have statements from the girls, the truth will come out sooner rather than later." He placed a comforting hand on her shoulder and left her, and after he'd said goodbye to Valentina, he went to see Salvatore.

***

Tentatively, Nadia opened the door and stepped into the kitchen and lowered her crash helmet down slowly, doing her best to avoid it making a sound. She flinched as her keys jangled on the countertop and heeling the trainers from her feet; she padded out into the hallway. Her shoulders hunched as she heard her father call her name from his room.

"*Papà?*" she looked around the door.

"Good day?"

"*Si, papà.*" She hoped he couldn't hear her heart hammering in her chest.

"Come in Nadia. I want to speak to you."

"I'm busy, *papà*, I need to make your dinner."

"It can wait. Come sit down." Seeing the trepidation on her face, he gently said, "Don't be afraid."

Nadia shuffled into the *salotto* and lowered herself into the seat that looked out over the garden. It was looking superb; the new borders were full of colour and the raised beds were overflowing with tumbling petunias. All that need to be completed was the rose walk that was waiting for the plants to be delivered.

They both sat in silence. The ticking of a clock and the hum of the air-conditioning overwhelmed the space, the heaviness pressing the anxiety deeper inside her.

"We need to talk."

Nadia blurted out, "I'm sorry, *papà*, I never –"

Salvatore held up a hand and hushed her. "Let me speak." He shifted in his chair, his face turned to hers. "I know. I have always known."

"You know?" she whispered.

"Yes."

"How?"

"I saw you. As the car skidded away from mine, I saw you leaning forward between the front seats."

"Oh *papà*. I dare not ask for your forgiveness. This is all my fault."

"How was this your fault?" Unconsciously, he patted the knee on which his left leg had been attached.

"I wanted to change the music on the radio. I distracted Luciano."

Salvatore wheeled himself over to his daughter and took her hand in his. "*Cara mia*, the fault is not yours. The blame lies with the person who was driving. If he had been sensible, then this would never have happened."

"Why didn't you tell me you knew I was there?"

"For the same reason, I have never told the carabinieri that there was another car involved. I didn't want this to ruin your life."

Tears started falling again, and she said, "But our actions have ruined your life."

"I ruined my life long before the accident."

"What will happen now?"

"Avvocato di Renzo will put together a fresh case for the

insurance companies. The police will want to speak with Gianni and Luciano and in a few weeks, hopefully, we can put this unfortunate episode behind us."

"Do you think we ever will?"

"We have to. How can we launch our new father and daughter business with this muddying our waters?"

Fifty-Two

Cinquantadue

In Perano, Riccardo was ending the telephone call he'd received. "You're doing the right thing," he said, "and I promise I'll help you both as much as I can."

"Good news?" Gabby said, joining him outside.

"Gianni. He's got Luciano to agree to come clean. I'm going to see them later to take a statement before I drive over to see the officer in charge of the case."

"Do you think this will help Salvatore's claim?"

"It should do. It's all straightforward now. Petrini's insurer should pay the claim and I'm assuming after they'll instigate a fresh claim to get compensation from Luciano's brother's company."

"So a happy ending all round. Then Salvatore can pay you for your time."

"I guess so."

"You don't sound so sure."

"I'm not sure. At the moment, he needs every spare euro to put towards his new business. Maybe I'll defer payment until he has sufficient funds."

Gabby kissed him. "I love you, Riccardo di Renzo." She was proud of him and his enduring empathy.

"I think I ought to shower and change out of my overalls and head off to get the boys' statements."

"Perhaps I could join you in the shower."

Riccardo grinned and placed his phone on a window ledge and lifting Gabby into his arms, he carried her inside, heeling the door closed behind them.

***

In Laroscia, the roses had arrived three hours earlier than expected. The delivery driver had unloaded them outside the Pasquini villa and left. Trays with pots stood outside the driveway, half of them on the road, the other inside the property boundary. Nadia kept looking out of the window, hoping that Issac would arrive before someone saw the opportunity to drive up and steal some. Salvatore had told her she was worrying needlessly, pointing out that usually weeks could pass without a single vehicle coming into the piazza. Issac had been at the villa the previous evening to dig the holes ready for planting, but Nadia had had no contact with him. Sporadically, she had looked through the bedroom window to watch him, dismayed to see that he wasn't looking up towards her room. "Here I am, once again staring out of windows," she said to herself as she spotted Alina walking into the piazza. The girl gave her a wave and Nadia went to open the front door. "Hi Alina."

"Hi, I'm helping Issac today."

Nadia's hope of being available should Issac want to speak to her sunk as she heard those words. Alina and her endless questions would occupy him too much for him to notice she was home today. *Maybe I should offer to make lunch,* she thought as she saw his pickup pull into the piazza. Alina rushed to the front door before Nadia could stop her and, opening it, she bounded out to greet Issac.

"I got here before you."

"The boss always arrives later," he laughed

"Nonna told me the boss should always set a good example," Alina shot back with humour.

"Well, I had to stop off to get this." He held up a paper bag.

"What is it?"

"*Formaggio e prosciutto su ciabatta.* Our lunch." Hearing this, Nadia's morning grew a little gloomier. *What else can I do to get him to notice me?*

She watched Issac load the roses into a wheelbarrow, and wheel them away.

Peering around the drapes that covered the *porte-finestre,* she watched as Alina and Issac appeared in the rear garden, the wheel on the barrow squeaking. Nadia observed as they both positioned the potted roses in place, stood back, moved them and then stepped back once more and checked Issac's design before rearranging them again. Once satisfied, they began the planting.

With her father in his studio, Nadia escaped upstairs and sitting on the end of her bed, she watched as Issac planted the roses, heeling them in while Alina followed on with the watering can. "They will look beautiful," she told herself, "Just like when mamma looked after them, but now they'll always remind me of Issac."

Looking over the garden, she could see that it was almost complete and Issac would have no more need to visit the villa. The old *frantoio*, now a decorative ruin with a small table and chairs in its shade surrounded by low growing flowering plants, made the perfect space for relaxation and reflection. Their fruit trees would give shade and produce for the table. The old mill stone was a triumph; she knew that she'd share many meals at its upcycled tabletop with her friends. "That's if I have any friends left, now that I've betrayed them." Suddenly, she had a rush of anxious worry. "What will people say when the truth becomes public knowledge? Will Valentina fire me? Will neighbours shun me?" she lowered her head into her hands and weeping didn't notice that her bedroom door had silently opened.

"Issac has asked if you'd like to come and see the finished rose beds?" Turning around, Nadia saw Alina standing in the doorway. "Why are you so sad?"

"It's nothing. Just boyfriend trouble."

"Why do people say it's nothing when it obviously is something?"

"You'll understand when you're older."

"If getting older and having a boyfriend means I have to cry alone, I'll stick with looking after plants and my orto."

Nadia gave a small laugh. "You seem to have everything sorted out."

"Well, I don't want to be sad like you and Issac."

"Issac is sad?"

"Of course he is. Can't you tell?"

"No, we haven't spoken to each other for a while."

"There's your answer then... Do you want to come see the roses?"

For someone so young, you've a wise head on your shoulders, Nadia thought, then after wiping her eyes, said, "Okay, lead the way."

Fifty-Three

Cinquantatré

A thin shawl of cloud drifted in the morning sky, diffusing the sun's brightness, and a gentle breeze was keeping the heat at bay as the tables set out were being filled by the stallholders.

Ennio had paid over the going rate to have the work at the stables completed before the summer took hold. He knew workers didn't enjoy manual work under a scalding sun. His project manager had secured trades from all over Abruzzo; some even travelled in from as far afield as Teramo. *It was worth it;* he thought as he surveyed the hustle and bustle in the courtyard.

Nadia and Salvatore had spent the past few days selecting their wares and now, as she laid out the pieces of china on the simple blue tablecloth, Nadia saw the brilliance of her father's work as a stranger must. A sweet dish painted with periwinkles the colour of the sky above shone in a beam of sunlight that escaped the cloud cover.

On the table next to theirs, an old woman was laying out handmade lace items. Handkerchiefs, filigree edged photo frames and small hearts filled with lavender. "Those look lovely," Nadia said, and the old woman held up a book jacketed by an intricate lacey cover. "I hope you have a good day selling."

"You too," the old woman said, before going back to organising her stall.

Alina waved to her. She had already set up her stall with plant pots filled with flowering plants and some trays of 'cut and come' salad vegetables.

Sonny rode out of the stable. Ferro's hooves clopping on the driveway as he gave his horse a walk before he would take up position at the gate to welcome the visitors and hand out leaflets.

Enio was calm and sailed slowly between stallholders, caterers and the grooms, asking questions and giving instructions in his calm manner. Valentina was on the opposite side of his dial. She was fraught with worry.

"Do you have the timings correct for the opening presentation?" she asked the caterer for the third time. "You know where the fire exits are?" she enquired again with the waiters, and for the umpteenth time, she grilled the grooms about their duties.

Quickly the morning ran away with the organisation of the event, and the public started arriving. Ennio had the idea for Sonny to ask people where they had come from as he handed them an advertising flyer; this way he could gauge the distances people had travelled to aid future promotions.

Valentina gave a welcome speech as families came through the gates and accepted a complimentary glass of frizzante or orange from the catering staff. As soon as the speech had finished, children eager to visit their dedicated area ran to play in the brightly coloured playground. Squeals and laughter raced through the air, mixing with the chatter of the grown-ups and the occasional whickering of a horse, hoping to be given a candy peppermint as a treat.

The visitors congregated around the stalls and Salvatore was busy talking about the processes he used to produce his pottery creations; he talked about underglazes and oxides and even had his sketch book available for browsers to look at. Meanwhile, Nadia was wrapping their sales in tissue paper and taking payments. She glanced over at Alina, whose stall was also busy and in a moment of calm gave her a wave. Luca and Rachel had arrived earlier with Ben and Louise and as they sauntered around the site, Luca hung back to help Alina with her stall, giving gardening advice and taking the cash for her sales.

Because the bar interior was still incomplete, they'd set

up a temporary bar outside, where two waiters filled glasses with beers and wines. The drinks queue mirrored the congestion outside the stables, and at one point an angry old farmer complained he couldn't get to his land; a free glass of ice-cold Peroni settled him down and his tractor joined the cars parked with their wheels on the grass verges.

Nadia watched as Gabby and Riccardo came into the yard. Riccardo stopped to speak with her father and as she wrapped a bowl for a customer, she spotted Issac walking over to greet Luca and Alina. He spoke to her and she hugged him before he took over her stall, letting her skip off to join Sonny, who was now giving pony rides to children in the paddock. Observing Alina's innocence and exuberance, Nadia wished *she* could go back in time to a place when life was less fraught.

"Your stall has been busy," Valentina said, bringing Nadia back from her thoughts.

"Yes, more than I thought it would be. We've sold quite a few pieces."

"Be sure to put one of these aside for me." she handed Nadia a vase decorated with cornflowers, then said. "You look happier today."

"I am," Nadia said. It was a half-truth as she couldn't stop glancing over at Issac who was never looking over in her direction.

***

Issac enjoyed helping Luca at Alina's stall. His friend had told him to use it as an opportunity to introduce himself to people and sell his gardening business. "I can't use Alina's stall to feather my own nest," he said.

Luca didn't understand his Scottish friend's idiom, but replied, "I'm sure she won't mind. Besides, she'll be helping you, no doubt." Issac nodded and removed a stack of business cards from his jacket pocket and laid them out on the table.

He'd seen Nadia across the courtyard and a melancholy mood blanketed him because every time he looked across at her, she wasn't looking his way. *She's definitely no longer interested in me*; he thought as a woman nudged him to swap a euro coin for a pot of yellow calendulas.

The day turned out to be a success. Everyone who had visited complimented Ennio and Valentina on what they had achieved, with many promising to return once the bar and restaurant were open.

Families with tired younger children began leaving to be replaced by older teens eager to watch a local band made up of teenagers from Casoli that had set up outside the bar.

Older men assembled their long slim charcoal burners ready for the evening, when the air would fill with the tempting aroma of *arrosticini* and a horn sounded as a van selling porchetta arrived to take over the spaces vacated by the stallholders.

Alina returned to help Luca and Issac pack away the leftovers of her stall and, seeing the plastic box filled with coins, she gave a squeal of delight. "What will you do with your takings?" Issac asked her.

"Half will go towards some new plants for my garden and I shall use the rest for a birthday present for my nonna."

"That's good of you."

"Shall I carry these over the road for you?" Luca said.

"No you will not!" Alina said loudly, her hands on her hips. "I know your game Luca," she gave Issac a wink and smiled, "You just want to see my if my watermelons behind the compost heap are bigger than yours."

"Hah!" Luca exclaimed with great humour, "You've rumbled me."

"Who will judge your competition?" Issac asked.

"We could ask Valentina?" Alina said as signora Barone walked across the courtyard.

"Ask me what?" Valentina said, putting a hand on

Alina's shoulder.

"Our watermelon competition, would you judge it?"

"Yes, I've heard about this challenge that Luca set last year. I'd be happy to be the judge."

Alina clapped her hands with glee, picked up the tray of her remaining plants and ambled off across the road promising to come back with Nonna, who was partial to *arrosticini*.

Looking up, Issac saw Salvatore put the last of the boxes of unsold china onto a sack truck, ready for Nadia to wheel home. "Salvatore," he called out, "Let me put your boxes in the back of my pickup and drive you back home."

***

Nadia stood in silence and watched as Issac loaded the boxes and her father's wheelchair into his truck and drove away to the top of the village, leaving her standing at the side of the road. *He didn't even look at me;* she thought, *he must really dislike me.*

Feeling dejected, she walked over to watch the band, who had just started playing. The surrounding crowd swayed and cheered, but she wasn't in the mood to enjoy herself. She was happier dwelling on her sadness.

The smell of the sheep's meat skewers on the barbecues couldn't tempt her and leaning against the bar waiting to be served, she watched as Alina ordered a half-dozen of the *arrosticini* for her nonna, who was tapping her feet to the band's cover version of, *Sarà Perché Ti Amo*.

Taking her drink away from the crowd, she leant against the paddock fence and, lost in thought, didn't notice Gabby approach her. The conversation started with chit-chat about the day and how the stall had sold a good amount of ceramics, until Gabby said, "Have you spoken to Issac since you fell out?"

"We didn't fall out," Nadia said defensively. "We split

up." Seeing the shock cross Gabby's face, she apologised for the outburst and said, "No. Issac doesn't want to speak to me."

"I'm sure that's not true," Gabby said before Nadia told her how the day had been a collection of empty glances across the courtyard and his taking her father home without even so much as a glance her way. "You know Issac is painfully shy. My guess is he doesn't know how to react in this situation."

"Maybe. But I thought he'd have apologised for betraying my trust."

"He thinks he already has, and you pushed it aside."

"I was angry with him."

"You do understand, he had no choice?"

"What do you mean?"

"Issac cares deeply about your father. Salvatore gave him the opportunity to develop his business, and he knew that telling Riccardo about Luciano it would bring a favourable resolution to his insurance claim."

Nadia nodded and then told Gabby that her father had known all along that she had been in the car, "He was protecting me."

"I understand that, but sometimes secrets don't protect. They only delay a resolution."

"So, what shall I do?"

"It's not for me to say. I made enough mistakes of my own at your age. What I will say is, work out what outcome you want and decide how you'll achieve it." Gabby squeezed Nadia's hand. There was nothing more to say and with a comforting smile, she made her way over to Riccardo, who was also buying *arrosticini*.

Nadia finished her drink before she walked home, tucking herself into a hedge as Issac's pickup drove past on the way back to the stables. "Perhaps I should have stayed," she said aloud as the band's audience cheered and, looking up at the stars, she wished things had been different. "Life would certainly have been much easier if I'd never met Issac."

Fifty-Four

Cinquantaquattro

Hannah and Gabby were sitting beneath a striped awning at a bar on the coast at Lido Riccio, with the tall commercial hotels at their backs and the beach in front of them. As they waited for Rachel and Louise to join them, they sipped tall glasses of lemonade with ice and submerged sprigs of mint. Gabby was talking about the open day at the stables when two long shadows inched their way towards the table. "The girls are here," she said.

"Would you like a drink?" Hannah said as she reached for the jug in the centre of the table.

"Thank you," Rachel said.

"What are you having?" Louise's face crumpled when Hannah told her it was a virgin mojito. "Virgin, I think I can remember a time when…" she paused, then with a wide grin said, "No, I can't remember that far back. Do you mind if I pass?" Hannah shook her head and Louise went to the bar to choose something stronger.

"I was just talking to Hannah about the writing courses we'll be hosting in Palombaro next year."

"Would you like me to put a link to your place on our website's 'places of interest' page?" said Rachel.

"That would be very kind," Hannah replied. "I was thinking about Salvatore's business."

"What about it?"

"I wondered, if he was willing, maybe he could host pottery workshop visits for our guests."

"Let me ask him for you." Rachel said.

"Sounds interesting," said Gabby. "Keep me in the loop."

Louise returned with a large glass of chilled pink *cerasuolo*, plonked herself down at the table, and asked the others about the plan for the day.

"There's a great fish place along here," Rachel pointed along the boulevard, "I thought we could have lunch there, then maybe a stroll looking in the tourist shops before spending the rest of the day soaking up the sun on the beach."

"That suits me fine," Louise said. "So we'll have time for another drink?"

Rachel rolled her eyes and with a smile, shook her head. She called over a waiter, ordered a bottle of wine and because she and Hannah were driving another jug of the virgin cocktail.

The conversation centred on the open day once more. Rachel commented on how fabulous Valentina had looked.

"That woman could wear an old blanket and still look exquisite," said Gabby.

"I thought Nadia looked a bit detached," Rachel said.

"Hasn't she made up with Issac yet?" Louise asked, pouring wine into Gabby's glass.

"Not yet." Gabby lifted her glass in a silent toast across the table.

"What a waste. He's one hell of a hot guy." Louise laughed.

"Have I met him yet?" Hannah said.

"If you had, you'd remember. Tall, broad, pale and interesting."

"Red haired and rugged," added Rachel, and the table detonated raucous laughter.

***

Issac was at a loose end. Riccardo was in Gabby's office working while she was out with her girlfriends, leaving him alone. There was nothing that needed his attention in the vineyard, and his services weren't required at the hotel.

Bored, he opened a magazine Gabby had left on the table and flicked through it; nothing grabbed his attention. He picked up his phone and thumbed through his social media, but nothing there interested him, either. He thought about uploading some photos of the roses he'd planted at Salvatore's villa, but he couldn't drum up enough energy to push the buttons. "I need to shake myself up and get over this... whatever this is," he told himself.

He got up from the table and walked outside; he stood for a while looking down the valley towards Quadroni and tapping his pocket for his keys, got into his pickup and drove down the hill.

A solitary *Ape* buzzed on the other side of the road as he drove, not knowing where he was going until he arrived at the industrial estate at Saletti.

The parking area was vast, a place where lorries stopped overnight and people came to visit the huge discount store, bar and pizzeria that remained a popular meeting place for young people and those who frequented its weekend open-air market.

He ordered a zero beer and took his slice of pizza to a table outside and watched the cars that arrived and departed with regularity. His mind whirred, going over everything that had happened to him since he'd returned to Abruzzo. His mind punctuated memories of the garden at Laroscia, first seen four months prior, with images of Alina helping, Nadia smiling, and Salvatore approving the changes Issac wanted. So much had happened. He'd settled down quickly and living with Gabby and Riccardo was easy. The work he'd secured was fulfilling, and he felt that his business could have a chance of becoming successful. If only his relationship with Nadia had turned out the same. Her smiling face swam before his eyes and a memory of her laughing in Campobasso flooded his head, threatening to break the dam, holding back his tears. He thought about the day he'd planted the roses. He'd known she was home. S*he'd been determined to keep her distance,* he thought.

Shaking his thoughts away like a bird scarer, he took a deep breath and let it out slowly to prevent himself from shedding a tear. He picked up his beer; it had warmed in the sunshine and lost its bubbles, and his pizza was now lukewarm and unappealing. Leaving them untouched, he got up from the table and climbed back into his pickup. "I need to take action," he said aloud. "Pining won't solve this mess."

Issac was determined to win Nadia back and as he drove, he rehearsed what he was going to say, and each recitation bolstered his courage.

He pulled into the driveway at Perano and, leaving the truck's door open, he raced inside the villa and upstairs where he changed his clothes and doused himself with a liberal amount of cologne before returning and setting off for Laroscia.

***

"We had a lovely afternoon at the beach," Rachel said as Nadia fixed them both a cold drink, mixing sparkling water with *sciroppo di ciliegie*. "Louise had one too many glasses of wine, so I dropped her back at the hotel to have a nap." Rachel accepted the glass of cherry flavoured water and asked how she'd been.

Nadia told her about the conversation she'd had with her father and also said that she'd started speaking with Pina again. "Flavia's parents have banned her from associating with any of us."

"I hear you were successful at the stables."

"Yes, we sold more than we expected. It means *papà* can buy more oxides and glazes and we have enough to pay someone to build us a website."

"Let me speak with Louise. She'll probably know of an

e-business with templates you can manage yourselves."

Hearing a vehicle outside, they both looked up and Nadia said, "It's Issac."

"Would you like me to leave you to talk? I can go next door to speak with your father in his studio."

"No, stay here, please. I don't think he'll have come here to see me."

"How can you be sure?"

"He worked in the garden yesterday and ignored me for the whole time he was here."

The front door opened and Issac walked into the hallway and said, "Nadia, there's something I –" He spotted Rachel in the kitchen and mumbled, "I... I need to check in the garden." He turned around and left the villa and disappeared around the side of the property.

"You see," Nadia said, "he came to see his flowers, not me."

Rachel looked into Nadia's face. A sadness crept over her features and so she made her excuses and went to speak with Salvatore in his studio.

"What will it entail?" he said.

"Whatever you want it to. Maybe just hold sessions for the guests to decorate their own pieces. You must have some that aren't quite the best grade for your own work."

"Well yes. But I'm not sure I can give up too much time."

"Hannah says it'll be just a couple of days every three or four months. It's not a continuous thing. Mostly holiday season and think of the extra income."

"Very well, let me think about it."

"You'll let me know your decision?"

Salvatore nodded and Rachel told him she needed to get back to the hotel. After bidding him a good night, she stepped outside to find Issac climbing back into his pickup.

"You going back to Perano?"

"Yes," Issac said, as he spat out the word.

Aware that he wasn't in the best of moods, she said, "Drive safely," and climbed into her own car and gunned the ignition.

Fifty-Five

Cinquantacinque

The June temperatures had been higher than previous years, with some days being so oppressive, the heat felt physically heavy. As the month wound down, the skies had become darker with threatening rain and people were predicting a storm to clear the air, ready for the next temperature increase in July.

Issac had loaded his pickup with empty sacks and headed out to Salvatore's villa. Pulling up outside, he noticed Nadia's scooter was gone and thinking she must be at work; he breathed a sigh of relief. The last thing he needed was to face up to his *faux-pas* yesterday.

Last night the plum coloured sky had crept into his bedroom and he'd lain awake staring through the window at the stars, his mind churning like a whisk mixing cake batter. *What would I have done if Rachel hadn't been there? Would I have delivered my rehearsed speech?* He sighed loudly. How would Nadia have reacted? *Have I crushed my chance now?* He rolled over, closed his eyes, but sleep didn't come. All he could think about was what a failure he was.

Salvatore said hello briefly before he headed into his studio and Issac began working in the garden. There was very little to do now. It was mostly tidying up, removing a wayward weed and making sure everything looked perfect. He scooped up fallen leaves and pruned some of the older shrubs; it was out of season but he wanted it to look perfect because he'd booked a professional photographer to take shots for his website and future promotions.

Alina arrived as he was raking the gravel path between

the two rose beds. She called out to him and asked if she could help. "Sonny is taking some holidaymakers trekking this morning."

"Can you tidy up the mill stone feature?"

"Yes, I've bought some left over petunias from the open day. I can put them in the raised beds?"

Between the two of them, it didn't take long for the garden to look pristine and standing back, they admired their work.

Issac had divided the garden into three sections. To the left were fruit trees, their canopies giving privacy from the piazza and neighbouring houses. Below he'd put in raised vegetable beds, their heights easier for Salvatore to manage in his chair. An oval bed closed this section with a mix of tall ornamental grasses and floribunda rose bushes.

To the right where the old frantoio had stood was the new ruin flanked with succulents, its brickwork now a breathing wall of green that created a cool area for the small bistro table and chairs surrounded by fragrant lavender.

Issac was especially proud of the giant stone olive wheel that now had three wooden benches around it. Through the central hole where the thick wooden spindle had been, gurgled and bubbled water, its soothing sound welcoming the birds that drank from it. Leading to it was a gravel path from the stone patio where on either side he'd planted the lower growing persica roses that Salvatore had wanted and a mix of hybrid teas and floribundas.

"If I could, I'd pat myself on the back," he said to Alina.

"Let me do it." Laughing, he stooped for her to thump him between the shoulder blades as she told him he'd done a good job. "Shall I set up the hose?"

"No, I think we're going to have some rain tonight," Issac said as a raindrop landed on his nose. "Come on, let's get these sacks of rubbish onto the pickup and we can let Mother Nature look after it tonight."

The falling rain was quite pleasant in the warm air and

without urgency they loaded up the truck and afterwards Issac dropped Alina home as Sonny was returning with his guests.

"I will see you again, won't I?" Issac turned to look at Alina. She looked small in the pickup's passenger seat. Her face had lost its shine and her bright eyes their lustre.

"Of course you will. We're friends, aren't we?"

Alina's smile returned. "Yes. And don't forget me if you need any help with other gardens."

"You'll be the first person I call on."

She opened the passenger door and before she hopped out, she dived across the cab and planted a kiss on Issac's cheek, then off she skipped towards Sonny, leaving the burly Scotsman with tears in his eyes.

Driving back to Perano, the rain went from spotting to a light shower; he watched as women came out of their homes to remove washing that had been drying outside. People huddled in shop doorways along the road at Quadroni, their summer attire not suitable for a sudden shower.

Driving up the lane to the villa, the rain found it difficult to penetrate the green canopy of trees. Issac liked the lane. He slowed his truck and wound down the windows to breathe in the earthy scent, the mixture of damp earth, decaying leaves and pine needles. The rain would slowly drip down and add to the moisture trapped beneath the trunks, and the perfume would be more intense in a day or so.

Reaching the villa, the rain stopped, and the sun shone again, illuminating raindrops on the vine's leaves. He locked up his pickup and strode into the house with a smile on his face. His morning had turned out much better than he had imagined.

"You look happy," Gabby said.

"I am. The garden is complete and a few showers of rain will do it good."

"Riccardo said the vines could do with it, too."

"My photographer is coming the first week of July, so hopefully the showers will pass and the flowers will be at their best."

Gabby told him there was some leftover salad in the fridge before she went back to work in her office. Issac had a fixed smile as he prepared some lunch and after eating, he spent the afternoon walking through the wilder parcels of land behind the vines. He tried to clear his mind, but the situation with Nadia kept bullying his consciousness. *Maybe I should pack up and start again somewhere else*, he thought, looking down at some tracks, darkened by the rain. "Deer," he said. The tracks diverted his thoughts away from his romantic, or lack of, situation. He followed them through the trees until they disappeared into the long grass. The view out of the trees was breathtaking, a lush expanse of green leading down into the dip of a small village before the mountains pushed their peaks, now minus the snow that had crowned them, up into the heavens. Looking out over the landscape gave him a feeling of belonging. He loved being in Abruzzo. Apart from Scotland, this place felt like home to him. "I've worked too hard to give up everything and move away," he said to himself. "I'll just have to man up and face the end of our relationship, head on."

With a renewed vigour he strode through the grass, wet from the rain, making his way around the villa until he reached the road on which it stood. He looked down at the road through Quadroni. The early evening brought more cars, and the pavements filled with people absent during the day. Walking into the driveway, he saw Riccardo's car and removed his boots before stepping inside the villa to prepare the evening meal.

Over dinner, Gabby talked about her latest feature for the magazine, telling the men that Nolan was coming over the following day to go through her schedule for the next couple of months. "I think I'll miss *Ferragosto* this year. I have interviews in England lined up in August."

"That'll be a shame," Issac said.

"It'll mean your August alcohol intake will drop." Riccardo said with a smile.

"That can only be a good thing." Gabby cleared their dishes and took a tub of gelato from the freezer.

"There's been deer in the woodland," Issac said, "we need to take precautions otherwise we'll wake up one morning to find they've eaten the vine shoots."

"What do you think we should do?"

"I suggest putting up a fence?"

"Temporarily? I'd hate to have a permanent barrier."

"You know how much Riccardo loves his wild residents." Gabby placed a bowl of ice cream in front of him.

"This is their land as much as ours."

"I'll make a start tomorrow," Issac said, used to the friendly banter between Gabby and Riccardo about his love of the local wildlife. "There are fencing poles in the shed."

Relaxing over digestivi, another shower came. Raindrops drummed at the windows and, with the house still warm from the sun, the atmosphere was comfortable and relaxing. The three of them spent the evening talking; inconsequential chatter that side-stepped the important issues in their lives. *It's nice to just sit and chill out*, thought Issac.

The first crash of thunder shook the villa, waking everyone. Issac got out of bed and looked out of the window. Streaks of lightning were spearing the indigo sky, momentarily lighting up the landscape before it plunged it back into darkness. The rain was lashing down like stair rods, noisily and with determination, it battered against the roof, sounding like troops invading a foreign land.

"Issac?" Riccardo's voice sounded on the landing.

"I heard it," he said, opening his bedroom door.

"Gabby's making coffee. I need to check I've locked the door to the winery."

They both padded downstairs.

"It's a monster," Gabby said, setting down three coffees, while another thunderclap swept over the villa like a giant wave.

Riccardo pulled a coat over his vest and shorts and slipped his feet into Issacs boots that were still outside where he'd left them. A gale wrenched the door from his grip as he opened it, straining the hinges and banging it against the outside wall as giant raindrops invaded the hallway. Issac grabbed his coat from a hook and, wearing suede moccasins, he stepped outside and fought against the wind to close the door.

Rainwater washed the soil from around the vines, sending it rushing in a deluge down the terraced land. Feeling useless, he knew they would have to wait until the storm had blown itself out, hoping the damage would be minimal. Worried that the newly planted younger vines would wash away, he clutched his coat around himself and prayed silently.

"Come inside," Riccardo shouted in his ear. "We can't do anything until it's passed."

Back inside, Gabby had lit the wood burner and poured them each a large glass of grappa. And together the three of them sat in the sitting room as the storm roared.

***

Outside, the sun was high and not a single cloud blotted the agapanthus blue sky. The sound of birdsong trilled into the room through the open window and, as Issac rubbed sleep from his eyes, the smell of strong coffee invaded his senses. "Morning," Gabby said, putting down a cup. "We must have all fallen asleep down here." He looked down to see he was still wearing his coat and sodden moccasins. "Riccardo's outside assessing the damage."

After changing into his overalls, he found his boots in

the hall and went outside to join Riccardo. The vines looked battered, but they were still standing, albeit with less soil around their roots than the previous morning.

"Look." Riccardo pointed at the mound of earth that had washed away. Down the slope Issac looked at a mound of mud and knew that it would take some hard graft to shovel it all back up the terracing. "I've checked the weather and there's no more rain imminent."

"Well then. We'd better get started before it dries out and hardens into one giant rock."

"Issac!" Gabby shouted. "You're wanted on the phone."

"Tell whoever it is I'll call them back."

"It's Nadia."

He went into the villa and saw his phone on the kitchen table; the screen lit up.

"When I saw her name on the screen, I answered it," Gabby said.

Issac put the phone to his ear, "*Pronto.*"

He listened, and his shoulders slumped. When the call ended, he turned to Gabby and said, "I have to go." And after he'd picked up his keys and apologised to Riccardo, he drove away.

When he arrived at Laroscia, Salvatore and Nadia were on the patio surveying the damage. Nadia's eyes were ringed red and Issac guessed she had been crying.

Sludge covered the patio where the rain had washed soil and stones towards the villa. Ferocious winds had strewn the new rose bushes around the garden, ripping them from their positions and discarding them where they landed. Petunias and geraniums lay flattened, blooms tattered by the pelting rain. "Where is the patio set?" Issac asked, pointing to the frantoio ruin where he'd positioned the table and chairs.

"We don't know." Nadia said, the words catching in her throat.

Leaves, torn from branches in the rear woodland, were

scattered everywhere like ripped-up sheets of paper and over in the orto, the storm's invisible hands, hell bent on destruction, had pulled out the vegetables growing there.

"It's ruined." Salvatore turned his chair around and headed up the ramp inside the villa before he said, "I'm sorry Issac, all your hard work gone overnight."

Rooted to the spot, Nadia looked at the mess as tears tumbled over her cheeks. Issac reached out to her and she accepted his hand.

He pulled her into him, her face against his chest, her tears soaking his shirt as he ran his hand up and down her spine in the same way a father would soothe a disquiet baby.

"It'll be all right," he said. "I can fix this."

Nadia moved away from him. Looking up into his open face, she said, "Can you?"

Issac wanted to speak but instinctively their mouths met and as they kissed, his heart lifted and a quiet determination became fuelled within him.

Fifty-Six

Cinquantasei

The alarm rang, and Issac dragged himself out of bed and made his way into the kitchen. The Moka pot was cold and there was no sign of Gabby or Riccardo; they hadn't told him they would be going out last night. He made a coffee and grabbed a hunk of dry bread and smothered it with slices of salami before he climbed into his pickup. He wasn't looking forward to the day ahead and the devastation waiting for him. As he drove to Laroscia, the sun was low in the sky, casting a golden hue over the rolling hills and olive groves that held onto no memory of the storm. *How unfair*, he thought, *that everywhere holds onto its picturesque charm, yet my garden has been destroyed.*

Sludge had washed down the hill, edging both sides of the road to the top of the village; the brown mess had an umami aroma, and he saw half-buried young wild garlic plants with roots too weak to hold their positions. He made a mental note to gather some to take back to plant in the woodland behind the villa as the smell repelled deer.

Coming into the piazza, he was astonished to see it crammed with people who had gathered around a multitude of vehicles. Trucks, cars, and a tractor or two. He recognised Rachel and beside her, Luca was holding a clipboard. *Who is that he was talking to?* Issac delved into his memory and their names returned to him. It was Ivan and his wife, Mole, and beside them, he saw Cosmo and Massimo. Small fists banged on the driver's door and, looking out of the window, he saw Alina and Sonny.

"You're late... Again." Alina said.

"What's going on?"

"What do you think?" she said as he got down from his

seat. "We're all here to help put Salvatore's the garden back together."

"How come?"

"My fault, I'm afraid," Gabby said, approaching him. "I sent out a WhatsApp plea last night asking for willing volunteers." A car tooted, and she saw Queenie and some ladies from her creative writing group, all of whom clambered out of Beattie's Fiat brandishing trowels and hand forks.

"Cake," shouted Beattie, holding up a plastic box. "Queenie's got sandwiches."

Overwhelmed by so many people gathered there to help, Issac sniffed and fought back tears. Salvatore reached up and placed his hand on his arm and said, "Come inside and help me with the coffees. Let them get on with what Luca has asked them to do." Issac was about to protest but something in Salvatore's eyes told him it was best he took a break to pull himself together.

In the kitchen, the two of them were making jugs of coffee and carrying them outside to the hordes of people who were rebuilding and repairing the garden. One of Cosmo's builder friends who had come along stepped inside and placed a bottle of grappa on the kitchen table. "I think some of us would welcome a *café corretto*."

Salvatore's eyes widened when he saw it, and Issac reached over to remove the bottle. "It was inappropriate to bring this," he said.

The builder looked perplexed, and Salvatore lifted the bottle and poured a measure into a jug of coffee. "It's okay. I can deal with it. I'm not going down that road again." The builder put the bottle in his back pocket and carried the jug outside while Salvatore returned to filling the Moka pot with more ground coffee.

After their refreshments, everyone who Luca had arranged into groups and made responsible for sections of the garden set to work.

His plan was for everybody to work from the villa upwards to the end of the garden. "This way," he called to them, "we can clean as we go and any waste can go into the compost at the top or be spread out under the trees."

Issac was in charge of the roses. First, Nadia, with Alina and Sonny's help, rescued them from the places the wind had distributed them and put them into buckets of water. Issac and Alina then trimmed away any damaged shoots as Sonny and Nadia dug new holes for the roots.

Issac and Nadia passed the occasional comment to each other but kept themselves some distance apart. They had decided that today wasn't the time for people to know they had rekindled their romance; it was a day to restore Salvatore's garden.

The sun was now high in the sky, its warmth helping to dry the land and plants that the wind had flattened reached up, standing straight and proud. Ivan and Mole had found the missing bistro set in the woodland and reinstated it in place beside the *frantoio* ruin. Gabby's creative writing ladies replanted petunias and geraniums and when everyone took a break and they shared out the lunch they had bought along. Rachel went to her car and returned with two cool boxes filled with cans of soft drinks for the thirsty workers.

Issac and Nadia had slipped away on the pretence of making fresh coffee and as the pot bubbled on the stove, with Issac's back against the door to keep it closed, they kissed for the first time that day.

"Do you think we'll get the garden finished today?"

"Yes. Everyone is doing such a good job. It would have taken me many days to complete the work that's already been done." Issac kissed her again. "A few days of sunshine and it'll be blooming again."

Knocking broke them apart, and the door opened to reveal Luca in the hallway. "I've come for the coffee."

"Yes… it's… almost ready." Nadia stumbled over her words and Luca gave Issac a wink.

"When Rachel fetched the drinks from her car, she saw you both through the kitchen window." Luca told them and they both blushed, looking at the window, its shutters wide open. "Your secret's safe with us," Luca added, leaving the room and left alone again they both laughed.

As the day stretched on and dusk took over from daylight, the workers began leaving. There was a lot of back slapping and self-congratulating. It had been hard work, but now the garden was almost returned to Issac's original planting scheme and, as he had said, it needed a few sunny Italian days to get back to its best.

Rachel and Luca gave him a knowing smile as they said goodbye and Gabby promised that she and Riccardo would order take-away from the pizzeria on the way home.

"Okay, there's just a few last-minute things I want to finish up, then I'll head home."

Everyone shared their goodbyes, and once they were alone again, Issac cupped Nadia's face and kissed her.

Fifty-Seven

Cinquantasette

Riccardo felt it was too hot to be wearing a suit in town. But needs dictated. The Lanciano courthouse stood on an unremarkable street and, when compared to the town's elegant palazzi and old buildings, it looked unappealing. An unattractive rectangular structure with brutal corners and an ugly rectangular edifice attached to the middle where the entrance was. The interior fared no better; a dreary, faceless waiting area sporting a bland wooden door to the courtroom. Riccardo made his way along a corridor to a room that was just as drab. The walls were a nondescript colour and the furniture inside, dark and oppressive. He lay his briefcase down on the large central table and waited. He was ready for the meeting, the purpose of which was to put to rest the claim made by Salvatore Pasquini against signor Petrini's insurers, and those of Luciano's brother. Fortunately, the insurers and lawyers had pre-agreed on the claim beforehand, and the meeting was merely a formality.

Issac had driven Salvatore to Lanciano. He opened the door, nodded a brief hello towards Riccardo, and waited as Salvatore wheeled himself inside, followed by his insurance representative. Everyone stood in silence as the other parties arrived and Issac excused himself and left.

The meeting was cordial. A court clerk read aloud every word that was contained in the documents and finally, with a few scribbled signatures, the claim was complete.

Outside, the day felt hotter than earlier when they had entered the air-conditioned building.

Everyone shook hands for one last time and Riccardo no longer felt the need for formality and, after loosening his tie, he removed his jacket.

"I think I need to buy you a drink." Salvatore said.

"No, that's okay." Riccardo didn't know how to handle the invitation. "There's no need to do that."

"Relax, man. I'm buying *you* a drink, not having one myself. Unless it's a lemonade." Seeing Issac waiting, he beckoned him over. "And young Issac deserves one after waiting outside in this infernal sunshine."

The three men made their way up *Via Monte Grappa,* where outside a small bar was a collection of white tables and chairs. "Here will do," Salvatore said, while Issac made a space for him to wheel his chair into the shade. Handing Riccardo a ten euro note, he said, get yourself and Issac a beer. I'll have an orange juice.

Returning to the table, Riccardo could hear them discussing the meeting and hoped that following his advice, Salvatore made no mention of his payout.

"I think it was a satisfactory conclusion," said Salvatore. "Don't you agree avvocato?"

Riccardo nodded and removed his loosened tie and tucked it into his trouser pocket. "It went as well as I expected."

Abruptly, Salvatore changed the topic of conversation. "So what's next for our garden, Issac?"

"Our garden?" Issac replied, taking a drink of his beer.

"Well, now you and Nadia are back on track I'm assuming your intentions are honourable and marriage is on the horizon."

Issac coughed and sprayed the air with beer as he choked and stammered, "Yes… I… Honourable, of course. I… I…"

"Pull yourself together. I'm joking with you."

Issac breathed a sigh of relief and Salvatore caused him to panic again. "Besides, you've not asked my permission to marry my daughter yet." Salvatore winked at Riccardo, who joined in with the laughter.

Once the mood had calmed down, Salvatore repeated his earlier question and Issac told him that over the past few days, the garden seemed to have settled down and the flowers had recovered. "There are some new vegetables that Alina has grown from seed that she wants to plant in the raised beds in the orto section. Then I think it should be ready for the photographer."

"You must remind me what day the photographer is coming," Salvatore winked again at Riccardo, which confused him. "I'll need to make sure I shave and wear a clean shirt."

"Yes... But... she's coming to take photos of the garden... not..." Laughter once again distilled into the air as Issac realised Salvatore had ribbed him again.

***

Back at Laroscia, Nadia opened the front door before her father had got out of Issac's pickup. "Here, let me help," she said, lifting his wheelchair from the back of the truck. "How did it go, *papà*?"

"Just as the good avvocato here said it would. We have laid the unfortunate affair to rest."

"Alina is in the kitchen."

"Well, let's not keep her waiting. I want to hear what vegetables she's planning on putting in my orto."

Salvatore wheeled himself inside the house while Riccardo stood back, watching as Nadia did her best to keep her distance from Issac.

"Riccardo knows," Issac said, "In fact, it appears everyone seems to know."

"I never told a soul."

"You didn't need to. It was obvious by both of your demeanours when we were all helping in the garden."

"We wanted to keep it a secret," Nadia said.

"I think," said Riccardo, looking serious. "We've all had enough of secrets. They can sometimes do more harm than good."

Standing in the doorway, Alina shouted, "Are you coming Issac or standing gossiping like a housewife?"

Fifty-Eight

Cinquantotto

July was just a few days old and so far, it had delivered a storm followed by blisteringly scorching afternoons. Alina woke and smiled. The morning was cool with a promise of warm but not imposing heat. She had left her bedroom window open overnight, hoping the morning birdsong would wake her early and her plan had worked.

She moved around the kitchen quietly and selected two apricots, halved them and removed the stones before she sliced an apple, giving it a splash of lemon juice to stop it browning. After she'd arranged the fruit in a bowl and opened the oven where a cornetto had been warming, she added them to the tray alongside the small posy of flowers she'd picked the day before and had hidden in her bedroom. The one-cup *Bialetti* on the stove had finished gurgling, and she took the coffee pot and placed it alongside the other breakfast things and carried them up the stairs. She tapped on her nonna's bedroom door and called her name softly.

"*Si? Entrare.*"

"*Buon compleanno*, Nonna," Alina called before the door had opened fully.

"*Mia cara, grazie mille.*" Nonna shuffled into a seated position, and Alina placed the tray in her lap.

"I have made you breakfast."

"How kind. Thank you."

Alina ran from the room, calling out that she was fetching her birthday present.

"You shouldn't have wasted money on me," Nonna said, as she received the small cardboard carrier with a ribboned handle.

"Valentina gave me the bag it is in."

Reaching inside, Nonna removed a legendary dark blue box of *Baci Perugina;* the individually wrapped chocolate and hazelnut kisses. Alongside them was a small heart-shaped pebble; on its surface Alina had painted the words, '*Ti amo*' above a small painted flower.

"I'm rubbish at painting flowers, so Salvatore painted it for me."

"Alina. It's beautiful."

"That's just the first part of your birthday present. You'll have the rest at lunchtime."

"Sweetheart, this is more than enough for me." Nonna beckoned her close and placed a kiss on her cheek. "I love you, my darling girl."

"You eat your breakfast while I tend to the orto."

Alina slipped outside and was watering her tomato plants when a horn sounded. Skipping to the front of the villa, she saw Issac sitting in his pickup. She ran to him and he handed her an enormous bunch of flowers, "These are for your nonna. I'll see you later at Salvatore's."

"See you there."

Turning around, Alina saw Nonna standing in the driveway. "Issac has brought you some birthday flowers." Nonna waved to Issac and thanked him as Alina, almost completely hidden behind the blooms, delivered them to her. "A lady is coming today to take some photographs of the garden now it's finished. Shall we go to watch?"

"I'm sure signor Pasquini won't want us under his feet…" she paused, realising what she'd said, "You know what I mean."

"It'll be fine. He said to come along, and I'd like to show you the roses."

"I'll think about it. Now I must get on. There are dishes to wash and towels to put out to dry."

"I'll do that. You sit outside and relax. Birthdays are not days for housework. I'll go inside and see if we have enough vases for all of your flowers."

"Don't forget the posy you gave me with breakfast. Please, can I have it beside my bed?"

***

Salvatore had also woken early and when Issac arrived, he was out in the garden cutting out the faded geranium blooms and dead-heading the petunias.

The transformation of the tangled mess from a few months ago into the jewel of a garden still astonished him. Originally, he thought he wanted a replica of his wife's planting, but this was different and he liked it very much. The only things to remind him of Cristina were the persica roses, but with the addition of the teas and floribundas, these no longer took centre stage.

He'd taken to sitting outside in the evening as the sun set on Laroscia surrounded by the whirring of insects and the perfumed flowers. He often thought about how his life had changed that fateful day in January, but it was no longer a negative thought. "Who'd have thought losing a leg would be a positive thing?" he said aloud.

"Sorry, did you say something?" Issac said.

"Just ruminating." He dropped the spent flowers he was helping to deadhead into the bowl in his lap and moved along to the raised bed and continued with the grooming.

Issac was nervous and flitted around the garden, his mind taken over with trivial tasks that in the grand scheme of things made no difference. He looked up and understood Nadia was aware of what he was doing. She called them both over for coffee on the patio and told them to relax. "There's nothing more to do. The garden is perfect. Let's just wait for the photographer."

"Is everything else ready?" Salvatore asked her.

"Don't worry, everything is in hand. You concentrate on being the perfect host." Nadia kissed her father and reaching over and taking her hand, Issac gave it squeeze.

The two men sat in companionable silence looking over the scene before them until Salvatore said, putting down his coffee cup. "How so much has changed in a short time."

"It has. What was once wild is now tame."

"Rather like me." Issac gave Salvatore a puzzled look, and he continued. "I'd spent so long being an unpleasant individual until this." He patted the stump where his leg had been attached. "This changed me."

"How do you feel about it now?"

"Oh, believe me, I'd give anything to have my leg back, but living without it, I have become a better man. I've a chance to build a new relationship with my daughter and another with my neighbours." He looked at Issac, who nodded his understanding. "The circumstances I first lamented have allowed me the chance to once more strive for success, but more importantly, to see myself for who I really am and I like the new Salvatore Pasquini."

Another shawl of silence covered them, but the mood was one of stillness until sounds from inside the villa disrupted it.

Rachel, Luca and Louise stepped out of the *portefinestre,* delivering a jocund welcome to be followed by Riccardo and Gabby, also immersed in a cheerful mood.

"Everywhere looks fabulous," Rachel said.

"I told you it would perk up," Luca said.

"It's a real credit to you," Riccardo said.

Corks popped and Nadia carried out a tray and poured fizzing wine into glasses, the bubbles as ebullient as the mood. Handing one to her confused father, she said, "It's non-alcoholic. We can't celebrate properly without you *papà.*"

"*Grazie, amore mio,*" he whispered.

After the toast, Louise took out her phone and began taking photographs. Everyone grouped together, jostling for space as they smiled and cheered.

The photographer arrived and introduced herself as she

set up her tripod. Salvatore watched the animated conversation between her and Issac as he pointed and she made square shapes looking through her fingers.

After shooting the garden at different angles, she packed away her equipment and accepted a glass of fizz before swapping business cards with Rachel and saying goodbye. At the door, she passed Valentina, who was carrying a platter covered with aluminium foil.

"I have beer," shouted Ennio, putting down a case and nudging Salvatore said, "There's zero, my friend, for you."

The garden became a hub of activity. Riccardo and Luca set up trestle tables and Ennio and Issac unloaded chairs from his pickup. Gabby and Rachel laid the tables with platters after Louise and Nadia had covered them with tablecloths supplied by *Le Stelle*.

There was a shout from outside the new gate that Issac had fitted following the repair of the perimeter fence. Nadia opened it and Cosmo and Massimo entered, followed by Mole and Ivan, with Sprog trailing behind asking what time Alina and Sonny were arriving.

"This looks splendid," Mole said, kissing Salvatore and passing Gabby a box containing homemade English scones. "I saw Beattie and Queenie in the piazza, their arms laden with trays of sandwiches."

With the garden packed with everyone who had come along to help after the storm, Sonny ran in through the gate and shouted, "She's here! She's coming."

Everyone shuffled to the sides of the patio, legs pressed against raised beds with the overspill on the gravelled paths.

"Shush!" Sonny hissed, and a hush fell over the garden.

Inside the villa, Salvatore said, "Come this way. It's so lovely to see you. I'd like to show you the excellent work that Alina has done." His voice carried outside to everyone waiting, and a giggle from Alina travelled out of the *porte-finestre*.

Nonna's hand went to her mouth in surprise when she

saw everyone gathered in the garden, and before she could speak, a rousing chorus of 'Happy Birthday' rang out.

Nadia passed Nonna a glass of prosecco and after she'd said happy birthday, she took her by the arm and, with Alina in tow, showed her around the garden as the others unwrapped the platters of food.

Cosmo produced a speaker from somewhere and music played as people gathered at the tables to fill up plates and retire to the seats that were set up among the borders.

Ennio was in charge of the drinks with Riccardo, who had brought along a case of both red and white wines, proudly pointing out to everyone his family name printed on the sides of the boxes.

The conversation centred around the garden, with Issac answering a multitude of questions about both the scheme and plant names.

Salvatore talked about his plans for the business, telling people about the website Nadia was setting up and a shop in Atessa that had placed an order for some pieces.

Nonna enjoyed her surprise birthday party, with its mood as bright as the sun. She almost cried when Salvatore presented her with a vase that he had painted specially for her, with the same flowers as her pebble from Alina.

***

As the afternoon slowed and people began talking in muted tones, Issac took Nadia by the hand and led her away from the party up to the top of the garden where they stood in full view of everyone talking and waiting.

"No one is looking." Issac said and grabbing her hand they ran into the trees where they dissolved into the woodland.

Stopping, Nadia bent at the waist, hands on her knees, as laughing, she tried to catch her breath. "We shouldn't have run away."

"Yes, we should." Issac said pulling her up and towards him, "Because I can't do this in front of everyone." He ran a finger down her cheek and kissed her gently as her breathing returned to normal. He tucked a strand of stray hair behind her ear before kissing her harder, with more commitment. As his tongue explored, Nadia's hands searched his spine, moving up to his shoulders and tracing the width of him.

They broke apart, and looking deep into each other's eyes, he said, "I've never missed someone as much as I missed you."

Nadia let a smile grace her face and replied, "I have never loved someone as much as I love you."

La Fine

Acknowledgements

Wow! Here it is book three. I never thought when I started writing Under Italian Stars that it would spurn a series, let alone this book. With others planned, they will continue for as long as the ideas come and my readers want them.

Books start off as thoughts and so much has to happen behind the scenes for those thoughts to become a story to share with others. And it's the people unseen that I need to thank for giving me the help and support I needed to deliver this story.

Heartfelt thanks go out to my beta readers who help me fix character gaffes and plots holes during the early stages of writing. Grateful thanks go to my editor, Georgie, who corrects my passive verbs and deletes my overuse of certain phrases in the manuscript.

Once again, I have to thank the Renegade Writers for their continued advice and critiques. To Faye and the people from Bomba who have given me their support, I say, *grazie mille*.

To 'the lovely' Annie, who has been instrumental in extra chapters being conceived and for being the inspiration for the next book in this series, I send a massive amount of thanks.

Undying thanks goes to **YOU**, the reader, for your well wishes and your support throughout my journey thus far… there it is, the J-word.

Finally, I have to thank my adopted Italian family for the valuable lessons they have taught me and for their love and friendship.

Devo ringraziare la mia famiglia italiana d'adozione per le preziose lezioni che mi ha insegnato e per il suo amore e la sua amicizia. Piero, Menina, Massimo, Nicoletta, Matilde per citarne alcuni.

Tutte le traduzioni sono mie e mi scuso con gli amici italiani per gli errori commessi.

***

As I have said before, the village of Sant'Andrea is fictional, but all other towns, street names and businesses are factual. I like to use actual street names etc to enable anyone who visits to see exactly where the story is set.

All characters are products of my imagination and any resemblance to anyone else is purely coincidental.

Grazie a tutti,
XXX

Coming soon from Barry Lillie

A new series of books set in Abruzzo.
Book one: **Second Chances at the Olive House**
Available to pre order now

Book four in the Abruzzo Series.
The Italian Retreat

For news and free content, sign up to Lillie's Letters at

https://barrylillie.eo.page/yz39v

Printed in Great Britain
by Amazon